Book 7 in the

Combined Operations Series

By

Griff Hosker

Published by Sword Books Ltd 2016
Copyright © Griff Hosker First Edition

A CIP catalogue record for this title is available from the British Library.
Cover by Design for Writers

Dedicated to my little sister, Barb, and in memory of my dad who served in Combined Operations from 1941-1945

Prologue

June 1944

My team had fought from June sixth until June thirteenth on the Normandy beaches. We had been there with the French when they had landed and we had helped the Paratroopers defend Bréville. For one week we had barely slept and had fought hard every day. That had not been the only price. Just Corporal John Hewitt and myself had managed to escape the hospital. We had been sent back to England mainly because my whole unit had gone. They had all suffered a wound or injury during the seven days of fighting. Our journey back had shown the price that the allies had paid. We had seen the graves as we were marched to the beach. After we had been taken by landing craft to the destroyer we had seen equipment still surging in the surf. There were sunken ships close to the beaches still and German aircraft attacked us constantly as we dodged them on our way back across the busy Channel. The destroyer in which we travelled had more holes than a colander! I was relieved when I saw the Isle of White loom up on our port bow. It had taken a few days for us to be given a berth on the tired vessel which now took us home.

When we reached England Reg Dean, the Regimental Sergeant Major, was waiting for us with a car. Southampton was a long way from Reg's billet in Falmouth and I wondered why we had been afforded such treatment.

"What's this all in aid of Sarn't Major?"

"Major Rose's idea sir. I have to say, sir, the adjutant has grown on me! Drinks too much but he is not nasty with it and he does worry about you lads."

"Sarn't Major!"

"Sorry sir, anyway with so many of the lads wounded he reckoned you and the Corporal here needed a leave." He leaned in, "Word has it that they are lining your lads up for another little jaunt and if you don't get one now then you might have to wait a long time."

I shook my head, "You mean a mission for the two of us?"

He shook his head as he started the car, "Sergeant Poulson, Lance Sergeant Hay and Private Beaumont will be fit for duty by the time your leave is over. Fletcher and Shepherd won't be far behind. Anyway the Major asked me to come here and pick you up. Where to gentlemen?"

I said, "London will do for me. Take me to the railway station."

"Aye me too. It'll take a couple of days but I'd like to get home to the Boro."

Reg rubbed his hands, "Good and I have a couple of travel warrants here too. Mrs. D packed you a couple of kit bags with clean clothes. They are in the back."

"Tell her she is an angel."

"Aye sir, I dropped lucky there. Well, settle down in the back and we'll have you in the station before you know it."

The leather seats seemed remarkably comfortable after two weeks of sleeping on the floor and sheltering from German bullets. I was tempted to close my eyes. The car pulled away from the kerb and Reg said, "Well we showed Jerry what's what eh sir? I reckon the war will be over by Christmas at this rate."

I opened my eyes and sat forward, "Don't you believe it Reg. We were supposed to have Caen by the end of the first week and it is still there. We have not taken Cherbourg either. This war has not run its course. We have a toehold in France and that is it!""

Hewitt, who rarely spoke, ventured his opinion, "The Captain is right, Sergeant Major, it has not finished yet and those Jerry tanks are better than anything we have. The only thing that kept us from being thrown back into the sea was the fact that we were too bloody minded. Isn't that right sir? We had to use anything we could find to fight back."

Reg nodded, "Then the papers and radio have it wrong again. That doesn't surprise me. It is like the Great War all over again. Well you two will have a pleasant week at any rate."

"When do we report back, Sergeant Major?"

"We have a new camp at Southampton. You are to report back on the twenty first of June. But I am afraid, Captain, that you have to give me a telephone number where you can be reached. Sorry. That order came from Major Foster when he suggested to Major Rose that you might need a leave."

"Not a problem Reg." I took out my notepad and the stub of a pencil. I wrote down the number of my father's flat. I would use that. I handed it to him. This made more sense now. Major Foster was keeping me close to hand. Reg was right. We would be sent back soon.

As the car pulled up at the railway station there was the sound of an air raid siren. Reg shook his head, "Since D-Day they have come over every day. The harbour is a right mess." He handed us both our travel warrants and then took the two bags out of the boot. He saluted, "Make sure you enjoy yourself, Captain. There won't be many more of these leaves."

An ARP warden came up to us, "Get in a shelter! You three should have more sense!"

Reg laughed, "I'll take my chances on the road, if you don't mind!"

Tutting the warden hurried us towards the sandbagged shelter. Corporal Hewitt turned to me, grinning, "I think Jerry has it in for us, sir! Two weeks in Normandy, all the way home and now in England!"

"Never mind John. We have seven days where we can forget it eh?"

Chapter 1

London looked weary. As the train stopped and started through the suburbs of south London you could see the effect of almost five years of war. Every window had tape upon it and every building was sandbagged. People still carried gas masks. They walked hunched and tired looking like the Morlocks from *'The Time Machine'*. The war was five years old and it showed. As the train pulled in to Paddington Station I saw rescue workers pulling people from a nearby bombed building. The war was most certainly not over. I shook hands with John after giving him money for a taxi to King's Cross. The train north could take twelve hours or more if there were air raids. The sooner he got to the station the better. I ran to the flat. I received strange looks but I didn't care. I was still alive and I was in England. Others lay on the beaches of Normandy and would never be coming home.

I did not have a key to the flat but there was a caretaker who had a spare one. Charlie also acted as a handyman. He had been wounded in the Great War and this had been the only job he could do. I knocked on his door. As soon as he opened it I was hit by a wall of smoke. It was the smoke from his pipe. He liked his St. Bruno. He recognised me straightaway and stiffened to attention. He was still the old soldier. "Captain Harsker, sir. I wasn't expecting you. Your dad isn't here, sir."

"I know, Charlie. I have just got back from Normandy. They gave me a short leave."

He nodded, "I understand sir. I'll get the spare." He hesitated, "Only the thing is sir I just have the one. You'll have to let me have it back when you go out."

"That's fine Charlie."

He went to a board and took one down. "Normandy eh sir? We knocked Fritz for six there eh? Papers say over by Christmas."

I took the key from him, "You know what they say about newspapers don't you Charlie? The only thing they are good for is wrapping your fish and chips in!"

He laughed, "Your right there sir. Enjoy your leave and if you need anything just let me know."

"Just one thing. Is the telephone still working?"

Father's work at the Ministry had meant we were given the luxury of a telephone. I did not know what effect the bombing would have had. "Not certain sir. We have had no raids around here since your dad was here last. Should be all right but if not let me know and I will get it sorted."

The flat had a musty, unused smell. I opened the curtains to let the afternoon light in. I saw the patina of dust lying everywhere. I dumped my bag in the bedroom and then went for the duster and polish. Mum liked order. She liked everything to be clean and neat. That was the nurse in her. After shaking all the cushions and curtains I quickly dusted and then I swept the linoleum and wood with the brush and pan. Finally I ran the Ewbank over the rugs and polished all the wood. It looked better. That done I went to the telephone and gingerly picked it up. To my great relief it worked.

I dialled the operator and asked for mum's number. I was tired and needed a bath but if I didn't ring her she would be upset. It rang for a few minutes before she picked up. I pictured her in the garden. "Hello mum, it's Tom."

"You're back! Thank God!" There was a pause. "You are all right aren't you? This isn't a call from a hospital is it?"

"No I am fine. They gave me a seven day leave but I have to stay around London. I am at the flat."

"It must be a mess. I'll come down and clean it for you."

"Don't be daft. I have dusted and cleaned already. I just rang to say I was safe."

"Well thank you for that. Your boys, are they....?"

"We were knocked about a bit but they are fine."

"And have you spoken to Susan yet?"

"Mum! I rang you first!"

"You should speak to her first! Don't you lose her. She is a treasure. You should be more attentive."

"She is up in Church Lawton and I don't know if they have a telephone."

"She isn't. She was returned to duty in May. With all this Normandy business they needed her. We arranged for her dad to have a nurse visit three times a week so you have no excuse. She is in London and you are in London. Now hang up and ring her."

"She might not be on duty."

"Tom Harsker! I love you to bits but sometimes...Ring Susan!"

The telephone went dead. Since Mum had met Susan my life had changed. Mum suddenly saw the prospect of grandchildren on the horizon. She had taken to Susan instantly. The feeling had been mutual. I was largely grateful but Mum and Susan seemed to be moving us forward a little too fast for my liking. I was going to put the kettle on and then I glanced at the clock. It was four o'clock. The day shift in operations finished at five. I sat down again and picked up the telephone and rang the Operations Room. As I had expected I was neither allowed to speak to her nor find out if she was on duty. The frosty voice of the operator left me in no doubt that the telephone was not to be used for any romantic liaisons. I

5

was about to hang up when I realised that I could kill two birds with one stone.

"Is Major Foster on duty? This is Captain Harsker and I was asked to ring him when I reached London."

"Major Foster? If you would hold the line I will find out for you."

The line went silent. If I could not get word to her then I could always walk around to Whitehall and wait for her to come from work. If I did without a soak in the bath and hurried I could just make it.

Major Foster's voice sounded in my ear, "Tom! Good to hear your voice. This is damned quick and fairly fortuitous! I needed to speak with you."

"Sergeant Major Dean implied as much. I was just ringing to tell you that I was in London. I am staying at my father's flat. It is in Belgravia, not far from the Caledonian Club."

"I know it. I take it you have just arrived?"

"I arrived an hour ago."

"Well look here, how about lunch tomorrow. Make it an informal chat eh? I don't want to spoil your whole leave."

"That sounds grand."

"Say twelve thirty at the Army and Navy?"

"I'll be there. Listen before you go could you do me a favour?"

"Of course."

"I don't know if Susan Tancraville is on duty today. I would like to meet her but they wouldn't let me pass a message on."

I heard him chuckle. "You are still keen on her then? I'll tell her you are in town."

"Tell her I will call down tonight to her digs."

"Will do. See you tomorrow."

I ran a lukewarm bath with the Government approved six inches of water. It cleaned off the salt, sand, grime and, I had no doubt, the tiny remnants of men's blood. There had been much of that. I put a kettle on to boil water for a shave. I would not risk cutting myself. By the time I had shaved and put on the clean uniform sent by Mrs. Dean I felt a new man. With a little of Dad's cologne I was almost presentable.

I hurried from the flat, remembering to drop the key off with Charlie. He grinned when he smelled me, "This has to be for a young lady! Don't you worry about disturbing me when you come back sir. I will probably be up and reading."

"I doubt that I will be late, Charlie!"

I hurried. Heading down Constitution Hill, past Buckingham Palace I went across St. James' Park. It was just over a mile and I did it in less than quarter of an hour. I could have run it in ten minutes but I did not want to undo the good work of the bath and shave. I reached her quarters well before the time she was due to finish work. I decided to go to the nearby Whitehall Grill and see if I could book a table. It was early and the restaurant was closed up. I knocked on the door and the head waiter, whom I vaguely remembered, arrived in shirt sleeves and smoking a cigarette.

His face showed he recognized me too, "Good afternoon sir. Good to see you."

"I know you aren't open yet but I wondered if I could book a table."

"Of course sir. The boss will be pleased to see you. Since Joe Cameron was put away profits have soared. What time?"

"That's the trouble, I am not certain. I haven't told the young lady and she is still on duty."

"Don't you worry, sir. Whatever time you get here there will be a table ready. We are open at six and, for you, the manager would stay open until midnight."

"Thanks."

I returned to wait outside her quarters. You could not stop a Commando preparing. It was second nature. It might just be a date with a girl but the only way to avoid disasters was to do a good recce and have a backup plan. The backup plan was a supper at the flat.

I heard giggling behind me and saw Susan, flanked by Doris and a girl I didn't know, linked arm in arm and walking towards me. Doris had the inevitable cigarette perched precariously between her bright red lips. She saw me and squealed, "Oh he is eager, Susie! Looking at him waiting there in his uniform with all them medals! You had better watch out or I shall have him off you!"

Susan blushed and disengaged herself, "I have no worries there!" She rushed up to me and, throwing her arms around me, kissed me hard on the lips.

As Doris passed she said, "If that Major Foster is free tonight we could double date."

I turned and smiled, "I am afraid he is busy."

The other girl said, "You knew that anyway, Doris. He was in that big pow wow with the brass."

"A girl can dream."

We were alone and Susan looked up at me with a smile as wide as the horizon. "When Major Foster told me I couldn't believe it. Seven days?"

"Yes but I am not certain how much of that will be leave. From what the Major said I may have to attend meetings."

She laughed, "As that will be at Operations I will get to see you. And a glimpse of you, even from a distance, is well worth the wait. What shall we do?"

"Dinner at the Whitehall Grill?"

"Can we get a table? It has become very popular and busy of late."

"I have a table reserved for us."

She looked at her watch. "Six thirty?"

"That will be fine. I will wait in the *'George and Dragon'*." I pointed to the old pub across the road. I kissed her again and she ran towards her quarters. I reached the pub just after the doors had been opened. The landlord looked at his watch and said, "You are right on time sir. I have only just opened."

"I have just started a leave so I am keen to make the most of it."

He went behind the bar, "What can I get you, sir? I am a bit low on spirits but I could let you have a single whisky if you wished."

"A pint of bitter will do. It's been some time since I had a pint."

He began to pull a pint and studied my face. Although I had not been wounded no one survived combat without cuts, scrapes and bruises. "Been in action sir?"

"Normandy."

He took in the Commando flashes, "Then this first one is on the house. You lads and the paratroopers did a cracking job from what the papers say."

"Everyone did their bit, landlord. The air force kept Jerry off the beaches, the Navy got us there and there were over a hundred thousand soldiers on the beaches. It was a team effort."

He nodded and then saw my ribbons. His eyes widened, "And you have a V.C." He wiped his hand on his apron. "Can I shake you by the hand sir? This is a privilege."

I shook his hand and then took myself away to a corner. I did not want to be anti-social but I disliked the word hero. I was not a hero. I just did my job and tried to keep my men safe. The beer was better than I could have hoped. The first pulled pint was always a risk. Before the war the landlord would have pulled a few pints first and poured them away. The war meant we could not afford such flagrant waste. My father and grandfather disliked what they called 'southern beer'. An Englishman is very parochial about his beer. I was used to it and, in truth, just needed the liquid. Commandos knew about dehydration. My spirits sank as more people came in, for the landlord pointed me out. I realised that the whole bar would be discussing me and making up, no doubt, stories which would have me as a Leslie Howard character or even David Niven; all stiff upper lip, neatly trimmed moustache and impeccable manners. That was as far from me as it was possible to get. The war had not changed me; at least I did not think it had. No one approached and, for that, I was grateful.

It was with some relief that I saw the doors open and Susan stood there. It was unusual for a woman to enter a pub on her own and every eye swivelled to take her in. She looked stunning. I fell in love with her all over again. She came through the clouds of cigarette and pipe smoke. I picked up my empty glass and took it to the bar, "Thank you for the pint, landlord. I enjoyed it."

Susan linked me and, as we walked towards the door the whole bar spontaneously began to sing,

"For he's a jolly good fellow,

For he's a jolly good fellow,

For he's a jolly good fellow and so say all of us!"

As the door slammed behind us she laughed, "What on earth was that all about?"

"I have no idea. Come on I am starving. The last food I had was on a destroyer fourteen hours ago and corned beef sandwiches made with stale bread pales when you have lived on it for months!"

As we headed towards the restaurant she said, "Well don't expect too much here. Rationing is getting tighter. I think all the troops need feeding first."

I was disappointed. I had been hoping for a good meal. I realised I was deluding myself. It would take many years for England to recover from this war and it was not even over yet.

Even though we were early many of the tables were occupied when we entered. The head waiter rushed over. He beamed, "Welcome! The manager will be out to see you soon. We have kept a little table in the corner for you, sir."

"Thank you...?"

"William, sir and it is an honour to serve you both again. Madam is looking particularly stunning tonight."

I nodded, "Isn't she just? I am a lucky man." The smile from Susan told me that I had said the right thing. I was heeding Mother's words.

When Susan's coat was taken and we were seated she smiled, "That is the nearest thing to a compliment you have ever paid me! It is a good job your mum told me all about you. She said you would be hard work like your father was but I should persevere!"

William returned with the manager. I had not met him before. He looked like a tired old man but he smiled when he saw me. "I have been eager to meet you and thank you for what you did the last time you were in, sir. The meal tonight will be on the house."

"No it won't. I am not Joe Cameron and you have a business to run. It must be hard enough with a war on without giving free meals. I shall pay. Now what do you recommend? Anything but corned beef!"

9

He leaned in, "Well sir, we have had some fresh fish delivered. I could have the chef prepare that."

I nodded, "Excellent. With chips, of course."

He laughed, "Of course. What else?"

"Any chance of a couple of sherries and a bottle of white wine to go with that?"

William said, "I am sure we can manage that."

They had put us so that we could speak without being overheard. "I was sorry to hear about your mother."

She nodded, "It was a relief. I think Dad was grateful that she did not have to suffer any longer. Your mum was terrific you know. She seems so quiet and gentle but when she decides something needs doing then nothing will stop her. She got things organized so quickly. I was grateful."

"She has always been like that. With Dad flitting here there and everywhere between the wars it was up to Mum to keep everything under control."

The waiter brought us our sherries. It was not the best dry sherry I had ever had but not the worst and there was a war on. Having drunk neat Navy rum I knew what rough was!

"Cheers! Here's to seven days leave!"

"Cheers! Chinking my glass, Susan lowered her voice, "I was on duty the whole time you were in action. I volunteered for extra shifts. It made me closer to you somehow. Every time I heard of one of your men being wounded my heart sank. I don't know how any of you survived the battle of Bréville. Even Lord Lovat was wounded."

"It was hard. That was something I wouldn't like to go through again." She sipped her sherry and lowered her head. "What? Do you know something?"

"Me? I am a lowly ATS. I know nothing." She tried to laugh it away but I knew that she knew something. I held her hand and gave it a gentle squeeze. When her eyes met mine I nodded.

"It's just that if it is Major Foster you have to see this week then I know it has something to do with an operation they have been planning since D-Day plus three. I think it has to do with Caen."

I nodded, "We thought that we would take it quickly and then have a solid base. It hasn't worked out that way."

William brought over the wine. He showed me the label. It was a Sancerre. It might be too dry for Susan but beggars could not be choosers. He poured me a glass. There was no way I would send it back; unless it had turned to vinegar, but I would not offend them. They were doing their best. It was on the sharp side of dry but I nodded. "Thank you William that will do nicely. What is the fish?"

He looked at me apologetically, "I am afraid is it just monkfish, sir."

I smiled. The English were funny about their fish. It had to be cod or haddock. At a pinch they might eat kippers but other than that they were extremely conservative. I had eaten the fish before the war in France.

Susan said, "Monkfish?"

"I am sure you will like it and I can guarantee there will be no bones!"

William smiled, "Yes madam and it will be a good sized portion too."

'Never mind the quality feel the width' was also an axiom in England.

The fish came and it was delicious. As Susan said, so long as there were chips with it then it did not matter. Dessert was a summer pudding. It would be the last of the summer strawberries but it was all the more welcome for that. I walked her back to her quarters feeling like a king. The meal had not been expensive and we had been looked after as though we were film stars.

As we neared her digs she said, "I am afraid I am on duty tomorrow from twelve until twelve. I won't be able to see you."

"Of course you will. I shall meet you after work and walk you home. You never know there might be some Joe Camerons about!"

"You don't need to."

"I know but I want to."

She suddenly stopped, "Where are you staying?"

"At my father's flat. It is the other side of Buckingham Palace in Belgravia."

She laughed, "Mixing with royalty!"

I gave a mock bow, "Of course, milady!"

We made it back with just minutes to spare and our farewell was perfunctory with a pair of armed sentries watching but I knew I would see her the next day.

I had the luxury of a lie in. I did not rise until seven thirty. I felt like the idle rich! After washing and dressing I gave the key back to Charlie and headed towards Piccadilly. I enjoyed a pleasant stroll through the parks before reaching the part of town which were busier. There were many small cafes where I could get breakfast. It might not be the full English from before the war but it would be better than the porridge we normally had. I had time to spare before meeting Major Foster and I headed towards Central London to see if life had changed. As I walked down Piccadilly I saw that the Ritz and Fortnum and Masons still did brisk business. I wandered down Burlington Arcade. When I discovered the date of Susan's birthday I would return here to buy her something ridiculously expensive.

The closer I came to Piccadilly Circus the busier London became. This was not the London of the Royal Academy. There were touts and their gangs with suitcases which were unpacked and their contents flashed before policemen arrived. They were popular for you did not require ration coupons to buy from spivs! There were those who had money and did not serve shopping for other goods which did require coupons. I saw Piccadilly Commandos also keeping watch for policemen but they were not on the street very long; there were plenty of servicemen who wanted to enjoy every moment of their leave. Life went on and, by the time I reached Leicester Square I felt uplifted. London was still a vibrant city and people got on with life. I might not approve of everyone's lives but they had not been cowed by the monster in grey who had come so close to ending British life as we knew it. After Dunkirk the days had been dark but after Alamein, Italy and now Normandy there was the glimmer of a tiny light at the end of a very long tunnel. I strode out as I headed to Pall Mall and, as it was known by the officers who used it, to The Rag, the Army and Navy Club, where I would meet Major Foster. I was not yet a member myself but I had been there with my father and, as a relative, I could use it. I waited in the lounge for the Major. I was on leave; he was on duty. It was me who had time to wait.

A Wing Commander wandered over, "I say, are you Bill Harsker's boy?"

I stood, "Yes sir. Captain Tom Harsker of Number Four Commando."

He shook my hand, "Thought you were. I am Wing Commander Roger Clayson. I served with your old man at the end of the Great War."

"Pleased to meet you, sir."

He tapped his pipe at my medals. "And I can see you take after him in other ways too." He waved over a servant, "Two whiskies." I was about to refuse and then realised how rude that would be. We sat down. "How is he by the way?"

"Haven't seen him for a while. The last I heard he was out east somewhere and I am kept a bit busy here, sir."

"Normandy?" I nodded. "Despite what the papers are saying that was a lot closer than it ought to have been. My chaps were flying sorties and they told me what the beaches were like. You chaps must have gone in first eh?"

"That's normally how it is with us, sir."

The drinks arrived, "Well here's to the Harskers. Thank God for them!"

We chatted a little about the war and he was about to order another when I saw Major Foster. "You'll have to excuse me, sir. I am here to meet with Major Foster."

In a flash he took in the uniform and nodded, "Intelligence eh? Be careful of them young Tom. They prefer sending in chaps like you and keeping their hands clean."

"Not the Major. He was a Commando until recently. Thanks for the drink, sir."

As I stood he said, "Say hello to your old man for me eh?"

"Sorry I'm late Tom. Let's get straight in. I am starving. We started at six thirty this morning."

I smiled as I thought of the Wing Commander's comments. Five was a normal start in the field for Commandos and frequently it would be a twenty hour day but I said nothing. Major Foster had done his part and I would not like to be responsible for planning the operations as he did.

We sat and he said, "I'll order if you don't mind. I've ordered the wine already. We have a lot to get through."

"So this is more than two old chums catching up eh sir?"

"No such thing as a free lunch Tom. No, I am afraid that time is of the essence. If your chaps hadn't taken such a beating we could have started this already."

I found myself becoming angry. We had lost men because we had been asked to go above and beyond what was expected of us. I was interrupted by the waiter who brought the wine. Major Foster ordered and then held up his glass, "Here's to a successful mission."

I just held my glass up and said nothing.

"What's the matter, Tom? You seem out of sorts."

"Perhaps it is the implied criticism of my men. They were wounded when we were asked to help out the Paras. We were glad to do it but surely there must be other sections you could call upon. Is a whole mission waiting just for us? Things must be pretty bad."

"Keep your voice down old chap. Look sorry about the comments. No criticism intended. You did a wonderful job and I know that the battle of Bréville was won because of you and your chaps as well as the other Commandos."

"Look, sir, we are not pet dogs to be patted on the head and given a treat because we performed a trick. I hate to say it sir but you are in great danger of becoming another Colonel Fleming. That cold attitude was his style."

I thought I had gone too far. He coloured and then downed his drink in one. "God you are right! It must be working in that damned sweathouse that does that to a man. But look, Tom, I meant what I said. We need you. There are other sections we could use but none have the skill set that you do."

"Skill set?"

"Sorry. That is the sort of jargon some of the intel wallahs use. You and your men have a perfect combination of sabotage skills, language skills and, most importantly, the ability to survive behind enemy lines. What we asked you to do at Bréville was not a good use of you and your section. I was against it but if we had not held then we might have been pushed back into the sea. It cost you and your men. I know that."

The food arrived and we stopped our conversation. We ate in silence for a while. "Look sir, at the moment there is just my corporal and me left. What the hell can two of us do?"

"By the time we need to send you... well when the time comes you will have eight men and we think that will be enough. This lunch was to say thank you and to ask you to come in to Operations on Friday. We would like to brief you. This is neither the time nor the place."

It would have been churlish to say that I would be cheated out of a day's leave and so I said nothing. I nodded, "What time?"

"Ten eh?" I nodded. He grinned, "I passed your message on to Private Tancraville. Is it serious with you two? The rest of the girls in Operations seem to think so."

"I think so, sir. She has met Mum and they get on and, well... yes sir. It is."

"Who would have thought I was there at the start eh? Every time I pass through that Doris winks at me. I tell you now, Tom, she scares me and no mistake."

I laughed, "She asked me if I would ask you to take her out. I guess the answer would be no?"

"Emphatically!"

Now that the air was cleared we were able to talk easier. We avoided the operation and spoke, instead of the Brigade. What became obvious to me was that my section was now seen as being discrete. We were no longer part of Number Four Commando. We were the strike force of the First Special Service Brigade.

Chapter 2

Major Foster drank more at lunch than I did. I just had one glass of wine. I walked back to Whitehall with him to make sure he got there and then I strolled back to the flat. I knocked on Charlie's door. "Have you got the key, Charlie?"

"You don't need it sir, you dad is home. He is upstairs now. I have sent to the locksmith's to get you a new key cut."

I knocked on the flat door and Dad greeted me. We had always been close but since my section and I had rescued him in North Africa there had also been that bond of men who have fought together and faced death. He hugged me. We had not done that before the war.

"This is an unexpected surprise, Tom! When Charlie told me that you were here it made my day."

"Likewise. What are you doing back? The last I heard you were out east somewhere?"

He laughed as he led me to the coffee table. "You are partly to blame for that."

"Me?"

"Well you and the lads who went ashore. The brass has decided that as we are now close to the area where I fought my advice might come in handy. As soon as we have captured a few air fields I shall be going over to coordinate close air support. My squadron pioneered that in the Great War. We now have the Typhoon, Mosquito and the Americans have the P47 Thunderbolt. With their rockets, cannon and Brownings they are a powerful weapon."

I took the drink he proffered and toasted him, "You might have a wait for that. Caen is still in German hands."

He nodded, "I know. I called in at the Ministry today. It appears to have stalled a little. Caen looks to be holding us up." He gestured at me, "And I haven't even said well done for the gong!"

I shrugged, "You know better than anyone, Dad, that a bit of braid just means you were lucky."

"You are right but I was going on to say I hear you have a young lady now, Susan, isn't it? Mum likes her."

"Yes she is lovely. I am meeting her at midnight to walk her home from work."

"You know that you mum is hearing wedding bells already?"

"I know but this leave isn't even a proper leave. I am here so that they can brief me to send me back behind enemy lines again. How can I get married until all of this is over?"

"Remember your Aunt and Charlie?"

"I have thought about that but if she had married him he would still have died and she wouldn't miss him any less would she?"

"You are right I suppose. So we'll pop out later for a spot of dinner and then we will have to find a time when the three of us can meet up. I am keen to meet her."

"My only commitment is Friday and you?"

"I am free for both lunch and dinner." He tapped his uniform, "The benefit of rank. Us old codgers have a little more leeway than you younger chaps. Now, tell me about your section."

He knew most of my men and he was one of the few people, outside of the Brigade, with whom I could have an honest and realistic conversation.

I waited outside Susan's building to see her home. Two military policemen asked for my papers. I was happy to show them. I had been behind the lines enough to appreciate security at home. When the shift ended and the girls came out I saw that two soldiers had been assigned to protect them. They saluted when they saw me. One of them said, "Well Jack, looks like we have an officer with us tonight."

Susan ran up and kissed me. The other girls wolf whistled and cat called. "Ignore them Tom they are jealous. The Wild West decided that we should have an escort home after the late shift. Sorry." I remembered that the Wild West was the ferocious warrant officer who made their lives a misery.

We followed the gaggle of girls and the two privates. "Just so long as I get the chance to see you then I don't care." I pulled her a little tighter to me. "Dad is here. He would like us all to go out. I am busy on Friday and then I will be back in camp on Sunday."

"My only day off is Thursday and I am on this shift routine the rest of the time."

"Then Thursday it is. I'll walk you home again tomorrow."

Our farewell was as chaste as ever. It looked to be that way for the whole of the week. As I walked back, through St. James' Park, I berated myself. What did I expect? There was a war on. I booked a table for the three of us at the Whitehall Grill and spent my days enjoying the sights of London. Air raids had now been augmented by the terrifying V-1 Flying Bomb. Londoners called them Doodlebugs. There would rarely be a siren to warn you but a high pitched whine would suddenly stop as they crashed silently to earth. I experienced my first one on Wednesday as I walked through Hyde Park. Although it landed some way away I was amazed by the explosion. I asked Dad about them and he told me that they had almost two thousand pounds of explosives on board and were doing as much damage as squadrons of aeroplanes had done in the Blitz. It was another savage reminder that, despite what the newspapers said, the war was not over.

The weather on Thursday was awful. It didn't just rain. It was a storm of Biblical proportions. The only good news was there were neither Doodlebugs nor bombers! Nature decided to bombard us! Dinner, however, was delightful. Everything seemed to come together as though it was meant to be. Dad loved the restaurant and became an instant fan. Both Dad and Susan got on well too. She loved his sense of humour and laughed at his lame jokes. When she went to the ladies' room he confirmed it, "Your mum was right! You had better marry her. I can tell you now there won't be a better one than Susan. You are like me, Tom, a one woman man. I only ever took out your mum and that didn't turn out so bad did it?"

I knew he was right and, as I walked her back to her quarters I said, "I know you think I am a little shy and reserved. I am and I can't help it but I do love you. I want you to know that in case..."

She stopped and faced me, "Now listen here Captain Tom Harsker! You are going to survive this war! I am not going to wear black for the rest of my life! I am not going to be like your Aunt Alice and remember the hero I lost."

"I know and when this is over we will get married."

She stopped again, "Is that a proposal?"

"I thought you wanted to get married."

"I do but a girl likes a proposal!"

I shook my head, "Sorry. I am not very good at this am I?"

"No but I forgive you because everything else is perfect. And we will wait until this madness is over because I know that you will survive. It will be worth waiting for!"

I headed for Operations the next day with mixed feelings. My leave would soon be over and the briefing was reminder that I would soon be at, as Reg Dean often said, *'The sharp end of the war'*. However I would, possibly, have the chance to see Susan for she began work at noon. I would still be there when she was.

Security was even tighter now than it had been. Intelligence had discovered many more German agents landing in Britain. Most were caught but some were thought to have escaped capture and so there were more checks than ever. It was reassuring. I was taken through the labyrinth of corridors to the room I had visited before. This time there was neither Colonel Fleming nor Hugo Ferguson there. Instead there was a sergeant who was laying out papers.

"Nice and prompt sir. You would be Captain Harsker. I am Sergeant Reeves. If there is anything you want then let me know. I know I wear these stripes but my real title is 'General Dogsbody'!"

I smiled, "Thanks Sergeant. I am fine." I noticed a map on the wall. It was a familiar one. It was Normandy. I saw Caen ringed and arrows pointing at it. I knew what that meant. The Sergeant had finished and he sat down. He was obviously responsible for keeping a record of the meeting.

"The Major said you were over there, sir. Was it rough?"

"Getting ashore wasn't as bad as we expected but when they counter attacked we were hanging on by the skin of our teeth."

"I thought as much when we got the reports. They just gave numbers. You will have seen the faces though, eh sir?" I nodded. "I am afraid the Major and the others will be a little late. There is some sort of conflab. Between you and me sir there has been a problem I reckon."

"I can wait. Any chance of a cup of tea Sergeant?"

He grinned, "Just the job sir. I could do with a brew myself!"

He left and I stood to study the maps he had pinned to the cork walls. I recognised the targets which had been set. It looked to me as though there was a sudden need to capture Caen quickly. I wondered if that explained the delay. It was noon by the time that the Sergeant and I were joined by Major Foster and the three officers with him. One was a colonel and the sergeant and I snapped to attention.

"Sit down, please, sorry to have kept you. I am Colonel Waring, Major Foster's superior. This is Lieutenant Wilson and Lieutenant Ross. They are the ones who deal with the minutiae of this operation. Major Foster and I have the bigger picture to contend with."

He looked at me as though expecting a response, "Yes sir."

"Now I dare say you are wondering why we called you in during a well earned leave." He glanced at Major Foster which told me that my outburst at dinner had been noted. I nodded. "You performed above and beyond the call of duty as did your men. The medals on your chest tell me that is not an unusual event." He stood and went to the map. "Caen. We thought it would fall easily it has not. The storm we had yesterday and today was the last part of one which has wrecked the beaches. The Mulberry harbour has gone! We have eight hundred ships stranded on the beach. There is a problem with supply and we had intelligence that the Germans are planning an offensive." He sat down and lit a cigarette. "Cup of tea please, Reeves. Anyone else?" We all shook our heads.

Major Foster spoke, "We are in great danger of being thrown off the beaches and back into the sea. If that happened it would make Dunkirk look like a minor inconvenience. I am not certain we would get back as easily."

Lieutenant Wilson who looked as though he was still at school said, "I don't think so sir. We did it once. Should be easier the second time around."

I would not have dignified that with an answer but the Colonel snapped, "Wilson do not try to pull the wool over Captain Harsker's eyes. He has been fighting the Germans since before Dunkirk as has Major Foster. Our job is to see that the Germans do not throw us off the beaches!"

"Sorry sir."

The Colonel smiled, "And that is where you and your chaps come in. Field Marshal Montgomery has devised a plan which will, we hope, release the Americans to the south while attacking Caen from the north. In effect we will surround it and, hopefully, trap a large number of Germans between us."

I stood, "Do you mind sir?"

"Help yourself Harsker."

I went to the map. "The attacks would come here and here?" I used my hands to represent the two allied corps. He nodded. "Then I can see three major problems. The Americans would have to capture the high ground between St. Pois and the River Sarthe and British and Canadians would have to cross the River Dives. I was at the Orne and if the Airborne hadn't captured the bridge we would not have crossed."

Major Foster smiled, "You said three, Tom."

"The elephant in the room, sir, is the Second Panzer Division. They are S.S. and they have Tigers and Panthers. We found it hard enough to stop their reconnaissance vehicles at Bréville. God knows how you stop a Tiger."

Major Foster smiled again, "That is simple, we use your section." For once I was stuck for words. "You are right we have no tanks which can face the Tiger in a tank battle. We are outgunned and they have the best armour of any tank but they do have an Achilles heel. Their fuel. They drink it like water and we know that the Germans are running out." He stood and went to the map. "They are all supplied through Trun. It is on the main road from Caen to Cambois and a cross roads from the north and south of Normandy."

He paused. "So why not have the RAF bomb the hell out of it sir?"

The Colonel said, "We have been but they have a ring of anti-aircraft guns around it. They are the eighty eights that can be used against tanks too. Besides it is not the crossroads themselves which are important. They have built a huge underground fuel dump. Their lorries come at night to fill it up and then the bowsers from the Panzer Division fill up there. We have a rough idea where it is, thanks to the underground, but our attempts to bomb it have failed."

I could see how that would be apparent. "So you want us to go in and blow it up? That is a lot of explosives."

The Major stubbed out his cigarette, "Not really, Tom. They have pumps to serve the tanks. They can be blown up and that will, effectively disable it. We hope that there will be a chain reaction and the dump will be destroyed but even a short timeout of action would help to run the tanks dry and give our Shermans and Churchills a chance."

"And when is the off?"

"Operation Totalize is due at the start of August. Operation Epsom will be starting in the next day or so. This operation is Operation Thirsk." He smiled, "Not as grand a racecourse as Epsom but important nonetheless."

"We couldn't get there by then sir! I don't have the men."

"We know. Operation Epsom is the encirclement of Caen. If the Germans were stupid enough to use open country tanks in the wasteland that is bomb torn Caen then we would have won and we wouldn't need to send you at all. Totalize is the big one. Epsom is Monty's brainchild and is only the British and Canadians. Operation Thirsk only begins when Epsom is over. You have three weeks to get there and get the job done."

"If I have most of my men then we should be able to manage that. How do we get in?"

"We will drop you by parachute."

"Sorry Major Foster, that won't work. It would be suicide. D-Day showed them that we can land airborne troops and there will be Germans crawling over the countryside. Besides there are too many opportunities to miss the target. Better to sneak in."

"Sneak in?"

"Yes sir. We have German uniforms. I can speak German and some of my men are not half bad. We pass through their lines."

Lieutenant Wilson said, "But if you are caught you will be shot!"

I tapped my Commando flash, "If we are caught wearing these gets us shot. Herr Hitler does not like us." The young officer looked stunned. "Besides we can take more equipment that way."

"How?"

"There are Kübelwagens all over Normandy. I know because we shot enough of them up. If we get one or two that are repairable I have a genius with engines. We will drive the thirty miles to Trun."

The Colonel smiled, "So your time waiting for us was not wasted then, Captain?"

"No sir. A Commando is always prepared!"

"Well we need detain you no longer. Major Foster and Lieutenant Ross will come down to Southampton at the end of next week. By then you should have all your men. If you need any more then Major Foster will expedite that." He touched my shoulder, "This has come from the top,

Captain. The Prime Minister himself wishes it to happen." He smiled, "I believe your name was mentioned."

"I am honoured sir but I don't think we need any more men. We are a tight team and that is how we have survived as long as we have."

The look he gave left me in no doubt who was running this operation. "Nonetheless this operation is too important to risk failure over a missing man. Major Foster will make the final decision about the personnel you will take."

"Sir."

Chapter 3

As I sat on the train heading for Southampton I reflected on the end of my leave. I had not seen enough of Susan but there was a war on. I had, however, got to talk to Dad for longer than I could remember, and that was an unexpected bonus. He would be based in London until the airfield at Caen was in our hands. That was partly dependent on me. As for Susan and our future we had made plans but there was nothing decided. We would marry but that would be as soon as the war was over. I was lucky. Susan knew as well as any that the war had a long way to go before it was over. I had taken her to Bond Street one morning before she went to work and bought her an engagement ring. She said I had spent too much while I did not think it was enough. I didn't say anything to her but in my mind I knew that if anything did happen to me then she would have something from me. It was little enough.

We had no digs at Southampton. Instead there was a warehouse which had been commandeered and we would be staying there. The advantage it had was that it was close to the harbour; the disadvantage was that meant it was quite likely to be the target of German bombers. We would not have long there. We had just a week before the final briefing and then we would be trying to get to Normandy. Until we had a port in our hands, getting ashore would have to be the way we did it on D-Day, by landing craft. I doodled plans and ideas all the way to Southampton. We made two unscheduled stops to allow trains the other way. The Germans had damaged one of the tracks. The delay helped me to formulate my plans.

The Colonel had given me the approximate start times of the operations. We had until the first week of August to damage the fuel dump. As he had escorted me from the building Major Foster had said there would be secondary targets too. That did not surprise me. If we were behind the lines then we would need to cause as much mayhem as possible. We would need at least a week in Normandy to get the vehicles and to gather as much recent information as we could. I did not like the vague nature of the information. A hidden fuel dump could be as big as a large village but the pumps could be small. It was another reason I had chosen to go in by land rather than by air. We would have more chance of finding it that way. I sketched Trun, without names of course, and studied the sketch map. We would take full maps with us but it was often easier to have a small piece of paper at which to glance. When I got my Bergen I would transfer the sketch map to my small notebook.

As the train pulled in to Southampton Central I knew that my biggest problem was not knowing who I would be taking with me. The only one I was certain of taking was John Hewitt. I needed explosives experts as well as mechanics. At the moment it felt like trying to pick a lock wearing mittens!

It was Corporal Hewitt who waited at the station with the staff car. "I didn't expect to see you! You have a far longer journey than I do."

"I came back early, sir. Mam and Dad were having to live with Gran. The house was bombed. There were eight of us living in a two up and two down." He shook his head, "Rationing is hurting them sir. I felt right guilty. I mean I let them have me ration book but there was nowt in the shops. I got back yesterday morning."

"Well I am sorry about your family but glad that you are here. We have an operation in the next month."

He slammed the door shut and sat in the driver's seat, "Good! I'd like to get back at Jerry for bombing my home town and me Mam and Dad!"

"Anyone else back?"

"Private Beaumont and Fletcher although they are both limping. Sergeant Major Dean said the Doc passed them as fit for light duties. He reckons it will only take another week for them to be back to normal. Although what normal is for Scouse I have no idea."

I sat back. It was a start. I had my radio man and Private Beaumont was a whizz with both explosives and engines.

We had to pass through a barrier with heavy security to get to our digs. I was happy about that. The last thing we needed was saboteurs. Hewitt pulled up outside a functional looking building. He took my bag from the boot and then rapped on what I took to be a wall. It was a huge door and it slid back. Inside it had been transformed by the clever use of canvas and wood into a series of rooms. "Funny looking isn't it sir? Follow me. There's officers' quarters. At the moment it is just you and Major Rose."

We went through a curtain and there was bare room with eight camp beds and eight metal foot lockers. I took my bag from Hewitt and put it on the bed nearest to the door. "Thanks Corporal. I will go and find Reg and see if he knows any more about the missing men."

"I'd better take you sir, this is like a rabbit warren. You ought to leave a trail of bread crumbs to make sure you get back here!"

Reg looked harassed. His in tray was higher than his out tray and that was not Sergeant Major Dean's style. He managed a weak smile when he saw me. "Good to see you sir." Shaking his head he said, "We are so short handed here you wouldn't believe it. The Brigade is due back in ten days. There is so much equipment to replace... and I only have two clerks. There are four of us trying to do the job of a headquarters' company."

"Well we shall be out of your hair in ten days."

He stopped what he was doing and said, "Going back then, sir?"

"Looks like it Reg. Back behind enemy lines. Is Daddy here?"

"Aye sir and he is as shorthanded as I am. He has one corporal to help him."

"Well I shall see him next. We need everything he has and a bit he will have to find! What I need from you is the SP on my men."

He took a manila file and began to read, "Fletcher and Private Beaumont have been passed fit by the doc but I reckon they need another week or so of light duties. Fred Emerson should be back by the middle of the week. He is in London so if they say he is fit he will be. Poulson, Shepherd and Hay might be ready by the end of next week but their doctor, they are here in Southampton, says they need a week's leave after that." He closed the file.

"And the others?"

"Crowe is still critical. Gordy and Davis will need a month at least. Sorry sir."

"Not your fault, Reg. Well I shall go to the base hospital tomorrow and see those three for myself. I can't afford to take crocked soldiers with me. Better to go with a smaller number of fit men than with a full section of walking wounded!" I turned to leave, "Oh, by the way, I'd like Hewitt promoting. See what you can do about that eh?"

"Will do." He scribbled something on a piece of paper. "This operation must be important if they aren't letting the wounded recover."

"It is and it won't be easy. Major Foster and a Lieutenant Ross will be coming down at the end of the week to brief us. We will have to have the final numbers by then. The Major has said he will draft in replacements."

"Which you don't like, sir?"

"I think I am becoming an old stick in the mud, Reg. I don't like change."

I eventually found Daddy Grant and the new Quartermaster's stores. It was in a separate building which he shared with the armourer. Neither were happy about it. They were both territorial! Daddy was pleased to see me. He had been my sergeant and regarded me as his own personal success. "At last a face I am pleased to see. Good leave, sir?"

"It was Daddy. Any leave is a good leave but this one was special."

"Good. You deserve it." Then he frowned, "And this is not a social visit is it sir?"

"No Daddy. We are off Jerry side again. I need a few things."

"I haven't got much here, sir, but I will do my best." He took a clipboard and a pencil. "Fire away."

"Germans uniforms, weapons and rucksacks. New Bergens and uniforms. Grenades. Explosives. Timers. Fuses. Camouflage netting and a radio."

"Everything but the German stuff I can manage, Captain Harsker. I gave you the last of my German equipment." He shook his head. It's a shame because there must be a ton of stuff lying around in Normandy!"

I slapped my head, "Daddy, you are a genius and I am losing my marbles. Of course. We will pick up the German gear over there."

There were no separate messes and, with so few personnel, no need. We all ate together but you could not change the habits of a lifetime and we sat in three discrete groups. I sat with Major Rose and Doctor Hanson. I received grins from Fletcher and Private Beaumont when I walked in. I now had three men on whom I could rely. If I had to I would go in with them.

"How are those two, Doc?"

"They had nothing broken and the bullet that hit Private Beaumont just nicked his leg but Hewitt will have to keep an eye on it." He suddenly stopped. "You aren't thinking of taking them back are you? I thought they were just going to be training."

"It is not me, Doc. These orders come from the highest authority. If it was up to me they would have a month off. They deserve it but that is not the way it is going to be."

He shook his head. "What are we going to do after the war when we have so many broken young men to fix?"

"The same as we did after the Great War, Doc. Nothing. They will have to fend for themselves."

Major Rose had managed to get a bottle of something alcoholic. I had to get back in training and so I declined his offer. "You need to learn how to relax, Tom. It isn't good for you, you know. I mean when you are behind the enemy lines you must be living on your nerves. When you come back you should let your hair down."

"Not my way, sir. I was brought up to keep on going no matter what the problems were. I am too old to change now."

The rest of my equipment was stored in the QM stores and I fetched that the next day. I stripped down and cleaned my Thompson, Colt and Luger. Daddy had the ammunition for the Colt and Tommy gun and I still had some German ammunition but it would need replenishing. Major Rose was surprised that I didn't use one of the section to do it. He didn't understand the war we fought. A Commando looked after his own weapons. It was safer that way. He only had himself to blame it if went wrong.

When Fred Emerson arrived under his own steam and carrying his kitbag then I began to feel hope. I now had five men and, at a pinch we would make an attempt at the job. I still didn't want to have any men drafted in and so I went with John Hewitt to visit the other three in the base hospital just outside of Southampton. It was filled to capacity with the casualties not

25

only from D-Day and the first week of the invasion but the casualties which had accrued since then. Poulson and Hay were in the non coms ward.

We interrupted a game of Nap. They jumped to their feet when they saw us. "I hope you have come to rescue us, sir! This is like a Chinese water torture."

"That depends on the doctors, Sergeant."

"Honestly sir our wounds don't bother us. My stitches are due out tomorrow. After that I will be tickety boo!"

"And you Hay?"

"My stitches came out yesterday sir but I was a bit stiff like. They said I needed physio."

"We'll get physio getting ready for the next operation. Come on sir." Hay looked at Hewitt, "Hey John, tell them you will look after us."

"I will but I don't think it will cut much ice."

"We'll do our best but don't get your hopes up."

We had the same message from Ken Shepherd. He was keen to make up for what he saw as slacking off. He had not been there at the end when we fought at Bréville. That was my section through and through. In the end it was easier than I thought. The doctor who ran the hospital was short of beds, "There has just been an offensive in Normandy. I have been told to expect hundreds of Canadians. Where can I put them Captain? You can have your three. They have been making the lives of my staff a living hell!" He turned to John Hewitt. "Are you the section medic?"

"Yes sir."

"I will give you their notes and medication. Come with me now and I will get it sorted. You will have to wait for Sergeant Poulson. He has stitches due out tomorrow but you can take the other two now."

There weren't many men in our warehouse but the addition of my two walking wounded made it seem much livelier. When Sergeant Poulson joined us the next day I gathered them around me. "We are being sent behind enemy lines again. I know you all volunteered to be in the Commandos but you didn't volunteer to go when you aren't fully fit. I only want volunteers for this operation. It is your call but if you think you might jeopardize the mission then tell me now. You know that this is not a game."

I looked at each one in the eye. They said nothing. Then Scouse Fletcher said, cheerily, "You know sir, with the gains we've made already we'll soon be going behind lines in Germany! That Adolf Hitler had better watch out eh lads?"

They were ready.

Bill Hay asked, "Where to this time sir?"

"This is too public a venue. We will wait until tomorrow. Major Foster will be down to give us a briefing and our final instructions. Then we have a week before we set off. All of us need to be fitter than we are. And a cross country run with full pack will decide if any of you go or not! We will have a warm up in the morning before the major arrives."

As we were not sure of the roads I took a map to plan the route. My section prepared their equipment and we assembled at six o'clock for a six mile run. I would have preferred a ten mile warm up but that would have been unfair on Poulson and Hay who were the most recently returned from hospital. For Private Beaumont and Fletcher it would be a good test of their legs. Before we left I had a quiet word with John Hewitt. "Today I want you as Tail-End Charlie. You don't need to hurry them up just make sure they are not hurting themselves."

"Right sir."

We took full packs and set off. There would be no hills on this run which meant that it should not be a lung busting run such as we enjoyed at Falmouth. It would be a good test of their fitness running in an environment such as we might find in France. I had a second hand on my watch and I would use it to keep a steady pace. I aimed for ten minute miles. I had, in my head, the mile markers from the map and I kept it steady. I soon discovered that a week's leave had not prepared me for this. I found it hard and I had no wounds. I knew they would be hurting but it was better to find out their weaknesses here before we met the Germans.

I stopped when we reached the barrier. I turned and saw that Ken Shepherd was thirty paces from me. Behind him there was a gap to Private Beaumont. Then Corporal Fletcher appeared closely followed by Emerson. There was a long gap to Hay and we had all recovered our breath by the time Poulson and Hewitt arrived. Hewitt gave a slight shake of his head.

"Well done lads, breakfast and then change. We will meet in the mess at ten."

I heard Corporal Fletcher say, as he wandered off, "I'll have to give up the ciggies!" The others laughed.

Poulson was still doubled over catching his breath. Hewitt was standing over him, "Just take deep breaths Sarge. You did well."

I said nothing for I knew that the big man would not appreciate any empty comment. He had not met our basic standards and he would know that. When he eventually stood he shook his head and said, haltingly, "Sorry sir. Had no breath. Let you down. I'll work on it."

"We have a week."

He nodded, "It'll be enough!"

I was not so sure but I owed my sergeant the chance. After a hot shower and a change of clothes I was ready for my breakfast. I went to the office

27

and checked in with Reg Dean. "We'll need somewhere quiet to talk when the Major gets here Reg. This is a top secret operation."

"We have too many civilians in here sir. Why not down by the docks? There are lots of empty berths. If he is just talking to you that would be perfect. The weather forecast is good for today." He grinned, "Just watch out for the birds eh sir?"

I was in the mess hall early. I had picked up a clipboard and I had made a checklist of the men and what we would need. I had question marks against Hay and Poulson. With Gordy Barker still on the sick I might be without a sergeant. The section all arrived early too. Their silence reflected their own disappointment in fallen standards and levels of fitness. I could have allowed it to stay hidden but that was always the most dangerous course of action.

"We all know that today was a shambles. I took the run two minutes a mile slower than when we used to run to the camp in Falmouth. However it was our first run. Hewitt and I found it hard and we had no wounds. But we only have a week or so. Will you be ready?"

They looked at each other. I could see that their confidence was shaken. Bill Hay nodded, "We will be, sir."

Corporal Fletcher said, "I am giving up smoking!" They all looked at him in surprise. He shrugged, "I can make a fortune selling my ciggy ration when I go home on leave!"

Polly Poulson nodded too, "It will be like Commando camp all over again, sir. We found that hard but we came through. At the moment I can't see how I can be fit but I thought that at Oswestry too. I'll get there."

John Hewitt said, "Just don't bust a gut trying eh Sarge? I am lousy at stitching!"

The Major did not arrive until noon. "Sorry we are late Tom. My fault. I wanted to get the latest intel on the latest operation." He looked up at the cavernous building. "This is not a secure place. Come with me I have something arranged."

I was intrigued as he led us in the direction I had been going to take us. He led us to the harbour. I said nothing as I walked with him and Lieutenant Ross who appeared to be laden under a mountain of papers and maps. I saw a line of landing craft at anchor. They were the ones we had taken on the invasion. When I saw a familiar face and LCA(I) 523 I knew exactly where we would be going.

"Petty Officer Leslie!"

"Morning sir! Morning Major Foster." He waved his hand for us to enter. "The crew are all on leave until tomorrow. There is just the skipper and me. He has nipped home to see his wife and I will stand guard here at the gangplank. No one can overhear you, sir."

Major Foster nodded, "Thanks Chief and thank the skipper for this intrusion."

"No bother sir." He grinned, "Looks like we'll be taking another little trip together eh lads? All aboard the Saucy Sue!"

When we reached the crew's mess Major Foster shook his head, "As Petty Officer Leslie has already let the cat out of the bag I will tell you that this is the ship that will take you on your next operation. She will stay with you while you are in France as a floating barracks. This will be your new home for a while. Make yourselves comfortable. This will not be quick. Lieutenant?"

Lieutenant Ross began to pin maps on the walls. I saw, as he did so, that Major Foster scanned the faces of my section. He was assessing them. When the maps were up he began the briefing. I took notes as he did so.

"Captain Harsker has already been told the aims of the mission and the location of the target. What he does not know are the secondary targets." He smiled, "That may come as a surprise to him too."

I looked more closely at the map and saw that there were three crosses close to Trun. One was a large one. I had seen that in London but the other two were smaller ones to the south of the small town.

"You are going to make your way from Ouistreham to Trun. You will pass through enemy lines. Captain Harsker has devised that side of things and I will let him brief you on that. However once you get to Trun you will locate the underground fuel dump and pumping station. Your first target is the pumping station. That must be destroyed. If you manage that then your second target is the dump itself." He allowed that to sink in. "If, by some miracle you achieve that your next two targets are the two bridges south of Trun. One is here over the River Le Douit. That is in open country while the second, here, the Le Meillon is close to a hamlet, Guêprei. Both targets are two or three miles from Trun. If you succeed then you will head back through our lines. We are hoping to stop the S.S. division getting to Caen when we capture it. That thorn has held us up too long as it is."

He stopped and looked at us.

I finished writing my notes and said, "Any questions?"

Private Beaumont asked, "What kind of bridges sir? Stone or metal?"

He looked at Lieutenant Ross who panicked and began to search through his papers. "Come on Lieutenant!"

"Sorry sir. Er both metal."

Private Beaumont had his own note pad out and he scribbled away. "And the fuel dump sir, I am guessing it is underground and the RAF have been unable to destroy it from the air?"

Major Foster gave a wry smile, "Very astute Private. Yes, it is underground."

"Is this fuel for tanks, trucks or both sir?"

"Mainly tanks."

Private Beaumont nodded, "Good."

"Why good, Private?"

"I am guessing that this is fuel for their Tiger and Panther tanks. Both have a petrol engine. Petrol is easier to set on fire than diesel. We just need to start a fire and 'boom'! It will not need a big charge. The explosive will be the target itself."

Major Foster looked down at his own clip board. "You would be Private Beaumont?"

"Yes sir."

"Thought so, you are right Tom, he is a whizz. Tell me Professor, the bridges, how would you destroy them?"

"If they are metal sir then you destroy the metal piers attaching them to the banks of the rivers. You don't need a big charge because any damage will weaken metal and make the bridge unusable. Especially if Tiger tanks try to cross them."

The Major looked puzzled. "Why not take more explosives and make sure they are destroyed?"

"Weight sir. I think the captain will agree that if we are behind enemy lines we cannot have too much ammunition and grenades. We use physics to do the damage. We put the explosives where they have the most powerful effect."

The Major nodded, "And if you succeed you make your own way out. I take it you will go in as Germans and come out as British?"

"That's the plan sir."

"And the German equipment?"

"In the pipeline."

"Now what you should know, but this is top secret so keep it under your hats, is that today we have launched Operation Epsom. The weather delayed it. The Highlanders and the West Yorkshire Division will be attempting to surround Caen. We hope that by this time next week Caen will be in our hands. That is your own D-Day. You leave seven days from now. This landing craft will take you down the Orne canal to Caen. You will have a week in Caen to get your equipment and you will be ready to begin your mission one week later. Lieutenant Ross here will be liaison officer and he will come with you. We have a second operation and it is the timing of that which will decide your actual start time." He looked around. "Any questions?"

My men knew that I would ask any important questions and they shook their heads.

"Then good luck. I will leave the maps with you Captain Harsker. Destroy them before you embark. The Lieutenant will return in six days time with the passwords and other details. I will make sure you have everything you need to get you what you need. He can act as your liaison."

"A bit like Hugo eh?"

"Exactly, Tom. Well, good luck. We'll make our own way back to town." He stood and I went out with him. Once on deck he shook my hand. "I know this is a hard one and I know you have not enough men. I am sending over another Commando from Number 2 Commando. He is a fair sniper and has experience in explosives. More importantly he can speak German."

"I don't need him, sir."

"I have seen the medical reports. Not all of these walking wounded are fit enough and you know it. I doubt that they will all go and the numbers you are taking are cut to the bone. You will take Lance Corporal Wilkinson and that is an order. It is only for this mission. His unit is being refitted at the moment."

I was not happy but I could do nothing about it. An order was an order. I nodded.

Chapter 4

I put the new lance corporal from my mind. As I descended to the landing craft's mess I thought about the hard decisions I might now have to make. I forced a smile. I owed these lads a couple of days to prove to me that they were fit enough. "So another jaunt behind the lines."

Scouse nodded, "At least we won't be dropping out of an aeroplane sir."

Bill Hay said, "How do we get through their lines though, sir?"

"As Germans. We have done it by accident before, when we stumbled upon those Jerries and took their vehicle. This time we don't steal them. At least not from Jerry. When we reach Normandy, Private Emerson, I want you and Private Beaumont to find a couple of German vehicles and fit them up so they work. Then we get some Jerry uniforms. I intend to drive through their lines. The hardest part will be where they meet our lines but there are so many little roads over there that it should be possible. And I have a couple of wrinkles up my sleeve. I am not worried about that part but finding the pumping station won't be as easy."

"It should be, sir."

"How so, Private Beaumont?"

"They can disguise the facility all they like and hide it from aeroplanes but if they have heavy lorries and petrol bowsers using it then the road way near the entrance will show clear signs of heavy traffic. The verge and ditches will be flattened by heavy vehicles and they will have had to clear the hedges to allow the trucks to turn. Given that it has to be on a road and we know to within a mile where it ought to be I don't think it will take long to find it."

"Your logic is impeccable. Let's hope that you are correct. I intend to use this as much as possible. While we have this LCA let's use it. Any more questions?"

We spent a good hour talking through what we would need. At the end I said, "I have already had a word with Daddy Grant. Head there now and collect what you need. We will have another run this afternoon but faster this time. Sergeant Poulson and Lance Sergeant Hay, if you hang back for a moment..."

Both of them knew what was coming. Their heads hung. "I know you two want to come with us and it does you great credit but I can't do you any favours. We can't afford passengers. At the moment neither of you are fit enough to come with us."

Sergeant Poulson knew his shortcomings better than anyone else. "I know we were poor this morning, sir. Give us a chance. I reckon we can turn it around in four or five days."

"We haven't got four or five days. In six days we get the passwords and in seven we go. In five days I want us practising not getting fit. You have three days."

They nodded and Sergeant Poulson said, "Fair enough sir. We'll be ready."

I gathered all the maps from the walls and allowed them to leave. They would want to talk. Bill Leslie was leaning over the bridge smoking his pipe as I came out. "Those two didn't look happy, sir. It's not like you to upset your lads."

"I know. I just told them that they weren't fit enough to come on the operation."

He nodded and tapped his pipe against his hand and then dropped the ash over the side, "I can see how they would be upset but you are right, sir. On this ship you can carry a wound and still do your job but you and your lads..." He smiled, "It comes with the rank eh sir?"

"It does but I am glad that it is the 523 we will be using. She is a lucky boat."

He looked over to the Oerlikon gun where the young gunner had had his head blown off on D-Day. "Not for everyone, sir."

I nodded. His death was a reminder that the margins between life and death were measured in inches.

Poulson and Hay were not the only ones who improved during the afternoon run. Everyone was aware that I would be true to my word. It think Corporal Hewitt had spoken to them and given them advice. He knew his job. Even though there was an improvement Poulson and Hay were still minutes behind us. I saw the two of them closeted together as we ate our evening meal and I wondered what they were cooking up.

The morning run saw another improvement but instead of going to breakfast when they had finished Hay and Poulson headed for the sea. Intrigued I followed them. They both stripped down to swimming trunks and dived in. Bill Hay had been a frogman with me in North Africa and I knew he was a good swimmer. I wondered what they were doing. I went to the mess for breakfast. I had finished and was with Reg Dean. I had put Corporal Hewitt in for a promotion to Lance Sergeant. With Poulson and Hay unfit I needed a second in command. John had said he didn't want to be a sergeant as it would mean leaving the section but I could have a second lance sergeant on the books. I wanted to see if it had gone through.

I was just leaving the office when I saw them, "What were you two up to this morning?"

Poulson looked embarrassed, "Bill said swimming was a better way to get fit sir. Less impact. He was right. I feel better after the swim and I think we will make the standard!"

33

"Good. We will see this afternoon. We will have a new Lance Corporal with us. He arrives this morning. Major Foster thinks we need another man until we get Gordy and the others back."

"A new man sir? Not a recruit?"

"No Sergeant Hay but make him welcome eh? Play nice."

"Of course, sir."

I was not convinced by their answers.

Joe Wilkinson was a big Commando. Sergeant Poulson was the biggest in my section and Joe was his equal. I discovered that he had been a rugby player and had represented the army against the navy. That meant he was fit, tough and agile. All great attributes for a Commando. He was a serious soldier and not given to smiles. That marked him different to my team. He was ramrod straight when he reported to me.

"Stand at ease, Lance Corporal." Even with his feet apart he looked rigid. "I appreciate your joining us. We were knocked about a bit at Bréville and we will need you on this one."

"Yes sir. I have heard of your section. Behind the lines a lot eh sir?"

"That's right. Leave your gear here and we will have a wander down to the landing craft. I will fill you in." I did not sugar the pill as I gave him all the details. He did not seem to be unhappy about any of the problems we might have to deal with. "And your German, how good is that?"

"Fluent sir. My mum ran a lodging house in Harwich, sir. When I was growing up we had loads of sailors staying with us. They were mainly German and Dutch. I can speak both. I enjoyed picking up the words and it seemed to come naturally."

"Good. And does your mum still take in lodgers?"

"No sir, she died last year. They were bombed."

I nodded. We had had digs in Harwich and even in the early days of the war it was an easy target for German bombers. "Sorry to hear that, Wilkinson."

He shrugged, "It's this bloody war sir. Everyone I know has lost someone. She is with dad now. He was lost at sea in nineteen forty."

I liked him. He did not feel sorry for himself and yet he had lost everything, "Look, Joe, I will be honest with you. We are a tight team and you know how Commandos are."

"Don't worry sir. It's not a popularity contest. We'll all do our jobs. If they don't like me well they can lump it eh sir?"

"A good attitude to have. We will be out for another run this afternoon. The two sergeants are both recovering from wounds. If they are not up to muster then they won't be coming on the operation. You ought to know that because if they don't that makes you third in command."

"Right sir. I won't let you down."

"Then let's go to meet them. It is about time for our run." They were all waiting with their Bergens outside the barracks. I introduced the new man. "This is Lance Corporal Joe Wilkinson. He will be with us for this mission. He speaks German and, I think you will all agree, that will be fairly useful."

Scouse quipped, "Yer mean I won't get to tryout me Scouse German again?"

"Hopefully not Scouse!"

My new Commando showed his mettle when we went for our afternoon run. He could have stayed at the front, on the run, with me. Instead he stayed at the back with Hay and Poulson. It was a good start. He was giving them what they needed, encouragement. The next morning I noticed that Hay was not at the back. He was keeping up with Fletcher and Private Beaumont. They too had improved. The swimming had helped. However despite everyone's best efforts Sergeant Poulson was not ready after three days. I took him with me to the landing craft to give him the bad news.

Before I had spoken he said, "Sir, let me make this easy for you. I am not ready to go behind the lines. I would jeopardise the mission. Bill and Joe Wilkinson have done their best. I am fitter than I was and I reckon in ten days or so I will be back to my best but that will be too late. You can't afford to have me in the operation."

I nodded, "Thank you for that."

"But sir, I can still come to Normandy with you. I don't need to be fit to help Fred with the vehicles. I can be armourer for the German weapons. I can still be useful, sir. And I'll be there on the boat when you come back." I was not certain and it must have shown on my face. "What's the alternative sir? Sit on my arse here and do bugger all?"

I smiled, "No, you are probably right. Then until you are fit you can be company clerk and armourer!"

"Suits me sir. I'll still be with the lads and you. That is all that matters."

"Don't forget you will have a fresh faced lieutenant to baby sit too!"

His face fell. "I had forgotten Lieutenant Ross sir."

"Sitting on your arse doesn't look so bad now does it?"

The Lieutenant arrived the day before we were due to embark. He came laden. He had maps, charts, photographs and a plethora of documents. We all moved on to the LCA. It was more secure and we would be leaving the next day. We had our new radio and the Lieutenant spent some time with Poulson and Fletcher going through the code words we would use. Equally important were the passwords we would need to get through our lines. The Canadians and Highlanders had taken heavy casualties and experienced the S.S. Anyone speaking German was likely to be shot first and questioned later. Having seen how the S.S. worked I could understand that attitude.

My section all smiled as we left Southampton. The young lieutenant donned his helmet. Scouse Fletcher said, "Is it going to rain then sir?"

The lieutenant looked confused as he realised he was the only one wearing a helmet. "I thought it was standard operating procedure, sir."

"We are Commandos and we don't normally wear them but unless Jerry actually attacks us we should be fine, Lieutenant, and ignore our Liverpudlian friend. He regards himself as the section comedian! If he continues this way he could be on pan bash for a week!"

"Sorry sir. Just trying to lighten the mood!"

I joined Bill Leslie and the skipper on the bridge. It had been a month earlier when we had last crossed this water and that had been at night. I was anxious to see the journey in daylight. The waterway was busy. We still had no port and Mulberry had been destroyed in the recent storms but landing craft could still make the crossing and deliver vital supplies. They would land on the beach as they had on D-Day. We were lucky that PLUTO still operated and our vehicles in France had plenty of fuel. We were in a convoy escorted by two Hunt class destroyers. In the two weeks since we had crossed back to Blighty the RAF had largely cleared the skies of the Luftwaffe but there were always fanatics who would risk almost certain death to strike a blow against the allies.

It was late afternoon when we entered the Orne river canal. I saw the ruined Casino where so much fighting had taken place and the beach was still littered with the last of the damaged vehicles from the battle. Little could be seen to the north where we had fought at Bréville. There were just some blackened scars amongst the trees and a few damaged farmhouses. I knew that if we walked it we would see a different story. We passed under the bridge which had been taken by the paratroopers. The last time we had seen it we were racing across to reinforce the Airborne Division. It seemed so far away and yet it was just three weeks since we had fought there. It was no wonder that Sergeant Poulson had not recovered from his wound.

Caen had only recently been liberated and isolated pockets of Germans were still being discovered hiding out in cellars, bunkers and half ruined buildings. The allied bombing had made the historic old city a mass of rubble and broken buildings. It was one reason it had been so hard to take. Someone had made a mistake in ordering the bombing! There were few which still stood and those that did were not whole. It was a depressing journey. The river, however, was under firm British control and we were assigned a berth by the new harbour master. He was an organized and elderly RNVR.

"Ah you must be the cloak and dagger boys we have been expecting. This berth is well out of the way." He pointed to a half ruined building. "You can use that over there. It has a roof and three walls. It should suit. Anyway if you need anything then let me know."

With that he was gone. "Lieutenant Ross and Sergeant Poulson we will leave you to organise that building. Hay and Wilkinson, you take half the men. You know what we are looking for. Emerson and Private Beaumont, you are with me and Corporal Fletcher. We will leave our gear on the LCA for the time being.

I knew that there had been fierce fighting around the town. Although most of the bodies had been moved already there were still enough for us to find where the fiercest fighting had been. That was where we searched for weapons. We looked for half demolished buildings which had yet to be made safe. We headed west. That would have been where the main assault took place, There was an area of houses which had been half flattened by the bombing. I saw something sticking from the rubble. When I reached it I saw that it was a hand. The smell told me it was a dead body. We began to lift aways the bricks and stones. It was an infantryman. We would not touch his uniform but his equipment would be handy. After we had moved him we found another three men beneath him. Two of them had Mauser rifles which still worked and one the MG 42. We found four grenades and a couple of daggers. I took on the grisly task of finding their papers. They were as valuable as their weapons.

We moved on. We began to find buildings which still stood and had avoided the bombing. One was a sandbagged, residential building which suggested German occupation. Bizarrely the door had been locked. Corporal Fletcher said, "I can have a go at picking it if you like sir."

"We don't need to be silent we need to be quick. Break it down."

When we broke in we were, at first, disappointed. I had expected it to be important but I saw that it was just a requisitioned house. The lounge showed that Germans had used it. There was a half empty packet of Rote Hande cigarettes. I did not smoke but I took them. They were popular amongst the German soldiers. There was also a box with three cigars. They had a swastika wrapper around them and I took them too.

Emerson shouted from the kitchen, "Sir, I have found some German rations."

"Grab them! They are like gold. Private Beaumont, Fletcher, upstairs and see what you can find."

"And a rucksack!" It was Emerson again. He was lucky.

I went into the kitchen. He was not there but the back door was open and there was a garden shed. Fred was about to open it. I joined him and we tugged it open. It was like Aladdin's cave. It was where the Germans, who had been bivouacked in the house, had stored their ammunition and grenades. These were obviously what I would term, 'old soldiers'. They had hoarded equipment and ammunition for the hard times. I wondered why they had not reclaimed their equipment and then realised that the lounge looked as though they had just left quickly. Locking the door showed that they intended to return.

"Gold dust eh sir?" He took another German rucksack from a peg behind the door.

"It certainly is, Fred. Let's get it packed."

I heard a shout from indoors but it did not sound as though it was a cry of pain. We gathered all the ammunition. It would fit both the Mauser and the MG. We had enough, if we found more weapons, to go to war! When we went back inside, Private Beaumont and Fletcher had come down stairs and they had German uniforms in their hands. There were six greatcoats and four complete sets of tunics and trousers. "Jackpot sir! They were all in the wardrobe."

"Right. We have ammo and grenades. Let's get back to the boat and we will see what the others have found." I decided that if we could get away with it we would wear the greatcoats and caps. We would be travelling in the dark and they would help with our disguise. Everything now depended upon getting vehicles.

We received strange looks as we hurried through the town. The French gave us wary looks while the British soldiers we met just looked at us curiously. The others had not returned but Lieutenant Ross and Sergeant Poulson had managed to make a rough fourth wall and sweep out the floor. Sergeant Poulson said, "We have slept in worse sir."

"It'll do. What is the upstairs like?"

"A bit dirtier than here, sir."

"Right lads take our ill gotten gains up the stairs."

When Bill Hay led the other half of our men back they too had had success. They had papers. Three rifles, two helmets and three caps. We already had some caps and now we had enough for everyone. It was coming together. "What about vehicles?"

"Sorry sir, we saw bugger all."

Private Beaumont said, "Sir we are looking in the wrong place. There was so much bomb damage that any vehicles hit in the town would be beyond repair. Fred and I can only repair so much. We need to look between here and Ouistreham."

"Good idea. That is our job tomorrow then."

We ate aboard the LCA. Our conversation drifted towards vehicles. It proved useful for the petty officer in charge of the engines said, "When I was talking to the harbour master about spares he told me that they are collecting all the old vehicles just along the canal. They are going to load them on a barge and ship them back to England to be melted down and made into new tanks and the like. Might be worth having a scavenge there."

I nodded, "Thanks. Lieutenant Ross, did the Major or the Colonel give you any authorisation?"

"Authorisation sir?"

"Yes, you know a piece of paper letting us take what we need. I am sure he will have done. The Major is not stupid."

The young officer coloured. "There might be, sir. He gave me some letters and documents. I was more concerned with the passwords."

"Well cut along and fetch them eh? They might come in handy!"

Bill Leslie smiled and rolled his eyes. We had both experienced young officers like Ross. They meant well but were born without an ounce of common sense. In time he might make a decent officer but that was the key phrase, 'in time'. He rushed back in clutching a handful of documents. He looked like Neville Chamberlain when he had come back from meeting Hitler. "Yes sir! We have it!"

"Good, then tomorrow you can go to this dump with Emerson and Private Beaumont and see what you can find. The rest of us will continue to search for any equipment that might be lying around."

The next morning we left bright and early. We headed for the eastern side of Caen. That had been the last to be liberated. It was a long shot but we needed more guns and grenades. We were on our way back, in the late afternoon, when we stumbled upon our greatest find. Just before noon we had met some Canadian soldiers. They were led by a sergeant and they were heading to the camp where the prisoners were being held before being shipped back to England. They were escorting ten soldiers. It had been tempting to ask for their uniforms but I knew that would not go down well. However I saw two Canadians pulling a handcart and it was stacked with weapons.

I pounced. "Sergeant, have you got a moment?"

He took in my flashes and grinned, "A Commando. My cousin was on the Dieppe raid. He spoke highly of you guys."

"Yes that was a hard battle. You had some good chaps there. Captain Friedmann, Sergeant Hutchinson, good chaps all."

"Jake Hutchinson! That's my cousin! What a small world! Sir do you mind if I shake you by the hand?" I held out my hand and he almost crushed it in his ham like fist. "Now then sir what can I do for you?"

"What are you going to do with those weapons?"

"These? We hand them over to the armourer." He shrugged, "After that ... Why sir?" I saw curiosity etched all over his face.

"You will have to trust me on this but we would like to take them off your hands. I can assure you it is for the good of the invasion but I can't tell you why."

He nodded, "Jake said that you guys got up to some weird stuff. I have your word that this is on the up and up sir? I wouldn't want to get my chops busted over this."

"Where is your HQ?

"By the Cathedral sir."

"Then I will pop along with a letter from my commanding officer. I will show it to your colonel. How's that?"

"You seem like a square guy captain and it will save us lugging this cart there." He turned, "Dwight, let the Captain and his men have the guns, grenades and ammo." He smiled, "Just for the record sir; not that I don't trust you but what is your name?"

"Captain Tom Harsker of Number 4 Commando; 1st Special Service Brigade."

His eyes widened, "The guys who came in on D-Day?"

"That's us."

He saluted, "An honour sir." He shouldered his rifle, "Right Corporal, these Krauts have sat on their butts long enough. Let's move!"

We were already in a good mood when we made our best find. We were passing a French garage. I had not noticed anything but Corporal Fletcher had. After we passed it he said, quietly, "Sir there's a rabbit away there."

"What do you mean?"

"As we came near they pulled down the roller shutter at the front. They did it really quickly like they were trying to hide summat."

"Nothing unusual in that is there?"

"There is sir. It is two o'clock. We have seen enough of the French to know that they like a long lunch. Now opening the shutters at two, that I could understand but not closing them. Besides they only did it when we were getting close. It was us as made them do it. Trust me on this one sir."

I had faith in Corporal Fletcher's instincts. "Hay and Wilkinson, get around the rear. Make sure no one leaves. The rest of you come with me."

I went to the front and banged on the shutter. There was silence and so I repeated the action. I then shouted, in English, "Open up! This is the British Army."

I heard French voices. One of them said, "What should we do?"

"I will go and speak with them. I will get rid of them. Shift it out of the back."

I heard the sound of exertions and then another shutter closed. A few minutes later the front shutter came up half way and a small man with greasy hands and wearing overalls ducked out from under it. He smiled and then fired a barrage of French at me, "What do you want? We are law abiding citizens. I shall complain!" He smiled again. Obviously he did not know I could speak French.

I said, in perfect French, "And to whom would you complain? If you like I can find a gendarme or perhaps we should go to the mayor? Maybe the Provost Marshal?" Just then I heard shouts from the rear. The man looked at me startled. "Yes," I smiled, "I have men at the back too. Corporal Fletcher open the shutter. Shepherd cover him!"

Corporal Fletcher flung the shutter up. The Frenchman tried to run but Shepherd smacked him on the back of the head with his rifle. He did not hit him hard; just enough to make him drop to the ground and hold his head. The garage had a long bay leading to the rear where there was another shutter. Fletcher flung that one open too and I saw a Kübelwagen and three men being covered by Bill Hay and Joe Wilkinson. A fourth man lay on the ground holding his bleeding nose.

I grabbed the Frenchman and snapped at him, "So, you are a collaborator! You help the Germans!"

He dropped to his knees. He was now petrified. Collaborators could be tarred and feathered and in extreme cases hanged. "No, sir! I beg of you! We found the car. It had run out of fuel. Please! Just take it but do not tell people that we are collaborators."

"Will it run now?"

He nodded; eager to please. "Yes we had just finished trying it out when you came."

"Shepherd, drive it back. Bill go with him. Put it behind our building and hide it with tarpaulin." I leaned in to the Frenchman as my two men jumped in the vehicle, "I am going to be around here for a while. If I come back and find anything German in here...." I left the sentence hanging.

"I promise you we are loyal Frenchmen!"

"Very well. I will trust you."

We hurried back to the landing craft. We had had a result I could not have imagined when we set out. We now had a perfectly working Kübelwagen and enough guns for the whole section. We could cobble together everything else we needed.

Lieutenant Ross and my two foragers looked dejected when we met them. "Sorry sir. We have one beaten up Kübelwagen and spares but it will take at least three days to get her running."

I nodded. "Come with me." I led them to the back of the building. Shepherd and Bill were there. I nodded and, like a pair of magicians, they whipped off the tarpaulin. "How about a fully working, recently serviced one then! We are in business!"

Our success buoyed everyone. Lieutenant Ross stopped being the schoolboy who was out of his depth. He threw himself into the work with the rest of my section. As my engineers worked on the vehicle next day and Polly had the men stripping and cleaning the weapons, I sent him to find as many aerial photographs of Trun as he could get. I went to the recently captured airfield. I borrowed a bicycle from the harbourmaster. I found an airfield that had been badly bombed by the RAF. There were more pot holes and bomb craters than runway. I decided to play the dad card. I found the officer who was in charge of the airfield pending the arrival of the squadron which would operate out of it.

Squadron Leader Betts was a harassed looking officer. He was in his shirt sleeves and puffing on a cigarette when I found him.

"Sir, could I have a word?"

He turned round and snapped, "Yes? What do you want?" when I approached him.

I smiled. That was often the best way. "I just wondered when the field would be operational?" I thought he was going to explode. I held out my hand. "The name is Harsker, Captain Harsker of the Commandos."

I saw him ready to tear me a new throat and then he stopped. "You aren't related to the ace from the Great War are you?"

I nodded, "He is my father." He obviously didn't know that the field he was repairing would be used by Dad.

He shook his head, "Sorry for my reaction but things are a little fraught here at the moment." He waved his hand. "We have at least six days work here. Why do you ask if the field is ready?"

"I need a favour. Have you a little spotter here?" This was disingenuous of me for I had already seen the Lysander on the far side of the runaway, The Lysander had a very short take off and landing. It was perfect; even on a field as damaged as this.

"Yes we have one over there. We use it to run errands back to Blighty. It is my little taxi. My job is to help engineers set up new airfields. Why?"

"I wondered if I could borrow it."

"I am far too busy to fly you anywhere. Sorry and all that."

"I can fly it. Dad taught me. I have a pilot's licence."

He laughed. "I have never met your dad but from what I have heard you sound exactly like him. What do you need it for?"

I felt I could trust this officer. Sometimes you had to take a chance. "Look sir. Me and my section are going behind enemy lines soon. We have the aerial photographs but I want to have a look see myself." He nodded, "Winston Churchill himself is backing this sir."

He hesitated then said, "Oh what the hell. It's only a glorified taxi anyway. The Typhoons arrive next week. Just bring her back eh? She's a nice little beastie!"

"Is she gassed up, sir?"

"You are keen aren't you? Yes she's ready."

"Thanks sir. I owe you a favour for this."

"Make it a whisky when the mess is open and we are quits!"

Chapter 5

It was a nice little bus to fly. It had an incredibly short take off and I easily avoided the craters and pot holes. As I headed north east I kept low. The reconnaissance photographs had shown the land from a higher altitude than I wanted. I needed to see it closer up and this was the best way. The problem would be the Germans. I would be an inviting target for any who had a rifle. I had forgotten to ask if the two machine guns in the wheel fairings were armed. I would have to rely on my skills as a pilot but with a fifty feet wingspan I was a big target. It was the same wingspan as the Gunbus Dad had flown in the Great War.

I kept high when I left the airfield. The front line was not far away. I crossed the main road and the aeroplane was peppered by German bullets. I was far enough away for most of them to miss but the Squadron Leader would have a few holes in his 'nice little beastie'! I turned east and followed the D13 road. It would be the road we would follow. I had crossed the front line and there was less gunfire. The road was bordered by hedges. I saw German vehicles on the road. There were not many. Dad had told me that the RAF Typhoons were causing mayhem to any vehicles which risked the road in daylight. They would be as great a danger to us as the Germans.

I knew there were anti aircraft guns ringing Trun. However I had to risk getting as low as I could. I turned north so that I could sweep over where the dump was supposed to be. I took the Germans by surprise. They heard my engine, the Bristol Mercury was not a quiet one, but they looked for me higher in the sky. When I zipped over at a hundred and eighty miles an hour just a hundred feet in the air I was gone before they could cock their rifles. I saw the nasty looking guns which were in sandbagged emplacements and then I was over their defences. I found the road which passed the dump and saw what Private Beaumont meant. The storms of a week or so ago had dumped a great deal of rain and the muddy churned up ground on both sides of the road by the sandbags and barrier were a clear sign. I had found the entrance. I could not see the pumping station but the two parked Kübelwagens, machine guns and barrier were enough. If we could get close then we would find them. I knew where the front door was. Of the fuel dump all I could see was camouflage netting. At this low altitude it was obvious.

I turned south as bullets smacked my tail. I headed for Guêprei. It was a narrow road but, flying at a hundred feet above the ground I saw that something big used it for there were broken branches clearly visible on the overhanging trees. The river at Guêprei was not wide but there was a steep bank. If the bridge was destroyed then tanks would not be able to use it.

The eighty eights around it would need to be taken out before we could blow the bridges. There were two of them and that meant at least twenty men; ten per gun. I was too low for them to hit. Their fuses would be set for aircraft at a higher altitude. Turning east I headed back for Caen and passed the second bridge. It was slightly wider but I could see it would not represent a problem. That too had two anti aircraft guns. Our biggest problem would be getting there.

As I flew back to the field I saw that if the bridges were destroyed it would force the entire German army to use the road leading to Argentan in the south and that was where the Americans were. The British and the Canadians would be the rock and the Americans the hard place. I saw the semblance of a strategy. Now that we had Caen and with the Americans surging from the south there was a chance that we could catch Jerry napping.

I climbed to avoid the gunfire at the frontline. I was helped by a squadron of tank busting Typhoons heading in the opposite direction. I began descending as they roared overhead. As I made my approach I couldn't help remembering the early, dark days of the war when I had dodged the Stuka dive bombers as the Loyal Lancashires had retreated. Then we had feared air superiority. Now we had it and I knew exactly how the Germans felt.

The landing was as short as the take off and I taxied it back to where I had found it. Squadron Leader Betts, pipe in mouth, strolled over and put his fingers in the holes of the tail. He shook his head, "My poor little beastie! What has this mad man done to you?"

"Sorry sir."

He smiled, "I got on to my superiors after you left. You didn't tell me that your father was coming over to take charge."

"Sorry sir. I wasn't told to tell anyone."

"Quite right too. I was also told to help you in any way I could." He tapped his pipe out on his heel. "I was told that Winnie himself approved this. You watch out for yourself eh?" He pointed to my battledress. "You are modest. You have the V.C. and M.C. and don't wear the fruit salad. Don't be a hero eh?"

"The battle dress is just for missions sir. I am proud to wear my ribbons but this is neither the time nor the place. Everyone here is a hero."

"Well I won't keep you. I put your bicycle in the office. There are black marketeers who would take the pennies from a corpse!"

By the time I reached the river it was late afternoon and there was no sign of any of my men. Bill Leslie came on deck and pointed. "They are round the back of your building, sir. They managed to get what you wanted. They are slaving away right now! Do you fancy a brew?"

"If there is one handy. I managed to miss lunch."

"I'll get you a corned dog buttie too. Skipper got some French mustard. It isn't as hot as English but it livens up the corned dog!"

I enjoyed chatting to Bill. We had watched this war together. From different services and different backgrounds we found it easy to talk to each other. Fate kept throwing us together. I thought it was a good thing as we seemed to bring each other luck. We had both seen men die but we had survived.

The Dijon mustard on the sandwich helped and the sweet tea washed it down beautifully. "Well I had better get back to work. Thanks for the tea, Chief."

"No problem sir." As he took the mug he said, "Did you hear about Lieutenant Jorgenson and the lads from the *'Lucky Lady'*?"

"No. I have not seen them since Italy and Sicily."

"Skipper said he heard they were either captured or killed off the Yugoslavian coast. They went out and never came back. The fly boys saw the wreckage of their ship. Skipper knew him and that's how he found out. Thought you ought to know."

"Thanks Bill. They were tough lads. They might have survived."

"Aye sir. Best to look on the bright side eh but it makes you think. Here we are in France. If the papers are right and we can get to Germany soon then the war will be over. It would be daft to get killed now wouldn't it?"

I pointed to the half demolished buildings all around us, "If the Germans fight this hard for a piece of France imagine what they would do in Germany! No Bill, the war isn't going to end any day soon and we have to keep on doing what we have been. The moment we think we are going to survive..."

"Is the moment you find a bullet with your name on it. You are right, sir."

As I approached the area behind the building I heard the sound of banging and clanging. I saw that they had rigged the camouflage netting and some tarpaulin over the back yard and beneath it the whole section were busy putting together our second Kübelwagen . Freddie Emerson was as black as the ace of spades and his hands were covered in grease and oil. He had a cigarette stuck in the corner of his mouth and he looked as though Christmas and his birthday had come at once.

"We found everything we needed, sir! We found one with a decent body and there was a spare engine. We even have spare tyres."

"Good. Well done lads. Now will it run?"

Private Beaumont looked offended, "Sir, do you doubt us? By the time we are finished we could win the Le Mans twenty four hour race!"

"Good. Where is Lieutenant Ross?"

Polly said, "In the office sir."

The office was just two packing cases with a piece of wood on top and an old armchair we had salvaged from a bombed out house. The radio was next to it and the walls were festooned with maps. He jumped up to attention when I entered. "I have told you before John we don't bother with formality here. You did well with the scavengers."

He smiled, "That Fletcher is something else, sir. He seems to have a nose for this sort of thing. They were more than happy to let us lift whatever we wanted. The Army even loaned us a lorry to tow the Kübelwagen back. Lance Sergeant Hay said we could fit the MG 42 to one of them."

I nodded, "That would be fine. It takes the same ammo as the other guns. I am not going to bother taking the MG 40 we found. Different calibre."

"Did you manage to recce sir?"

"Yes I took a Lysander up and scouted out the dump. I think I know where the entrance is but it is guarded. Do we have the same timetable?"

"It might be delayed, sir but not by much. We are still talking about the beginning of next week. We have only just secured the crossing of the Orne. The Germans are just on the other side of the river. I think they are still trying to land the tanks which will make the attack."

"That gives us four days then. Remember, John, that once we start we can't stop. If the attack is delayed after we leave you can't get in touch with us."

"But Fletcher has the radio."

"And we won't use that until the dump is blown. We don't want British signals to be picked up behind the German lines. Major Foster knows that." I could see he looked worried. This was not like the war games he had played when training. This was real life. "We have done this before. If we blow the dump up early it has the same effect. I have seen the bridges. When they are destroyed we will be in the driving seat. I can see now why this mission is so important."

When I told the men the new timetable they worked even harder. We worked after dark. While those with mechanical skills put together the repaired Kübelwagen I sat with Wilkinson, Hewitt and Fletcher. We went through the papers we had gathered and the uniforms. As Joe Wilkinson and I would be doing all the talking he would wear the sergeant's uniform and I would wear the officer's. I had already decided to hedge our bets by making two teams. We had Private Beaumont in my vehicle and Shepherd, the other explosives expert, with Wilkinson in the second. If one team was out of action then the other could complete the operation.

We had four complete sets of papers. I would take two for my team and Wilkinson could have the other two. Billy Hay would be with Wilkinson and so we fitted the machine gun to his vehicle. We only had four Colts with silencers. We would need those. The one weapon we had in abundance were grenades, both English and German. We had plenty of parachute cord and we had the ability to make booby traps.

The work on the vehicles was finished with a whole day to spare. That meant we could go through everything in detail before we left on the next night. I knew that the Germans would be using the roads and two more Kübelwagen might not be noticed. I had made a sketch map and the men all copied it. Lieutenant Ross had arranged for us to cross over at the sector guarded by the Canadians. They would open fire, using blanks of course, as we headed towards the German lines. We hoped that the Germans would believe that we had escaped by the skin of our teeth.

"All of you have a few words of German but let Lance Corporal Wilkinson and I do all the talking. The papers we have are for the 342nd Division. They are hard lads and were based in Caen. We say we had been hiding out trying to get back. Emerson and Fletcher will be bandaged as though they have head wounds." I smiled, "Your German is awful! The less you speak the better!"

Sergeant Poulson said, "Scouse's English isn't much better sir!"

They laughed and it eased the tension.

I pointed to the map on the wall. "You all have your own copies. I hope you remembered to leave off the names. If you are captured just eat them."

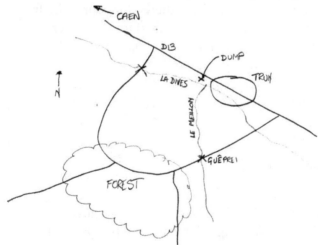

I used my Commando dagger to point out the pertinent features. "Our main target, as you can see, is the dump. I have flown over it. There is a small track leading off the main road to get to it. It is heavily churned up which means heavy lorries have been using it. The dump itself is invisible from the air. The only way I knew it was there was by the guards and sandbags. They have a couple of half-tracks there. We will drive up and use the silenced Colts to eliminate the sentries. I don't know exactly where the pumping station is but when we are on the ground we will have a better idea. Wilkinson, Shepherd and Private Beaumont will be in charge of the demolitions and the rest of us will stand guard. Private Beaumont?"

"We use a failsafe system sir. We use two sets of explosives and two sets of timers. It is unlikely that both will fail. You said ten minutes?"

"Yes. As you can see from the map we don't want to risk going through Trun. The road to the first bridge over the La Dives river is quiet. We drive there and set the charges."

"Sir, doesn't it make more sense to have one team setting the explosives on the bridge while the dump is being destroyed?"

"We can't take a chance, Joe. The main target is the dump. However, you are right about the two targets. While your team blows up that bridge I will take the other and we will blow the second bridge at Guêprei."

Sergeant Poulson said, "I know I am not going on this sir but I see a fairly major flaw in this plan."

I did not tell him that I already knew it. I let him explain. "Go on Sergeant."

"Well sir, it seems to me that you are burning all your bridges, quite literally. How do you get back?"

I nodded, "Quite right. To the west of the forest there is a road which heads north west. It is not a large road but it is straight. When I flew back I didn't see any signs of military there. Of course the front is fluid and there may be soldiers and units I failed to see. After we have set the charges we rendezvous in the forest where the road heads south west."

"Doesn't that lead to Falaise sir?"

"It does indeed, Lieutenant Ross, but we will have turned off before then."

Bill Hay nodded, "Seems fairly straight forward sir. If we leave after dark we have a good chance of travelling back in daylight. That might be a bit tricky eh, sir."

"That, Lance Sergeant Hay, is the problem. We either lay up during the day and travel back at night which just increases the risk of being caught or we cross early in the day."

Corporal Fletcher nodded, "Anyway sir we never know what problems are going to happen. We might have to lay up anyway. For me the plan is sound as a pound, sir!"

I shook my head, "Thank you for the vote of confidence, Corporal Fletcher. Fortunately this is neither a democracy nor a debating club. We go with my plan."

I had not put him out and he grinned, "Great by me, sir!"

Sergeant Poulson and Lieutenant Ross went, the next day, to liaise with the Canadians who would be making it look as though we were Germans. I had the rest of the men practise their German. It stopped them worrying about the mission and would, in the long run, help us. I would be in the

Kübelwagen we had taken from the French black marketeer. Fred Emerson was happy to be driving the vehicle he had repaired. Lance Sergeant Hewitt would drive ours leaving me to use the silenced Colt, if necessary, and to do the talking. Just before we left I had the men take out any papers which might be used by Jerry. It was second nature to us now but Lance Corporal Wilkinson was new. He just had one letter with him but it was from his young lady. We left it on the boat.

We had two military police motor cycles as our escorts but, as there was still a blackout and a curfew, we hoped we would not be noticed. Unless there was a German spy with a transmitter we would be safe. Our radio was in the back seat with Corporal Fletcher. There was not a great deal of space.

When we reached the jump off point the two motor cycles left us. We were just a hundred yards from the last houses and ahead of us lay hedge lined fields and the German front lines. A Canadian Major grinned when he saw us. "A good job you warned us. I would have taken you for Germans."

I smiled and, clicking my heels together, said in German, "That is good because we are Germans!"

He laughed, "Damned good!"

"By the way I wanted to thank your chaps for letting us have these weapons. I told them I would tell you."

"They mentioned it. As soon as they said you were Commandos I knew what to expect." He turned as a camouflaged sergeant and private came from the darkness. "Well McCormack?"

"There is a machine gun post four hundred yards up the road sir. I don't think the road is mined."

I nodded, "We will soon find out. "Well no point in hanging around. Thanks for your help Major and hopefully we will see you soon. Lieutenant Ross, Sergeant Poulson, have the kettle on ready eh?" I sat down. "Fletcher, start to play dead! Well Lance Sergeant, we might as well go. No lights and put your foot down. Don't stop unless I tell you to."

"Jawohl!"

He started the engine and began to drive. The Major shouted, "Open fire!"

All hell broke loose. They had rifles and machine guns chattering away. All of them were firing in the air so that there was no chance of them hitting us. They even took the opportunity of sending a grenade from a grenade launcher away to our right. In the back seat Private Beaumont fired his Mauser rifle in the air. It had a different sound to ours. Ahead of us I saw tracer as the Germans fired. Then the Major fired a flare high into the sky. It was a calculated move. We wanted them to see us. The sight of two Kübelwagen filled with Germans might make them hesitate. We just needed to be beyond their front line and then we would disappear. The firing from the Germans stopped and I saw the machine gun as we passed it. Then the Lance Sergeant stood on the brakes. There was a moveable barbed wire barrier before us.

A Waffen SS sergeant stepped out of the dark with a submachine aimed at us. Fletcher managed a moan. I said, "Thank God we have made it. Do you have a doctor? Schwarz here has been hit!"

"Where the hell have you come from? I thought the last of our boys escaped four days ago."

I nodded, "We broke down and had to hide up in a warehouse. We were lucky but we lost four men when they found us. We had to run for it. Have you a doctor?"

Lance Corporal Wilkinson shouted from the second vehicle, "Sergeant, Private Muller is in a bad way."

The Sergeant pointed, "The nearest is in Trun. It is twenty miles down the road."

"Then we had better hurry. Schwarz is a brave man."

The Sergeant shouted, "Move the barrier and then watch out. Those Canadians might take advantage of the situation."

As soon as the barrier was moved Hewitt put the accelerator to the floor. The French mechanics had done a first rate job and we sped into the night. The first part of our operation had been successful. Would we have as much luck for the rest of it?

Chapter 6

We made good time for the first ten miles and then we ran into traffic. It was all coming the other way. The roads were so narrow in places that we barely squeezed past the tanks and lorries heading to the front. It slowed us up. However each time the road was clear Hewitt put his foot down and we tried to make up the lost time. Once we had passed through the tiny hamlet of Le Marais-la-Chapelle I motioned for Hewitt to slow down. We were under two miles away from our target and I was looking for somewhere to stop before we reached the dump. We were helped by the petrol bowser coming towards us which had dimmed lights and turned off the road towards the dump. I jumped out. Bill Hay followed me from the second. We did not say a word. The rest of the team knew the plan.

Bill and I darted through the hedgerow. It was thinner on the ground than it looked from the air. Once through I saw the camouflage netting which was strung over the concrete. There looked to be concrete domes stretching as far as we could see in the limited light. We went back through the hedgerow and made our way along the outside. When we reached the intersection we dropped to our knees and I took out the silenced Colt. I peered around the side. There, two hundred yards from us, was the sandbagged entrance to the dump. The German petrol bowser was reversing in through the entrance. The attention of the sentries was on the vehicle. They were using torches to help guide the driver in. Moving in the shadow of the hedge made it easy for us. German efficiency was working against them. They had hidden the dump from the air and in doing so had provided us with cover.

We made it to within thirty feet of the sandbags. There was just one half-track now and the fuel bowser. We crouched in the bottom of the hedge. I saw the bowser as it backed down a slight slope. I wondered if it would disappear altogether but the cab remained visible. I saw the driver switch off the engine and get out. His assistant disappeared down the slope. Then we heard the whine of a motor. The driver came over to speak to the sentries who were close enough for us to hear. We were also able to count them. There were four sentries.

"You are going to be busy later. Another regiment of tanks has arrived in Flers and they are dry as a bone. More tankers are coming!"

The sergeant in charge laughed sardonically, "Well they better hurry or the Tommies will have them. They love to catch easy targets like tankers on the road."

"They are just an hour behind me. There will not be a problem."

"There will, my friend. You will need another fifteen minutes before you are fuelled. It is a thirty minute turnaround. The only way we can service a large number is if they arrive as soon as it is dark."

"You had better tell them at headquarters."

He laughed again, "The Generals are changed on a daily basis. My orders come from a Colonel in Falaise!"

I hoped that Hewitt and Wilkinson would have the sense to wait until the petrol tanker had left. If not then we were in trouble.

The sergeant was wrong. They managed to fill the tanker in ten minutes. It struggled to get up the rise and then passed us as it headed for the road. The sentries took the opportunity to light up now that the danger of igniting fuel had passed. The sound of the bowser could still be heard when our two Kübelwagens appeared. I pointed to the two men on my left and Bill nodded. He would take those two out. I would deal with the sergeant and the other. What we did not know was who manned the pumps.

The Sergeant angrily stubbed out his cigarette, "What do you want?"

Joe pointed to the back seat, "We have a wounded man here."

"What do you think we are, a damned hospital? This is a restricted area. Push off!"

As soon as Joe stood we both fired. Corporal Fletcher's gun came up as well and he fired two silenced shots. The four men that Bill and I had aimed at fell dead. They had been less than thirty feet away. It was harder to miss than to hit. We stood and ran to look down the slope. There were two dead soldiers lying at the foot of the slope. Fletcher had hit them. I could now see the pumps. They were well below the level of the road.

"Hewitt, Emerson get the vehicles turned around. Private Beaumont, Shepherd, do your stuff." The rest of us dragged the bodies away from the sandbags. We quickly took their papers and weapons. "Bill, booby trap the half-track."

"We should take it, sir. Handy vehicle."

"It will slow us down."

"Lance Corporal Wilkinson take Corporal Fletcher and get back up the road. There are more petrol tankers coming. Stop them and tell them there is a fuel leak and they will have to wait!"

"Right sir."

I went down the slope. Shepherd was already setting charges to the pumps. "Where is Private Beaumont?"

"He went down there to the tanks."

I walked down the slope. It was eerily empty. The camouflage netting worked. I had seen nothing from the air. I found Private Beaumont. He was standing on top of one of the concrete domes. "Can we do anything with them?"

"They are well designed, sir. But there is a chance. They have a metal inspection hatch on the top. It would have to be a direct hit on the actual top to blow them. We can rig something there and hope for a chain reaction."

"We have less than an hour."

"Then we will just have to set charges on two. Send Ken down when he has finished, sir."

"Don't hang about will you?"

"If we make a mistake, sir, then we will just kill us and hardly damage the dump. We have to do this right."

I nodded and ran back, "Shepherd take the rest of the explosives and join Private Beaumont."

The others had finished. Joe and Scouse were at the main road and the rest were waiting in the Kübelwagens. "It will take time. As soon as Private Beaumont and Shepherd arrive drive like the devil is behind us."

I quickly reloaded my Colt. I had only fired two bullets but two bullets could be the difference between life and death. That done I ran to the crossroads. "Anything?"

"A little bit of traffic, sir, but no tankers."

"Good. You did well, Lance Corporal. I was impressed with the way you handled the German sergeant."

He shook his head, "Sir, your whole team is the best I have ever seen. I thought our brigade was good but..."

I nodded, "We won't be long. Keep a sharp watch!"

I was beginning to worry. It was forty minutes since the tanker driver had said his colleagues were an hour behind. I saw that Emerson and Hewitt were ready behind the wheel. Bill Hay was watching the hedges as though a Waffen S.S. battalion might emerge. Emerson said, nervously, "So far so good eh sir?"

"Thanks for the work on the vehicles, Fred. They are a credit to you."

"I like working on cars, sir. When this is over I reckon I might open a garage. If that greasy Frog can do it then why not me?"

Private Beaumont and Shepherd came racing up. Private Beaumont nodded, "Fifteen minute fuses, sir. I reckon we should shift."

"Right lads, all aboard!"

I jumped in and Hewitt floored it. They raced to the crossroads. Joe Wilkinson pointed down the road, "Sir, lights! It is the tankers!"

"It is too late to worry now! Follow us!"

We raced down the road. It did not matter now if we made noise. It was four minutes since the fuses had been set. They could not be disarmed but we now had the pressure of getting to the two bridges. We only had a few more minutes on the road before we would turn off. Our turn off almost came too soon and Hewitt screeched the wheel as we spun onto the narrow lane between the high hedges. We had just over a mile and half until we rattled over the metal bridge. As Hewitt screeched to a halt an enormous explosion lit up the sky. It seemed to ripple and grow as the flames rose higher. The blast passed over us and we felt the concussion even at a distance of two miles. We even felt the ground shake as though there had been an earthquake. More explosions followed as the fire spread to other tanks. The air was filled with the smell of burning petrol. I wondered how much of it we had destroyed. There was no time for self-congratulation.

I pointed to the bridge and then held up my thumb. Lance Corporal Wilkinson held up his thumb. I turned to the Lance Sergeant, "Right John, we are on the last leg!"

We did not make such good time as we raced along the narrow lane. The forest seemed to be within touching distance. Hewitt had to drive carefully. A puncture could be disastrous. I noticed the road we would take later as we passed it. Guêprei was tiny. I counted four houses and all were well away from the bridge. That was good. I could hear the explosions from the north of us. The loop in the road had brought us around so that we were just a mile or two from it. The fact that no one had come from their homes showed that they were used to explosions in the night. The smell of burning fuel was wafted to us on the night breeze. I gambled on the fact that the Germans would be mystified as to the origins of the sabotage. Until they heard the sound of these two bridges being blown they might look elsewhere for us.

"Hewitt turn it around when the lads have set the explosives. Scouse, help Private Beaumont. I will keep watch." I walked back to the houses. I saw a flicker of a curtain. I stood in front of the doors. Eventually one of the doors opened and an old man stood there. He saw my uniform and his eyes widened.

I spoke French, "We are British soldiers and we are going to blow the bridge. If you stay indoors you will be safe. You will not be harmed."

He grinned, "The British and the Americans are coming?"

"Eventually. If the Germans asked tell them that you heard the explosion and that was the first you knew."

He nodded and held out his hand, "Thank you!" He shook my hand and closed the door.

I heard a whistle and ran back to the bridge. "All set sir. Ten minutes."

"It will be just the bridge won't it Private Beaumont?"

He shook his head, "Sir, are you doubting me? I promise you they will feel a slight breeze and that is all!"

I didn't believe that it would be as gentle as that but I trusted my young genius. "Right Hewitt, back to the rendezvous."

Even as we headed west we saw and heard the explosion from the other bridge. When ours went, as Sergeant Poulson had said, all our bridges would be blown. The other Kübelwagen was waiting for us at the road junction. Even as we pulled up there was the double crack as the carefully placed charges blew up the piers holding the bridge. Private Beaumont knew his business. He had used just enough explosives to destroy the bridge and no more.

We took the lead as we drove through the darkened forest. Dawn was not far away and we needed to be as close to our lines as possible. We took it steadily while making the fastest time that we could. Disaster came in the form of a laager of tanks which lay hidden in the forest. I saw the barrel of a gun jutting out. Hewitt saw it too and began to slow. This time the sentries did not have the benefit of a flare to see our German uniforms and vehicles. They heard the sound of the engines and they opened fire. Hewitt barely managed to stop the Kübelwagen as the front tyres were shredded. We were probably helped by the fact that two of them were hit.

"Out! Into the forest." Fletcher had the radio and Private Beaumont a Bergen. I just had grenades and my pistols. Those and my field glasses were all that I carried. We tumbled out of the Kübelwagen as quickly as we could. The small arms fired continued to rattle into the Kübelwagen even as we bailed out. I waved for the others to join us. Bill Hay led them from the second Kübelwagen. I just had time to jam a primed German grenade under the brake and then I followed my men into the woods. I did not fire back for the muzzle flash would give away our position. The Germans were firing blind. It was too dark to see us but soon it would be daylight and then the hunt would begin. When we were a hundred yards into the forest I whistled. The section stopped. We had run directly into the forest and were heading north but we had to make our way north west if we were to reach our lines. I tapped Private Beaumont's arm and handed him a German grenade. He opened his Bergen and began to take out grenades and cord. He and Shepherd made a line of them behind us. They would warn us of pursuit and slow it down. We were aided by the night. I pointed to Bill Hay and the rear. He nodded. I pointed to myself and led them north east. We stopped running and moved silently.

As soon as we set off I could heard the noise of pursuit. When I heard an explosion I knew they had found the booby trap in the Kübelwagen. I heard, too, the sound of a tank's engines being started. The noise of the heavy engine did not help us for it drowned out all the other noises. There could have been German soldiers all around us and we would not know. The silence of the night was shattered. I knew that the forest ended towards the north west and there would be open fields. We needed to cross into the fields in the night if we were to have any chance of escape.

As we hurried through the ever thinning forest I saw the black become a murky grey and knew it heralded dawn. Eventually we would need to ditch the German uniforms but I wanted to keep them for a little while longer. When we were spotted the slight hesitation when they saw German grey might just be the difference. I held my silenced Colt before me. It was fortunate that I did for otherwise when we stumbled upon the two Germans walking towards us, the sound of my shots might have drawn their companions to us. As it was I managed to lift the Colt and fire two shots into each of them before they knew we were there. I could not stop one of them crying out but I hoped that the sound of the tanks' engines to our left might mask his cry. The fact that there were men ahead of us now made caution even more imperative. Behind us was a double crack as two of Private Beaumont's booby traps were triggered. It was then that I saw the open fields ahead of us. There was a wire fence around the field and I saw dark shapes within. They had to be cattle. I took out my wire cutters and cut a hole to allow us through. We had less than twenty miles to go. On a good day we could run that in four hours. This was occupied France and it could take all day.

We sprinted across the field. The sun was rising behind us and was as good an indication of our direction as my compass. As it appeared over the trees I realised we were heading due west and I pointed to my right to take us in a more northerly direction. The cows obligingly moved out of the way. The farmhouse was to our left. I wanted to avoid that. I saw another hedge ahead and I put on a spurt to reach it. This time there was a farm gate and we clambered over it. Once on the other side I waved the men to the ground. I crawled back and lay beneath the gate looking back to the forest. The field we had crossed had been about two hundred yards wide. The cows moving back and forth helped to make it hard to see us but equally hard for me to see the Germans.

I took out the field glasses from beneath my German greatcoat. I saw the Germans as they found where we had cut the wire. One of them turned and shouted to his companions. Seven men headed through the field. I turned to the others and held up seven fingers. I pointed to my Colt. Fletcher, Hay and Shepherd all had silenced weapons. These were the last four in my section. If the Germans came close they would die silently. I watched the seven as they headed across the field. They were going to the farmhouse. Our booby traps came back to haunt me. The Germans did not bother to ask those within the farm questions; they used grenades and bullets. The fusillade and the cracks of grenades echoed to us. I could not see the result of the firing but the Germans would know we were not within. The French family whose cries we heard had paid the price for our sabotage.

I dared not move while the Germans were in the vicinity and so we waited. I was rewarded when I saw two heading back across the field towards the wire. That left just five Germans. I turned my field glasses back to the smoking farmhouse. I could not see the Germans. Then Emerson tapped me on the shoulder and pointed to our right. He cupped his ear. He was correct. There were Germans and they were walking towards us along the hedge. At first I could not make out their words but then I caught snatches of it.

".... Captain Sweinstiger."

"I know. He should have sent more men with us. Two Kübelwagens had to have more than four men in them."

One of the Germans laughed, "He said they might be deserters! The man is a fool. It was the resistance! Since the Amis came they have grown bolder. Shoot first boys. That is how you stay alive. When we have more men we can sweep up the rest of the locals and question them."

They were now almost upon us. I rolled over on to my back and held the Colt in two hands. As the first two Germans appeared I snapped, in German, "Drop your weapons!"

As the sergeant leading them swung his sub machine gun in my direction I fired two bullets at him and then swung to fire at the second. I heard the phut of the other's silenced weapons as my men fired through the hedge. The Germans died quickly.

"Get their grenades and let's get out of here quickly!"

I dumped my greatcoat. I would need it no longer and it promised to be a warm day. I kept my German field cap but jammed it in my battle dress. "We head north west and we need to run. They will miss these soon enough." Some of the others took the opportunity to shed their German greatcoats.

We ran. We kept to the sides of the fields. We had a start now and our running would extend that lead. They might have men on the roads but we would avoid them. Each time we reached another fence we halted to see if it was clear. We had two very small roads we crossed and they were both empty. It was eight o'clock when we heard the sound of aeroplane engines. It was a flight of Typhoons. They were diving to attack. For the briefest of moments I thought that they were attacking us but when I heard the whoosh of their rockets I knew they were attacking tanks. Their attack saved us for they hit something four hundred yards to the north of us. There was a loud explosion and a column of fire leapt into the air. We would have walked into them but for the arrival of the aeroplanes.

I heard, in the distance, gun fire and the sound of artillery and tanks. There was an attack. I wondered if it was Operation Totalize then I dismissed the thought. That was not due for at least five days. Whatever it was we were in the middle of it. "Ditch the Jerry uniforms. It looks like there is a battle ahead." The ones who still had greatcoats and caps threw them away.

Bill Hay shook his head, "And we are stuck in the middle of it! Every bugger will take pot shots at us."

"Corporal Fletcher as soon as we have an idea where we are get on the radio and tell Lieutenant Ross where we are."

"Right sir."

"Let's move. Hay, you can be rear guard."

I led them further west than we had been heading. The pall of smoke in the sky told me that there were Germans there. I knew we would have to pass by Germans at some point. I just wanted to be closer to our lines when I did so. We scrambled across fields and hid in whatever cover we could find. Above us were aeroplanes; Luftwaffe and RAF. We heard the chattering of their guns when they met. We took cover whenever we heard engines above us. We were behind the lines and fair game for the RAF as well as the enemy. What saved us was the river. We almost stumbled into it. We were forced to take cover when a diving pair of Spitfires took us for Germans. We dived through a hedge and tumbled down the bank of the Dives.

After they had gone we rose, dripping, from the water. "We'll follow this for a while. I know it is taking us away from Caen but we have cover from the trees. Corporal Fletcher, see if you can get a signal and tell the Lieutenant where we are. The rest of you eat and drink. We can fill our bottles from the river." I finished off the last of my water and then refilled it. I slipped in the water purification tablet and shook it up. I took out the biscuits I had brought with me. They were largely crumbs but the sugar in them would keep me going.

"Sorry sir. There is too much other radio traffic and they are using our frequency. From what I heard it was Canadians and Poles chattering away."

"That makes sense. They were holding the sector. Right, follow me."

I headed upstream. We were able to walk in the water at the sides where it was shallow and when it became deeper we scrambled up the bank. We made half a mile before we hit trouble. I saw a bridge ahead and realised it was manned. I moved ahead using the cover of the trees. There was a gap of twenty yards before we could reach the cover of the bridge itself. We would have to move cautiously. I watched the parapet and when the sentries' attention was not on our side I waved pairs of my men through. It seemed to take forever but eventually they all made it. I knew we would not be able to continue upstream so long as they were there. I had counted four of them but I knew there could be more. I took one of the German grenades and broke the porcelain top. I rested the bottom on a piece of driftwood from the bank which I propped against the trunk and tied the cord to a branch of a willow. It balanced. The weight of the falling grenade would set it off. I just needed something to trigger it. Picking up a stone from the river I watched the sentries and, when they turned, ran to join my men.

The grenade, hanging by its cord, was thirty feet from me. I was about to throw the stone when Corporal Fletcher grabbed my arm. Shaking his head he took the stone from me. I nodded. He had a good arm and a better eye for this sort of thing than me. He threw the stone and it knocked away the prop. The grenade fell and we dived to the ground. Shrapnel rattled into the bridge as the grenade exploded and we were all deafened. I stood and ran upstream. My men followed me. As I emerged I saw that the Germans had left the bridge to investigate the explosion. The river looped to our left and we made the shelter of some more trees within forty yards of the bridge. I looked back through the trees. The Germans were now scanning both sides of the river. We had a lead again. But we had also notified the Germans that there were enemies close by.

Chapter 7

We hurried up the stream. Shaded by overhanging branches and shallow at the edges, it made perfect cover. We travelled another mile or so and I checked my watch. It was almost two o'clock in the afternoon. I took out my map and realised that our deviation up the river had added six miles to our journey. We still had fifteen miles to go. I knew we would have to hide up. We had used up all of our luck already. I saw, on the map, a Château, Venduevre. It was more than likely to be occupied by Germans but it looked to have extensive grounds and we could hide there. It would be the last place they would expect to find British soldiers and we could then use the river to get to a road and back to our own lines.

The trees were much thicker the nearer we came to the Château. I guessed they used it for hunting before the war and I risked walking in the woods. It was faster going and we made better progress. I saw, through the trees, the German flag above and knew that we were close to the Château. I circled my arm signifying that we should make camp. I headed towards the edge of the trees. I crept to the eaves of the forest and took out my field glasses. The Château had sentries but they were over four hundred yards from us across neatly manicured lawns. There were many cars parked outside and they looked to be staff cars although there was one armoured car. I deduced the Germans had used this as some sort of local headquarters. As I watched I saw a great deal of activity. Officers left the building and jumped into cars. Others shouted orders to those who were still within. Then two German lorries arrived and soldiers jumped out of the back. I wondered if they were coming for us and then I saw them run inside. I had intended just to check on our safety but now I was intrigued. As soon as I saw the soldiers emerge with boxes I knew what was happening. They were evacuating the building. We had a chance to escape sooner than I had expected.

I went back to the men, "We have had a bit of luck. Jerry is evacuating the building. We will keep watch and when they have gone we will be able to head back to Caen in the confusion. Joe, go back to the edge of the forest and keep watch. Let me know when the lorries have gone." I gave him my binoculars.

"Right sir."

"Corporal Fletcher, try the radio again." He set it up and charged it. He put on the headphones and turned the dial. "The rest of you get food and take on water. Check your guns. We will be in action soon."

I took my own advice and drank some water. Fletcher shook his head. "Still nothing sir. Just a lot of German and Polish.

"Keep trying. I will go and check out the Château again." I went to the edge of the woods and found a camouflaged Lance Corporal Wilkinson. He was prone and peering at the Germans. "Three or four cars have just gone, sir, and the crew has just got into the armoured car."

"That means they are leaving."

Private Beaumont ran up and whispered, "Sir, Scouse has Sergeant Poulson on the radio."

I ran back with Private Beaumont and Fletcher put the headphones on my ears and handed me the microphone, "Poulson?"

"Yes sir."

"We are at the Château Venduevre. It looks like Jerry is evacuating it. We are going to head into Caen as soon as they do. Have Lieutenant Ross warn the Canadians and Poles that we are on our way and we are back in British uniforms. It is likely we might be driving German vehicles."

"Right sir."

I took off the headphones and gave the microphone back to Corporal Fletcher. "Get ready to move. Jerry is on his way out of the Château. With any luck we can use the confusion to head back to our lines."

I rejoined Wilkinson. He pointed, "There is still one truck left sir but the armoured car has gone to the gate."

I looked at my watch. It was almost four o'clock. "You have good eyes, Wilkinson." I took my binoculars from him and scanned the vehicles. I saw that he was right the other truck and the armoured car were waiting with a Kübelwagen at the entrance. There were still four cars and another Kübelwagen in front of the Château. When I saw the flag being lowered I knew that they would not be long. As Corporal Fletcher joined us I saw the soldiers emerge from the Château and this time when they had filled the truck they climbed on board.

"Right lads, let's move. Keep low and let's be sharpish eh?"

We spread out and ran through the formal gardens. The topiary and hedges would give us some cover and yet allow us to keep an eye on the enemy. I saw the truck leave. It disappeared from sight behind a line of Cypress trees and then reappeared again by the gate. I hoped that the convoy would leave and we might be able to get our hands on a German vehicle.

When we were a hundred yards away I saw that there were just two vehicles left, a Kübelwagen and a staff car. The soldiers taking down the flag were urged on by an officer standing on the running board of the staff car. Glancing to my left I saw that the other vehicles had gone. I drew my Colt. As we neared them the officer saw us. He began to pull his gun and he shouted to his men. I dropped to one knee and took aim. The rest of my section drew their weapons and did the same. I hit the officer with my first bullet. One of the soldiers managed to get a couple of shots off but there were eight of us with automatics and we rarely missed. All seven Germans fell.

"Sir, Wilkinson is hit!"

"Hewitt see to him. Emerson and Shepherd you two drive." I went with Hewitt to Lance Corporal Wilkinson. He had been hit in the shoulder.

"Sir, keep pressure on this will you while I get another dressing out."

I pushed the dressing into the wound. Wilkinson shook his head, "Just my rotten luck."

Hewitt said, "You'll be all right Joe. It just nicked your shoulder. It looks worse than it is."

"No, Sarge, it means they will send me back to Blighty and I like being with you blokes!"

"Sir, we are good to go!"

"We wait for Wilkinson!" Hewitt and I manhandled him to the staff car. It had more room in it. The building stood with doors swinging open. It had been truly abandoned. I shouted, "Have your guns ready. We are not wearing German uniforms but the car and the Kübelwagen might just slow their reactions." I patted Emerson on the knee, "Drive but remember the Kübelwagen will be slower than us."

"Aye sir. This is a nice little motor!" We drove out through the gates. I had seen the convoy head left down the main road. "Go straight across!" There was a minor road ahead and I had seen, on the map, that it twisted and turned but eventually it would take us to Caen.

It was a narrow road. The German staff car had a small flag on the front. It made the German lorry we met coming the other way pull to one side. As we passed I saw the look of surprise on the German faces as they saw the British passengers. One of them pulled out a gun but Bill Hay, in the Kübelwagen, sprayed him with his sub machine gun. Private Beaumont hurled a grenade and, as we disappeared down the road, I saw the lorry catch fire as the grenade exploded under the rear.

We would now be more likely to be spotted. Since the gun fire in the fields and the attacks in the morning we had heard little gunfire. Whatever had gone on had now stopped. I knew it could not be the offensive but something had happened. We were in the dark. It could have been a German offensive or the Canadians could have started early. It made no difference to us for either would make the Germans we encountered more nervous and likely to fire first. The machine gun and the grenade would alert those ahead of us. I took out my Luger and a Mills bomb. I made sure my window was wound down as Emerson took us down the narrow country Normandy lanes. If we met any more Germans I would be ready. We were so close to Caen now that it was almost in touching distance.

63

We left the narrow lane and found ourselves on a larger road when we reached Bellengreville. We were less than a mile from the front line. We would need to find somewhere to dump the cars and sneak across after dark. Although it was a larger road it was filled with Germans. This time they were more observant. As we turned a corner, there, ahead of us, I saw a machine gunner by the side of the road. He had to swing his machine gun towards us. I put the Luger out of the window and emptied the magazine. The gunner and his loader were less than twenty feet from me and both fell. I was not certain that they were dead. Ahead I saw Germans turning to face us. "Fred turn right!"

He threw the wheel over and we hurtled down a lane just as wide as the car. There was a tearing sound as the paint was taken from the doors and the rear wheel arches were torn off. The Kübelwagen was smaller but I saw that two wheels almost lifted as it took the corner. There was the rattle of gunfire but we were briefly hidden. The lane had houses down the side. It was heading north, away from Caen.

"Follow this road until we are out of sight of the Germans. The more twists and turns the better."

As Emerson took another bend I saw, to my horror, that it was a dead end. We were trapped. There was no point in bemoaning our ill luck. We were Commandos and we would work our way out of the situation.

"Everybody out!" I jumped out with my Colt ready. The Kübelwagen screeched to a halt but Shepherd applied the brakes too late and he slammed into the back of the German staff car. "Get Wilkinson out and head west. Corporal Fletcher, leave the radio in the Kübelwagen. I am going to blow them up. Now run. Bill, stay with me!" I saw that ahead of us was a wall. It would disguise us if they could get Wilkinson over it. He was a big man.

Hay had the German submachine gun. I took the pin out of the Mills bomb just as a handful of Germans raced around the corner. Bill gave a short burst with his submachine gun and I dropped the grenade to the floor of the staff car. "Run!"

When we clambered over the wall I saw that Shepherd and Hewitt were supporting Lance Corporal Wilkinson. The other three were heading across the field of wheat. It left five of us to fight the Germans. Just then there was an enormous double explosion. The second was far bigger than a grenade alone. The petrol tank must have ignited. It would slow the pursuit. I shouted, "Private Beaumont, take point. Find us a way through!"

"Sir!!

We hurried through the wheat field. It was tempting to drop into it and hide but that would be a mistake. We had to put space between us. I turned and saw two Germans climbing over the wall. I took a couple of snap shots. They were too far away to be certain of a hit but they dropped back on the other side anyway. I saw that Private Beaumont had reached the western side of the field. He waved us over. My shots had bought us a little time but not much. The problem was we still had the front lines to cross. In a perfect world we would wait until dark but we lived in the real world. As we neared Private Beaumont I saw that there was a gate through the hedge. When we got through I saw, on the other side, Caen in the distance. It was tantalisingly close.

"Lance Sergeant Hay, booby trap the gate. Private Beaumont, take it

steady. Emerson go with him." I threw him my silenced Colt. "Use that.

We have to disappear. Find somewhere we can hide."

Private Emerson said, "Sir, the place is crawling with Jerries!"
I shrugged, "Hide or face the firing squad." He ran after Private Beaumont. I looked at Wilkinson, "How are you, Joe?"
"I'll be fine sir. I don't need these two watching me."
"We never leave a man behind! You will not be the first!"
"Done!" Bill Hay was a master of booby traps.
"Right lads it is not over yet!"
We headed across the field. The ground dipped and we lost sight of Caen. At the other side I saw Emerson but no Private Beaumont. Fred said, "Sir, Rog said to wait here. There is a house ahead and he thinks it is empty."
I was not certain about that. The Germans would check such places but Private Beaumont was the brightest of my men. He would have thought this through. "Right, go!" I watched them as they all ran after Freddie.
Just then I heard the crack of the grenade we had left on the gate. They were close. As I slipped through the gap in the hedge I saw the house. It was off to the side. Private Beaumont was alone and he was sliding down the pebble drive which led to the road. He said, "I thought we would make them think we had gone this way. " He slithered down to the gate and opened it. I saw that the skid marks from his feet were clearly visible.
"Well done. Let's get under cover."
Once inside the house I reloaded my Luger. I placed four grenades, my last four, next to me and I peered out of the window. The last of the afternoon light was fading fast and soon it would be night. Reloaded, I stared at the gap in the hedge. There was a rattle of gunfire and then four Germans pushed their way through the hedge and stared around them with submachine guns at the ready. One of them pointed at the disturbed stones and the open gate. The four ran off and were followed just a moment later

by a full squad. They did not hesitate but ran after their comrades. I knew it was not over but we now had a chance.

"Shepherd, Fletcher, check out the house and see what you can find. We may be here all night."

"Sir!"

"Emerson, nip upstairs and see what you can see. Hewitt how is Wilkinson?"

As Freddie ran upstairs Hewitt checked the wound. "A bit of bleeding, sir, but nothing to worry about."

"I told you, sir, I don't need a minder!"

"You will have two until we see the British lines again."

Fletcher and Shepherd returned with some cans of fruit they had opened and two bottles of red wine. "The rest was all mouldy sir."

"Right, divvy it up but go easy on the wine. Make sure Joe has a couple of glasses. It will help with the pain."

"I can manage, sir."

"I know Joe."

The tinned peaches were a luxury. I let the juice drip down my chin. I knew the sugar in them would keep me going. The rough red wine tasted sour after them and I just had the one mugful. I needed to be sharp. Emerson whistled from upstairs and I looked out of the window. Two Germans were returning through the gate. They stopped outside the front door. I pointed to Private Beaumont with my silenced Colt. He nodded. Corporal Fletcher had a second Colt ready.

I heard one German voice, "They might be in here."

I was willing them to move on. If they did not then they would die. The second sealed their fate. "We might as well check inside. Besides there might be some wine."

We were all pressed into the walls as they opened the door and stepped inside. The two Colts sent two bullets into each of them. "Get them inside quickly and lock the door."

Bill Hay and Ken Shepherd dragged them inside and shut the door. A few minutes later, as the sun dipped below the horizon, I heard the rest of the patrol approach.

Someone tried the door. "It looks like Karl and Christian checked the house. Those damned Commandos must have escaped. They are slippery bastards!" Their voices receded into the distance.

We waited, after they had gone, until it was pitch black. "Time to go. Wilkinson and his nurses in the middle. Hay, you and Shepherd watch the rear. Private Beaumont, with me."

We went through the gate. It led to a lane and we followed it. The German patrol had not been away long and that meant that the front line was close. It was after dark and the Germans would be nervous but their attention would be on their front and not their rear. We almost stumbled upon it. A German soldier was walking towards us. Private Beaumont had quick reactions and the silenced Colt killed him instantly. I managed to catch him before he fell to the ground and I lowered him gently.

I mimed for Private Beaumont to stay there and I headed off into the dark. Now that I knew the Germans were near I used my nose to smell them out. Every nationality of soldiers has a unique smell. I think ours must have been corned beef and Woodbines. The German tobacco and the smell of cabbage identified the Germans. I walked twenty yards to my left and saw some shadows. The barrel of a machine gun could be seen. I took out two grenades. I pulled the pins on both of them. I tossed one into the machine gun post and then hurled the other as far to my left as I could. I dropped to the ground and the two grenades went off in rapid succession. I shouted, in German, "The Canadians are attacking! Stand to!" I ran back to Private Beaumont and waved my men forward.

There was a fusillade of bullets as the Germans reacted to my shout. The Germans thought that we were reinforcements come to their aid. As my men burst through we fired on both sides of us taking the Germans by surprise. We clambered over the sandbags and rolled down the other side. My fear now was that the Canadians would open fire. I hissed, "Keep low!"

There was a cry of pain. I turned and saw Lance Corporal Wilkinson and John Hewitt lying in a heap. Running back I saw Hewitt stagger to his feet. "I am fine sir."

Wilkinson was holding his leg which was bleeding. He had been hit again. "Leave me sir!"

I handed my gun to Hewitt and heaved Wilkinson over my shoulder. He was a dead weight! The rest of the section were squatting , waiting for us. Bullets were still being fired and how we avoided being hit was a miracle. I lumbered on and my men formed a human shield behind us. I saw the barrel of a tank ahead. It was facing me. I guessed it was Canadian and I shouted, "British Commandos coming in!" I trusted that Lieutenant Ross had passed on our message and I ran ahead of my men, expecting a bullet at any second.

When a grinning Canadian sergeant stopped me I breathed a sigh of relief, "You guys sure live dangerously!"

Chapter 8

The Canadians got on the radio as we were taken past the Sherman tanks which blocked the road. We left Joe with their doctor. His leg had bled all the way back. As he lay on the cot he said, "I owe you my life, sir."

I shook my head, "I told you, we don't leave one of our own behind." I shook his hand. "Thank you for what you did on this operation. We couldn't have done it without you."

The doctor said, "Captain..."

"I know. We are going. See you Joe."

We walked through the Canadian lines. I heard a shout from the dark. "Sir!"

I looked up and saw Sergeant Poulson and Lieutenant Ross. They were standing by a German half-track. We went over and Private Emerson ran his hands over the machine. I said, "Where did you get it?"

Lieutenant Ross pointed to the Canadian lines. "Jerry launched an attack yesterday at dawn. They tried to break through our lines. They captured this. We said we would take it to the collection point." He smiled, "We will won't we sir?"

I smiled, "Lieutenant Ross, we might make a Commando of you yet. Right lads, all aboard!"

I sat in the back with my men. Those who smoked lit up their first cigarette since we had started the operation. I was amazed that any of them still smoked. They had been able to give up for almost forty hours and yet they all sucked greedily on their first cigarette. The glow of their cigarettes seemed like fire flies. I just looked up at the sky. There had been more than one occasion when I thought we were not going to make it back. Had it not been for the German sudden offensive and its defeat we might not have had the confusion which aided us. I hoped that we would not have to go as far behind the lines in the future.

Bill Hay, one of the non-smokers, said, "What will happen to Wilkinson sir? He was a good lad."

"We only had him for this one operation. He is due promotion and when I write my report he will get one. We already have a sergeant in this section."

Bill nodded, "I wasn't sure that an outsider would fit in with us sir, but he did."

I knew what Bill was thinking. He had found it hard to be accepted by the section but then he had come from a section where he had been treated badly. It had taken capture by the Germans of the two of us for him to have his St. Paul's moment.

"Hopefully we will have Barker and Davis back soon."

"And then what sir?"

"Oh I daresay they will find more jobs for us. We keep doing the impossible."

When we reached the LCA it was close to dawn. Sergeant Poulson parked the half-track out of sight. We would take it to the scrap collection point ... eventually but it was still serviceable and we wasted nothing. We collapsed into our beds.

I was the first up. I only needed a couple of hours sleep. I needed a change of uniform. The blood from Wilkinson's leg had hardened on my battle dress. In addition I had reports to write. I had a good wash and changed into a clean uniform. I put my battle dress in a bucket of river water to soak the blood out. I went to the mess. The rating whose turn it was to be cook said, "You missed breakfast, sir. I can do you a cup of tea and some toast if you like. One of the lads liberated some jam! The French have nice jam sir; big bits of fruit!"

"That'll do nicely."

I took the mug of steaming tea and the plate of hot toast and jam up on deck and then across to the building we used. I had work to do. Lieutenant Ross was there busy writing. He looked up, "Sergeant Poulson has gone for a run. He said something about getting fit enough to go with you the next time."

I nodded and bit into the toast. The rating was right, the jam was good. "He is a soldier who likes action. Most of my men are the same. I am not certain how they will get the same thrill when the war is over." I rinsed my mouth with tea. "What are you writing?"

"I thought I would make a start on the reports for you, sir. I have topped and tailed the report and written the parts I knew."

"Thanks. That is good of you."

"Will we be back to England after this sir?"

"I don't know. Officially the mission is not over until aerial photographs confirm that we blew up the dump."

"You must have, sir! We heard the explosion from here. The sky was lit up by the burning fuel."

"It was a well-made complex and bigger than I thought. We will see. The camera boys will get a better picture. The camouflage netting will have been destroyed that is for certain."

It took an hour or so to write the report. By then Sergeant Poulson was back from his run. "How is the wound?"

"Hardly bothers me, sir. I can keep going longer these days. I am not ready yet but I will be."

"I am not certain we will be in action any time soon so don't push yourself too far." He nodded. "Come on let's go and wake the sleeping beauties. I have some dhobi to do."

Lieutenant Ross looked up, "Dhobi sir?"

"Washing! We don't have servants out here, John. We all do our own washing,"

He shook his head in disbelief. He was learning about life on the front. Most of the men were already up. The exception was Fletcher. Bill Hay organised breakfast. They fried corned beef and had it with powdered egg. It was as close to a fried full English as they could get.

Private Emerson wolfed his down. "Sir, can I have a look at the German half-track? You never know when it might come in handy."

I smiled, "Of course, Fred, and I dare say our young engineer will want a shufti too!"

Private Beaumont grinned, "Yes indeed, sir."

"The rest of you; make and mend. We have had no more orders yet but you never know."

I took my washed battle dress up on deck to dry it. I saw Bill Leslie approaching. He did not look happy. "Just had word from the skipper, sir. We are back to the beach. A troopship has arrived and we are to ferry them ashore."

"So he would like us off his boat eh Bill?"

"Like yesterday, sir. Sorry."

"No problem. We have enjoyed your hospitality. Lance Sergeant Hay, we are leaving LCA 523. Have the men take all our gear ashore."

"Right sir."

Bill Leslie looked around and handed me a lemonade bottle with a brown liquid. "I managed to put you and your lads on the books for rations, sir. You didn't manage *'up spirits'* and I saved it for you and the lads."

"Isn't that against King's Regulations, Petty Officer Leslie?"

He gave me an innocent smile, "Well you know the King better than I do, sir. You have met him. What do you reckon?"

"I think he would approve. Thanks Bill." I took the bottle.

He said, quietly, "It's neaters sir. I would water it down!"

Laughing I said, "I will miss the old 523."

"In this war you never know. We may see each other again."

"I hope so."

It was mid-afternoon when the landing craft headed downstream. It had been a comfortable berth. The half derelict house would take some work if we were to stay there for any length of time. Sergeant Poulson and Lance Sergeant Hay soon got the men organised to clean up the rooms we had not used. Even Emerson and Private Beaumont were dragged away from their half-track. The only one not involved was Lieutenant Ross.

He burst into the maelstrom of dust and mayhem as excited as I had ever seen him, "Sir, sir! It worked!"

Everyone stopped, "What worked?"

"The raid, sir. London has just been on the radio. The aerial photographs just came back. It looks like half of the dump has been destroyed. London said there were tankers taking the remainder and heading east! The RAF have been shooting them up!"

The men all cheered.

"Good and are there any orders for us? Our lift home has left so what does Major Foster have in mind for us?"

"He said to sit tight, sir. He is coming over himself in the next couple of days. He said to take two days off."

Fletcher rubbed his hands together, "That'll do for me!"

Sergeant Poulson said, "We have to get this place ship shape first, Corporal Fletcher!"

In the end it was four days before Major Foster arrived. Part of that was due to the fact that the work on the airfield had slowed. German counterattacks had prevented it being ready. It suited us for we now had better quarters. We scrounged and we collected so that we could be both secure and comfortable. All the time more troops arrived from the beaches. We knew that there would be an offensive at the end of the first week in August. Ominously the Germans must have known it too. Every tank we had seen when we had been trying to evade the Germans had been either a Tiger or a Panther and they were S.S.

As we sat one night on the river bank, watching the sunset in the west, Lieutenant Ross said, "Surely, Captain, the fact that you destroyed so much of their fuel means that their tanks will not be able to move. The war in this part of the world will soon be over."

I shook my head, "These are S.S. divisions; the Das Reich and the Liebstandarte Adolf Hitler. They are fanatics. If they run out of petrol they will become static obstacles and will pick off our tanks one by one. They will not surrender. They will fight to the death and take a lot of brave men with them."

Sergeant Poulson said, "You know what their crews call the Shermans don't you sir?"

"No, Sergeant."

"Ronsons, because they light up as quickly as a lighter. They are death traps and the German guns tear through their armour as though it wasn't there. You need a point blank hit with a twenty five pounder to stop a Tiger or a Panther. The Captain is right. This will be bloody."

Just then, as though to prove the point, more Shermans trundled up the river road towards the jumping off point for the offensive in two day's time.

We were woken next morning by the sound of gunfire and it was German eighty eights we could hear. I rushed outside and saw, to the north, smoke. We had no orders but the firing was so close that I could not ignore it.

"Stand to! Get your weapons. I want everyone here in five minutes."

I grabbed my battle vest, already festooned with grenades and ammunition, and put it on. I took my Thompson and my Colt. I was outside before the rest. Emerson was the first to reach me. "Freddie can your half-track go?"

"Of course sir."

"Then we will get to the front line quicker in that."

"Yes sir!"

Lieutenant Ross was the last one to join us. "What do I do sir?"

"Find out what the hell is going on. We will take the half-track and head for the front line."

We boarded the half-track. Bill Hay cocked the heavy machine gun, the MG 42. We would have some serious firepower. As we headed north we received some strange looks but we were all wearing British uniforms and Private Beaumont had painted over the German cross. We saw ambulances carrying wounded men as we neared the front lines and the road became clogged. "Fred, take us down a side street." We were able to move faster. We could still hear the sound of tank shells hitting buildings and then the sound of hits on tanks but we saw nothing.

As we turned left the houses disappeared and we were in the open land to the north of Caen. I saw a burnt out Sherman and a disabled Churchill. The Sherman was a blackened shell. The Churchill had lost a track. The smoke from the tank made it hard to see beyond the two vehicles. The Canadians were manhandling a six pounder anti-tank gun into position. "Stay here and I will find out what is going on."

I jumped out. Bullets pinged off the armour. Bill fired a burst from the German machine gun. I guess he must have seen where the gunfire came from. Shells were still hitting the buildings behind me. I ran from side to side with my head down until I reached a partly demolished building. A Canadian Major looked up when I entered, "Where the hell did you and the half-track come from?"

"We were by the river and I heard the firing. What is going on?"

"We had a message at midnight that the Germans were planning to attack us this morning. We were ready for them but they had Tigers. We are holding them but only just. More men are coming from the beaches right now. If you and your men can block the road you are on and cover the six pounder that would be a help."

"Will do. How many tanks have you left?"

"Two Churchills and a Sherman. We lost five tanks already and we haven't even dented the Tigers. I think it is just the wreckage of our tanks that is stopping them."

I dodged and ran back to the half-track. "Right lads we are on a holding mission. We stop them here. Emerson, Hay and Shepherd, you stay here with the vehicle. The rest of you grab your weapons and we will join the crew of the six pounder."

I ran to the anti-tank gun. Even as I reached it a bullet struck the layer in the head and he fell at my feet. "Corporal Fletcher, act as gun layer." I fired a burst from my submachine in to the smoke. Both sides were firing blind. The Canadian gun layer had just been unlucky.

"Thanks sir." The sergeant looked at my flash, "Commando eh?"

"Don't worry we know how to stand and fight too. Can you see any targets?"

He shook his head. "The Germans have laid down smoke and the tanks just appear out of it. The only advantage we have is that when they are that close we can do some damage."

I nodded. "Sergeant Poulson get some sandbags erected around the gun. Private Beaumont, come with me."

I crawled along the ground towards the German lines. I counted on the fact that any bullets would be at waist or head height. "Where to sir?"

"Let's head for the Churchill. It might be disabled but the gun looks like it will fire. Besides it will safer inside rather than out!"

"Looking at that Sherman I am not sure, sir."

Bullets zipped over our heads but they seemed too high to cause us damage. The Germans could not see us for we were below the smoke. I saw two of the tank crew. They had been shot after they had evacuated the damaged tank. When we reached the Churchill I climbed up the rear. The turret hatch was open but if I just went in blindly then I risked a bullet. I raised my head over the top. I could see, a hundred yards away, the German Panzer grenadiers. They were advancing alongside two Panthers. A Tiger was stationary some two hundred yards behind it but its gun was still traversing and it was still firing. Glancing to my left I saw two Tigers and to my right another two Panthers. I saw my chance when a breeze suddenly blew some smoke in front of our Churchill. I scrambled into the hatch and dropped down. I landed on the body of the headless driver. There was a large hole in the front of the tank where the shell had blasted through. Inside the turret was blackened. There had been a fire but it had gone out.

I moved towards the gun as Private Beaumont dropped down beside me. "Do you know how this works Private Beaumont?"

He looked at it and nodded., "I think so. We won't be able to traverse the turret but we can raise and lower the gun by hand. If you can load, sir, we might give Jerry a shock!"

I saw that there were shells behind me. It was a miracle they had not exploded. Then I realised that the German shell had been armour piercing and not HE. I saw the difference in the two types of shell. The armour piecing had a more tapered tip and was made of harder steel. Private Beaumont said, "Give me an armour piercing first, sir, and then if you want to get on the machine gun. Those grenadiers are getting a bit close to us."

Getting to the machine gun involved moving the torso out of the way. I could not be squeamish about it. The poor driver was well out of it anyway. I cocked the Besa machine gun. "Ready when you are, Private Beaumont."

"This will be tricky sir. I have to wait until the Panther moves into my sights. If you have to fire then go ahead sir and I will do my best."

The Panzer grenadiers were now less than sixty yards from me. I could see the nearest Panther was traversing its turret to fire to our right. I opened fire moving the gun left to right and back again. I could not depress it too far but the range was perfect. I hit some of the grenadiers and the others hit the deck. The Panther's gun began to traverse. It now saw us as a threat. I left the gun and grabbed another shell. Private Beaumont fired the Churchill's seventy five millimetre gun and struck the Panther just below the turret. The barrel stopped traversing. The shell had done some damage.

"Quick sir, another! I have him!"

I loaded another armour piercing and he fired. This time it penetrated the turret. There was a whoosh of flame and the crew began to bail out.

"HE sir."

I loaded one of the other shells and then went back to the machine gun. I was just in time as the infantry was advancing again. I fired a burst and then the gun jammed. Before I could clear it Private Beaumont had fired and hit the tank with high explosive. There was an enormous explosion. The Panther's turret flew into the air. We had no time to congratulate ourselves as our tank was rocked by a tank shell which smashed into the left side, low down. It too was armour piercing but it was hot enough, as it struck, to start a fire.

"Right Private Beaumont. Time to bail out."

I jumped up and, grabbing my Thompson held it above the turret and sprayed blindly. I pulled myself out and dropped behind it. I put it on single shot and began to aim at the Panzer grenadiers. I saw the second Panther lining up to take a shot as us.

"Hurry up Private Beaumont!" He tumbled out and I yanked him over the back. We fell in a heap. I grabbed his collar and pulled him up. "Run!"

We were just forty feet from the Churchill when the shell hit it and exploded the petrol tank. We were thrown to the ground and I could smell burning hair as the flames singed us. I could barely hear anything but I pulled Private Beaumont to his feet and stumbled back towards the half-track and the six pounder.

I could not hear but I could shout, "A Panther two hundred yards away!" I dropped behind the sandbags my men had put up. I put a new magazine into my Thompson and placed a Mills bomb before me. My hearing would come back but it would be gradual. I turned and shouted, "Lance Sergeant Hay, Panzer grenadiers and a tank!" He waved his acknowledgement and began firing into the smoke. With a range of two thousand yards he might get lucky.

I saw the flash of the muzzle of the Panther and, tapping the gunner on the shoulder, pointed. He nodded. The shell exploded behind us. I turned and saw the headquarters' building crumble. Part of the stonework crashed onto the back part of the German half-track. Bill Hay waved. He was still standing. The gunner fired and immediately the six pounder was reloaded.

I saw the Panzer grenadiers as they darted, as I had done, from cover to cover. They were good. One man fired while the other covered. We needed a grenade launcher but we had none. I fired a short burst to make them go to ground. The rest of my section used their own automatic weapons to lay down a wall of fire. The Canadians around us had Lee Enfields. A good rifle, it did not have the rate of fire of our Thompsons. Then I saw the barrel of the Panther. The gunner saw it at the same time. The range was less than a hundred yards and the shell slammed into the front. It did not do as the Sherman was prone to do and catch fire but it was stopped.

"Hit it again Sergeant!"

I stopped shooting blindly and looked for the officers and sergeants. If I had had my sniper rifle then I could have been more accurate but I had to use the machine gun. I saw an officer raise his arm and I fired three shots. One of them hit him. Then the Panther's machine gun began to chatter. The Canadian sergeant fell. Bullets had torn into his chest. Private Beaumont leapt to replace him. I took my grenade and stood. It was risky but I needed the maximum flight. I pulled the pin and threw it as high and far as I could. "Grenade!"

I dropped to the ground as Private Beaumont fired the anti-tank gun and joined me. The shrapnel from the grenade scythed through the air at head height. As soon as it had passed I rose to my knee and fired again. I saw that the Panther was smoking and the turret had been damaged. The crew began to clamber out and Bill Hay cut them down.

Just then there was a whoosh from behind us followed by the roar of a pair of tank busting Typhoons. I saw an explosion in the distance. They had destroyed the disabled Tiger. "Right lads, at them!"

I led my section and the remainder of the Canadians and we ran at the Panzer grenadiers. Already badly shaken and without their three tanks they turned and ran. They were S.S. and this was no time to be noble. We shot then. When we reached the burning Tiger I stopped. We had held off a major attack. The question was, would we be able to launch our own attack or had the Germans forestalled it?

Chapter 9

Hay , Emerson and Shepherd were covered in brick dust and had minor cuts and bruises but otherwise they had survived well. Fred Emerson was more concerned about his half-track and he had my section remove the bricks and stones so that he could see what damage there was.

The Major and his headquarters' staff had all been killed when the building collapsed on them. Captain Thomas was the senior surviving officer from the battalion. He looked shaken as he watched the bodies being brought out from the rubble. "Thanks for the help Captain Harsker."

I nodded, "We were lucky this time."

"I know. We had warning but it didn't seem to do us any good."

"Are you involved in the offensive tomorrow?"

"No. It is an armoured attack. The Poles are going to assist our boys. Thank God. It will take us a few days to get back in some sort of order."

"I am afraid that time is a luxury we do not have." I shook his hand. "If my chaps have repaired the half-track we will get out of your way." I pointed to the battalion which was marching to relieve them. "New uniforms. You had better tell them what they are up against."

I reached my men, "They nearly hurt Bertha sir but she is a tough old lady!"

"Bertha?"

"Like the big gun from the Great War sir, Big Bertha."

"Right Freddie, let's get your new girlfriend home. Well done everyone, especially Private Beaumont here. Two tanks is an impressive score for your first time."

"It would have been nice to get a hat trick, sir."

When we reached our base Lieutenant Ross said, "Major Foster is arriving tomorrow, sir."

"Good."

"How did it go?"

"We won but the Canadians picked up the butcher's bill."

Private Emerson and Private Beaumont did not do as the rest did and find some food. They began tinkering with their new toy. I cleaned my weapons and reloaded my magazines. After I had done so I had a thought, "Lieutenant Ross, just in case Major Foster takes you back to London with him, could you spend the afternoon trying to get us some ammunition? Use your magic letter while we still can and while you are about it see if there are any American rations kicking about. They are always better than ours."

He looked perplexed. Scouse Fletcher volunteered, "Should I go with him sir? Show him the ropes, so to speak."

"Just don't get him arrested."

"As if I would and if we took the half-track sir it might be easier to carry the stuff back."

"Very well."

Scouse looked happy, "Great, come on, sir, and I will open those baby blues of yours to the real world of bein' a soldier!"

With Shepherd doing some washing that left me with my three NCOs. "Sergeant Poulson, how is the wound? You seemed to cope today."

He looked at John Hewitt, "I feel fine, sir, but sometimes my chest feels tight."

Hewitt nodded, "To be expected. I know you are running and that will build up your stamina but you need to build up your chest muscles too." We all looked at him. He shrugged, "When I went home I went to the library to find a bit of peace and I read up on the wounds the lads had suffered. Until we are attached to a unit with a doctor I guess I am it."

"There you are Sergeant, you have a starting point."

"That's all I want. I need to know how to become as fit as I once was."

"What next sir?"

"I don't know, Bill. I can't see the Major coming all the way over here just to tell us we can go home. There will be another job for us. Of that I am certain. Why, do you want to go back to the Brigade?"

He shook his head, "This suits me. We all get on. Life is never dull and there is no spit and polish here. It's just that I heard his lordship wanted us to be more like regular troops."

"Like Poulson here he is wounded and appears to be out of it for a while. We have the support of the Prime Minister and that seems more important than the fact that generals like Monty don't approve of us and our tactics. They think they are a distraction."

Bill Hay shook his head, "With respect, sir, that is a load of bollocks! Pardon my French! In terms of cost we get better results than large numbers of other units. Look at today. If we hadn't been there then Jerry would have walked through. You and Private Beaumont took the initiative and destroyed a tank and slowed up the advance."

"The fighters were on their way, Lance Sergeant."

"By the time they got there the whole of the Canadian company would have been dead or in the bag."

"Well it is not our decision. We just do what we do and hope for the best." I stood, "Anyway we had better make arrangements for Major Foster."

"Will he be staying here?"

"I have no idea but better to be prepared. Rig something up. Put him near Lieutenant Ross."

"Should we put a curtain around him or something?"

"No Bill, he is a Commando. He knows how to rough it but see if you can scrounge another mess kit for him. He won't have thought to bring one."

"He can have Joe's. His stuff is still here. I wonder how he is."

Hewitt said, "His wounds were straightforward. A week of sick leave and he will be back to normal duties."

"Just my luck to have something that has taken two months to heal."

"What about the other lads? They are worse off. They are still in Blighty. I bet Gordy is climbing the walls!"

"You are right Bill." Sergeant Poulson chuckled. "He will be giving those nurses hell! I miss his miserable face."

It was early evening when we heard the sound of our captured vehicle. We went outside to see them. Corporal Fletcher said, "The Lieutenant is a natural sir! We were stopped by some redcaps who asked why we were driving a German vehicle. Mr Ross here whipped out his magic letter and put them in their place. They were all, 'sorry sir, just doing our job sir'! Proper Jobsworths!"

"As much as I enjoy listening to your jaundiced view of the world did you get what we needed?"

Lieutenant Ross smiled, "Oh yes sir. We drove a fair way down the coast and found some American landing craft. They were landing supplies. They were quite keen to be shown around the half-track and let us help ourselves. Jolly obliging."

Emerson lit a cigarette, "And we even got some petrol." He slapped the half-track affectionately. "Bertha got up to thirty five miles an hour!"

Bill Hay said suspiciously, "How do you know that? The speedo is in kilometres."

Private Beaumont smiled, "I had a bit of acetate and I made him one in miles. Fred thinks it is more British."

"You can't beat Imperial. None of this Continental nonsense. Litres and kilometres! You know where you are with miles and gallons!"

I saw that Fletcher was lifting out what looked like a large icebox. "What have you got there, Corporal Fletcher?"

"The pièce de résistance! Steaks!"

"They gave you steaks?"

He shook his head, "Not exactly gave, more swapped. You remember when we captured that staff car sir? Well the German flag was in it. I swapped it for the steaks. We have enough for two days!"

Bill Hay shook his head, "We are fighting in the wrong army, sir! Let's join the Yanks!"

"Wasn't the flag worth more than a few steaks Fletcher? It isn't like you to let something like that go cheaply."

"I figure we will get another, sir. The war isn't over yet. Easy come easy go."

Sergeant Poulson said, "Well how are we going to cook them? We have a petrol cooker which can take one pan at a time! We will be here all night."

I remembered the large oil drums we had found when we first arrived. We had dumped them with the other rubbish. "Private Beaumont, go with Emerson and fetch in two oil drums. If we cut them in two we can make a barbecue."

"A what sir?"

"At last! Something our Liverpudlian friend does not know! It is an open air way of cooking. Trust me you are in for a surprise tonight."

Private Beaumont and I were the only two who knew what a barbecue looked like but the others enjoyed the challenge of making them. Shepherd went off and returned with some heavy duty wire mesh. It made a perfect grill. We had plenty of wood and we soon had a fire going. I let them choose their own steak and then showed them how I prepared mine. We had often had food like this when using our French home. Corporal Fletcher had also managed to liberate some red wine and the evening proved a great success. Lieutenant Ross found the wine a little rough for his taste.

"Trust me, John, when you have been over here long enough this will taste like nectar. I bet you are remembering wine from before the war."

He nodded, "Yes sir. My parents allowed me to drink wine from the age of thirteen. My father had a fine cellar."

"We all remember those days but since the war started?"

He thought for a moment, "You are right sir."

"We all do it. The past is a lovely place to visit but don't stay there. The world changes, John, and we change with it." He nodded sagely and when he drank his wine he smiled a little more. "So, will you be off to London with the Major tomorrow?"

"I hope not sir. I like it here." He leaned in and spoke quietly, "To be truthful these chaps scared me when I first met them. There was only Private Beaumont I understood. But they are damned good chaps. And they are damned good at their job. You have a good unit. I envy you."

"Have you done any combat training, John?"

"Just when training to be an officer. It was damned exciting. War games, teams, ambushes; I loved it."

"None of us had training like that. I trained by joining up as a private and the rest learned on the job. These are good chaps but every one of them is a killer. They can kill with a gun, a knife, a rock and even their bare hands.

None of them would hesitate to kill and they wouldn't lose any sleep over it. You, I think, would. What you see here is the tip of the iceberg."

"I know I could never be in combat with you, sir, but it would be good to be doing something useful."

He reminded me of Hugo Ferguson. "And the lads all appreciate you and what you do here but Major Foster may need you in London."

"Perhaps." He did not sound convinced.

We were awoken, in the night, by the sound of shellfire and tanks as the Canadians and Poles, to the north of us, began their offensive. I wished them luck. Just before dawn I went around to shake awake the section. There were thick heads when I woke them but no one shirked the run I had organised. Lieutenant Ross asked to come but, as I pointed out, he had to get to the airfield and pick up the Major. "Besides these lads take no prisoners! They will all try to beat me and it will be a hard run."

We set off before six. We would run to Ouistreham and back. It was seventeen miles all told and would be a good test of Sergeant Poulson's wound. We did not run with weapons and Bergens. We just ran in our battle dress. I wanted to it to be a real run. When we had covered six miles I worried that Polly would hold us up for he was a good fifty yards behind us. Bill Hay looked around as though contemplating dropping back. John Hewitt said, "It will do him no good if you do drop back Lance Sergeant. He either has to keep up with us or realise that he is not ready."

Hewitt was right. We kept our steady pace. There were road blocks along the road but I think it was obvious we were Commandos from our shoulder flashes. We were jeered and we had catcalls but it was all in fun. We turned around at the mole. It was just over two months since we had come ashore. How things had changed. As we turned to return I noticed that Sergeant Poulson had closed with us. He was less than fifty feet from us now and his breathing looked better. I saw Hewitt nodding.

With five miles to go he ran next to me and managed to say. "I have my second wind now sir."

"Good man."

Private Beaumont began to open his legs, Shepherd joined him and the pace was picked up. I knew that I could have overtaken him but I wanted Sergeant Poulson to be part of the team again. It had been a long journey for him. With our quarters in sight Roger looked around and saw the rest of us keeping pace with Sergeant Poulson. He and Ken began to slow so that we all reached home as one. That was their way and I was proud of every single one of them.

Bill Hay said, "Well I am hungry! Let's see what else Scouse got from the Yanks!"

There were tinned peaches and powdered pancake mix. The Americans had different rations to us. They were both novel enough for us to relish the prospect of an exotic breakfast. As we ate a well deserved breakfast washed down with Sergeant Major's tea I said, "This afternoon and tomorrow morning will be your last free time. I can't imagine the Major letting us sit here enjoying the sun. Make the most of it."

Fred said, "Sir we managed to get some paint. We thought of changing the colour scheme on Bertha."

I shook my head, "It's your free time. Waste it how you want." I received my answer when he, Private Beaumont and Ken Shepherd leapt to their feet.

Scouse said, "I will have a wander down town, sir, if you don't mind. I'd like to see a bit of it."

The others found things to occupy them so that, at one o'clock, when the truck arrived with the Major, I was alone. I was overjoyed when Gordy Barker and Pete Davis jumped from the back of the truck. "Well you two are a sight for sore eyes. All signed off?"

"Yes sir. They had a dragon at our hospital. She would have made a belting Sergeant Major. Where are the rest of the lads?"

"They are around. Three of them are round the back with Bertha!"

"Bertha?"

"You'll see." They saluted and sped off.

Major Foster shook his head, "You do run a unique section here, Tom." He waved a hand at the roughly repaired quarters. "I like what you have done with the place."

"Sir, do you need me?"

"Not for a while John, why?"

"I thought I might go and give them a hand with Bertha."

"Of course." The Lieutenant ran off and Major Foster asked, "Who the hell is this Bertha?"

"It is not a who it is a what. We picked up a German half-track."

"A German... I won't ask." He opened his briefcase. "Before I forget I have this for you." I recognized Susan's handwriting as he handed me the letter. "I hope she was careful. It did not pass through the censor!"

"Thanks for this."

"Oh and your father said hello. He arrived on the aeroplane with me. He is taking over from tomorrow."

I put the letter away for later. That was a pleasure I would savour. "Thanks. Things are a little precarious here right now. The Germans attacked yesterday which nearly made a mess of the offensive this morning."

Major Foster nodded. He glanced around, "I know Tom. We had intelligence of the German attack and we thought we had prepared for it. Obviously we didn't. You and your lads did well. This operation, Totalize, is just the first part of a two part operation. The second, Tractable, will begin almost as soon as we have met our objectives. The Americans will join up with us and, with any luck, we will have a German army in the bag."

"Sir, these are S,S. They don't roll over and play dead and they do not surrender. This will be bloody."

"Tom, be more positive, your mission was a huge success. The German attack would have been much more dangerous yesterday had they had more fuel. From the reports I received they only had seventy five Panthers and Tigers to use in the attack. It was not their full strength."

"They will just dig them in. Hull down they will be almost impossible to destroy."

"And that is why your father is here. His experience in the desert has given him an insight into close infantry support. He has Mosquitoes and Typhoons. The Americans have the Lightnings and P-47s. The air is ours. They have rockets and we know they are capable of destroying tanks."

"With respect sir the Mossy and the Tiffy are both very good against the Mark IV but a dug in Tiger is a different prospect."

"I am disappointed, Tom. I thought you would have been more optimistic. Your father is in command."

"Sir, I was there yesterday when three tanks, one of them broken down, almost broke through our lines when we were expecting an attack. If he arrived today then my father will not have a handle on the situation." I pointed north. The sound of the battle could be heard. "Right now Sherman tanks are going against Tigers!"

He smiled, "The same old Tom. Well you are part of the Tractable offensive. Trun is one of our targets. You are familiar with the area."

"Sir we knocked out the bridges and the dump has gone. What possible value does it hold for us now?"

"Ah, they rebuilt the bridges or replaced them, at least. When Tractable begins we want you to go in with the Fourth Canadian Armoured Division. You will go ahead of them when they near Trun and hold at least one of the bridges until you are relieved. We have a Kangaroo for you to use."

"A Kangaroo?"

"Yes they are a Churchill tank without a turret converted to a troop carrier."

I shook my head, "No sir, we will use Bertha. The Churchill is slower."

"But it has better armour."

"What you need, sir, is speed and besides my lads know our half-track. You have to trust me on this one, sir."

"Very well. Here I will show you the overall picture and it might help you to understand the importance of your mission." He drew me a rough map and I could see that the high ground to the north of Trun and Falaise was perfect for holding the Germans but the Canadians and Poles they would be using would have to hold out until Monty brought the Second Army in support.

"Right sir. I can see how it would work. I am still sceptical but... When does it begin?"

"That depends upon Totalize. I will be based at the airfield. I will go there tomorrow and I will take Lieutenant Ross with me. He will liaise with you. Are you happy to stay here?"

"We are comfortable, sir."

"Good. How is Lieutenant Ross? He is a bright lad. He has a great future on the staff."

"He has shown himself to be resourceful sir. He will be sorry to leave us I know that."

"Your band of pirates has that effect. I hear that your Sergeant Wilkinson has asked for a transfer back here."

"Sergeant?"

"Yes in light of your report it was decided to promote him. Hopefully the Second Brigade will have a section like yours eventually. We will go through the details when your lads return."

It was their stomachs which dictated their return. "Private Beaumont go and light the barbecues. We will have the briefing from the major while they are heating up and then we can eat."

"Barbecues? You are barbecuing corned beef?"

Lieutenant Ross smiled, "Oh no sir. We are having steak tonight... again!"

Chapter 10

My men were quite happy with the operation. I watched as they discussed various aspects of it They, like me, recognised the dangers but we were confident in our own ability. The questions were for clarification rather than whingeing and whining. It was obvious that they knew their jobs.

Major Foster was impressed by both their attitude and the food. "You certainly know how to make the best of a bad job! Steak! In wartime!"

"We are Commandos. You know how we operate. We live off the land and make do and mend. It is second nature to us."

"I think I am regretting accepting your father's offer of accommodation."

"Don't worry sir. You will be more comfortable there. I expect they will have an officers' mess with waiters and bar men. Besides the steaks cost Fletcher a Nazi flag! We won't eat as well again for some time! We were just lucky that some American brass had requisitioned steak and the deliverymen were happy to barter it. Such is war. We just try to make the best of what we have."

He laughed, "You mean neat navy rum as a nightcap?"

"I watered it down!"

He nodded, "But, I fear, no steaks Tom!"

"Sorry about that, sir. Let's just say my lads are good at scrounging." I knew the rum would help him to sleep in the dusty half derelict building that was our home.

I had not drunk as much as the others and I read Susan's letter while I listened to the snores from my men.

July 1944
Tom,
Major Foster has just told me that I can write a letter to you. Joy of joys, it won't be read by Wild West!

I know about your last mission. I barely slept and I have an idea what your next will be. Take care. I have the bigger picture here and I know that the war can't last a great deal longer. You are fighting fanatics!

Your mum came down to London and she and your father took me to the Ritz! You are lucky. Your mum and dad are the best. We had a lovely time. I showed them the ring and your mum burst into tears! I did too. I hope you don't mind but your mum and I began planning the wedding. I know we will have to wait until the war is over but your mum seems so keen.

On my next leave your mum has invited me to your home. I hope I can meet your sister.

I will have to close now as the Major has just come back.
I love you,

Take care,
Susan
xxx

It was a brief letter but I read and re-read it until I could recite it. It was a connection with home. I did not think that the wedding would be any time soon. It had taken us a month to reach the objective Montgomery had set for the first few days of the invasion. We were travelling like a snail. As I turned out my light I could still hear, in the distance, sporadic gunfire and the sound of tanks. The advance was heading east but how successful would it be?

The Major and Lieutenant left early for the airfield. We now had a timetable and a focus. Despite what Gordy had said I knew that most of the men were woefully short of the high standards before D-Day. I gathered them together the next day.

"Private Beaumont, Hewitt and I will be gathering together what we need for the mission. The rest of you will get fit. "Private Shepherd is the fittest of you. When he finishes toward the back of the runs then you are ready. Sergeant Poulson, how are the chest exercises coming along?"

"It is working, sir. Don't worry. We will be ready."

I had the letter which Lieutenant Ross had used and I wore my battledress with the ribbons. I would use any means possible to get what we needed. "Where to then, sir?"

Private Beaumont had changed since he had joined us as the shy young recruit. Scouse Fletcher had much to do with that.

"We need at least one sniper rifle and a grenade launcher. We also need some tin lids."

"I thought we didn't wear them sir?"

"We don't when we are sneaking around and we will not need them until we get to the bridge but if we have Jerry shells flying around I would like to have my head protected. And we need explosives."

Private Beaumont looked puzzled, "Aren't we supposed to hold the bridge?"

"We are but if the cavalry is late and there are German tanks trying to get over then we will blow it. Besides I would like you to be able to set off some little surprises on the south bank of the river."

As we had plenty of petrol for Bertha we took her down to the beach. This time we were not heading for the American sector, we needed the British area. It was still landing craft which were bringing in supplies. We left Hewitt with the half-track and we walked down the beach feeling like beachcombers. I saw men of the Warwickshire regiment and they were unloading, not from a landing craft, but from a lorry. I wandered over to the young Lieutenant. "What is going on here, Lieutenant?"

I saw him take in my rank, flashes and ribbons. He saluted. "Sir, we have come from the graveyard sir. This is the spare equipment from those who we buried."

"What is there here?"

"Mainly helmets, boots, webbings and haversacks. They are going home to be reused."

"You would be doing us a great favour if you would let us have a dozen of the helmets."

"What for sir? If you don't mind me asking? You chaps like your comforters."

"True but we are going up the line and I would like to see the end of the war."

"Help yourself sir. The dead won't mind."

He had one of his men help us carry them to Bertha. When the private saw the German vehicle he said, "Are you certain you are British army sir?"

I nodded, "Oh yes Private."

I was about to leave when John said, "Look there sir, the 523."

I saw the familiar landing craft as Bill Leslie nudged her on to the beach. We wandered down to speak with him. I watched as ratings began to carry the boxes of ordnance down the gangplanks. Bill waited until the boat was secured and then, pipe in hand came to the beach to join us.

"What have you got here, Petty Officer?"

"Bren guns, Lee Enfields, Mills bombs and grenade launchers."

"Any chance one of the grenade launchers and grenades could get lost?"

"Are you trying to lose me my stripes, sir?"

"No Bill." I looked around and saw that the ratings were carrying the boxes up the beach to a waiting lorry. "How about this then. Private Beaumont and Hewitt will help your lads carry a box up the beach. Which ones would be the best for us to carry?"

He grinned and went to identify the boxes. "These two look a bit heavy for my lads sir. Thanks for the help." He turned, "Jenkins, the Army will give us a hand!"

Able Seaman Jenkins grinned, "About time they did their share."

As we neared the lorry Private Beaumont managed to fall. The box broke open and the contents spilled. There were eight grande launchers. "Clumsy! Here let me help you." I grabbed a launcher and hid it behind my back. "I'll go back to the truck." Walking backwards I slipped the launcher into the back of the truck and then climbed aboard. Hewitt and Private Beaumont joined me. I could not see the grenades.

The two of them climbed in the back. Hewitt closed the door and then they opened their battle dress and grenades clattered to the floor.

I shook my head, "You two have been around Corporal Fletcher far too much."

As we headed back to the house with our treasure trove Private Beaumont said, "Pity about the sniper rifles."

"We did well enough. I'll see what the Major can conjure up."

The next morning I had Emerson drive me to the airfield. I was keen to know how the offensive was going and it was a chance to see Dad. Since I had last visited it had been transformed. There were now fences and runways. There were aeroplanes and anti aircraft guns. And there was the reassuring presence of RAF troops guarding it. We were here to stay.

"Drive round to the place where all the cars are."

"Right sir. Is it okay if I do a bit of scrounging?"

"Whatever for?"

He pointed over to one side of the airfield where there looked to be burned out German vehicles. "Gold sir. Pure gold!"

"I'll come and get you when I am done." I saw an airman, "Excuse me where can I find Major Foster?"

"He is in the mess sir with Squadron Leader Betts."

He didn't need to tell me where that would be. I followed the smell of tobacco and stale alcohol. Surprisingly they were not drinking but were studying a map. Neither Lieutenant Ross nor my father were anywhere to be seen.

"Ah Tom, just in time. It seems that this time the first part of the operation has gone smoothly. It looks like the Canadians might just make their deadlines and the Americans' Operation Cobra has been successful. The net is closing around Jerry." Major Foster stood and pointed to Trun. "That ridge that runs along there will be like a dam when the Americans join up with the Canadians. You can see why your mission is so vital."

"Yes sir. Where is Dad?"

Squadron Leader Betts chuckled, "He is just like you. He and Lieutenant Ross have gone up to see the front for themselves. He asked where the bullet holes had come from and I told him."

I nodded, "We have got almost everything we need now. We still need explosives and a couple of sniper rifles."

"What do you need explosives for?"

"If you expect a section to hold a bridgehead then we need some firepower. We can make the road on the other side of the bridge impassable. There are some big trees there."

"Ah. I will get Lieutenant Ross to get you some."

Squadron Leader Betts went over to the telephone and dialled, " I think I can help you there Captain." Someone answered, "Jones, this is Squadron

Leader Betts, there are a couple of rifles in my office. Be a good fellow and fetch 'em eh?"

"Rifles?"

"Sniper rifles actually. When Jerry attacked the other day they came here and tried to take back the field. The first of the Typhoons had just arrived and they shot them up. When we cleared the bodies we found these." At that moment Jones came in with two Mauser Kar 98K sniper rifles complete with 4x telescopes. "I know it is the wrong calibre for you chaps... I was going to take them home as a souvenir but if you can use 'em."

"They are perfect sir. We have plenty of German ammo and these are a good rifle." We heard the distinctive sound of a Lysander. "Mind if I go and watch the old boy land?"

"Be my guest. Jones put the guns in the back of the captain's vehicle please."

You mean the German half-track, sir?"

The Squadron Leader laughed, "Why am I not surprised?"

I saw the Lysander as it made its approach to the field. I admired the way my dad flew. He did it instinctively. I could fly but he seemed to be at one with the aeroplane. He had told me that he had learned while being an air gunner. His old comrades said that they did not know how he did what he did with a Sopwith Camel. I watched as he brought the Lysander in effortlessly. He managed to stop it ten yards shorter than I had and he landed closer to the main building. I smiled as I saw an animated Lieutenant Ross walking across from the Lysander.

"Your dad took us right over the battle, Captain! It was splendid."

I shook my head and said, "What would Mum say?"

He laughed as he shook my hand, "I'll tell you what, son, you don't tell your mum about this morning and I won't tell Mum and Susan about the bullet holes in the Lysander."

"Deal! Is the offensive going well?"

"It is but those big tanks are hard to stop. They are hiding in the woods We will have to get the big boys to bomb them."

"Remember what happened in Caen."

"I know. That was a disaster. So I hear you are off behind the lines again?"

"Not quite. We are with the spear head."

"And how is that different?"

"We don't have to spend too long cut off. With any luck the Canadians will get there almost as quickly as we do." I turned to Lieutenant Ross. "The Major wants you to get some explosives and detonators for us. Can you do it?"

He nodded, "Tomorrow soon enough?"

"We have a couple of days yet."

"Splendid then you can both stay for dinner." We had reached the main building. "How are you getting home?"

I pointed to the half-track, "In that."

He laughed, "Then I can see that the conversation will be anything but dull!"

It was an enjoyable meal. Dad and I caught up with events and then Major Foster saved the best news for coffee. "I forgot to tell you. There was an attempt on Adolf Hitler's life on the twentieth of last month. Lucky bugger survived but it was his generals who made the attempt!"

"Is that good news or bad?"

I looked at my dad, "What do you mean?"

"He survived and that means he may be like a cornered rat. We know he ordered the Sixth Army to fight on at Stalingrad well beyond what was reasonable. The Russians lost thousands. What if he does the same here?"

"I hadn't thought of that."

"One piece of good news is that he is culling his generals. And the ones being shot or sacked are his better generals."

I didn't ask him how he got his information. One thing about Major Foster his news was just that, news, it was not gossip.

Chapter 11

We joined the Canadians on the afternoon of the thirteenth of August. Our exploits during the German attack meant that we were not entirely unknown. Major Hamilton was our liaison officer. Three of his Shermans each had the seventeen pounder gun which was capable of penetrating the German armour. The bad news was that it had to be at a closer range than they would have liked. The other tanks had the standard 75. They were accompanied by some infantry in their Kangaroos.

"So you guys have been here before?"

"Yes sir. We blew up a dump here."

"Well we are not the main thrust. That will be to our right. The Colonel will be heading for Falaise. We have the Poles to our left. With any luck we will surprise the Heinies and catch them with their pants down."

"What time is the kick off, sir?"

"Kick off?"

"Sorry sir, when is zero hour?"

"Twelve noon. You guys are sending bombers over to soften them up and then we will attack on a wide front. The Americans will drive from the south and their nuts will be in our crackers!"

He sounded confident but I was not sure. Plans often went awry. The planners were used to the sterile world of the war game room. Accidents did not happen there and men behaved predictably. We and the Airborne had not done as expected at Bréville and we had won. We bivouacked with the crews of the Shermans but slept in the half-track. After breakfast we were ready for the off. We heard the bombers as they droned overhead and, not long after they had passed, the artillery started.

"Right Fred, get Bertha ready. She needs to start first time." It was some time since I had worn a tin lid and it felt uncomfortable as I put it on. I knew, however, that it might save my life.

At ten the Major was summoned to Headquarters. I thought that was unusual. "Corporal Fletcher get on to Lieutenant Ross at the airfield. Ask him if there is anything we should know. I'll go and see if their chaps know anything."

I wandered to the lead Sherman. A sergeant was smoking a cigar oblivious to the danger inherent in a tank renowned for fires. "What's going on sergeant?"

"Don't know, sir, but the Major took off like a jack rabbit. I guess something has hit the fan."

I nodded, "You are probably right."

When I reached the half-track Corporal Fletcher had just turned it off. "A bit of a cock up sir. One of the Canadians is missing and he had a copy of the plans on him. The Lieutenant says that Jerry is blocking our line of attack. There are a line of tanks and anti-tank guns backed up by grenadiers and they are along the Dives."

Sergeant Poulson said, "That puts the kibosh on our little trip then sir. Do we scrub?"

"We wait and see." The Sergeant was right. This was never foreseen by planners and why an officer was carrying plans around was beyond me. We had not even started and disaster had struck.

The Major returned at eleven and I was summoned to a meeting by his tank. "It seems that they will be waiting for us. We still go in but the Kangaroos will have to come in behind us. Your part of the operation is in doubt, Captain. I was told to say it is up to you if you come with us. There is no way that you can sneak past Tiger and Panther tanks."

There was a heartbeat when I thought about it. Mum and Susan would say no but the soldier in me made me answer, "Of course we will still come. If I might suggest we act as a scout? Travel ahead of you? The Germans might hesitate, seeing a half-track, or, more likely than not, they will not waste a shell on us. Your Shermans are a much more tempting target. We have a radio and we can let you know where the enemy are."

"Sounds good to me. You had better get in position then."

I went to the half-track. "Corporal Fletcher keep the radio on. We are going in ahead of the rest. We might surprise them."

Gordy said, "And whose bright idea was that sir?"

I smiled, "Actually, sergeant, it was mine!" The others laughed at his discomfort. "Right Freddie, take us to the front of this line. We have five miles an hour over their top speed. Let's use it."

"Actually sir it is a little more than that. Private Beaumont and I worked on the engine and the carburettor."

"Good! Bill I want you and Shepherd to keep that German gun firing. Gordy you take charge of the grenade launcher." Alan Crowe was our expert with that piece of equipment but he was still in Blighty recovering from D-Day wounds.

The Poles would have to cross the Dives but we would be using the road which ran alongside it. It meant we knew which side the tanks were likely to be. As soon as it was twelve we set off. We had seen the bombers returning. They had done their job. We headed towards the crossroads of Saint-Sylvain. The roads around there were narrow but the fields were undulating. It was to the north where the ridge rose. That was the objective of the Poles. We had the windscreen down and we wore the goggles we had found in the half-track when we had acquired it. My Thompson lay across my knee and there were grenades on my webbing.

I was reassured by the flights of Typhoons which crisscrossed above us. There was also a squadron of Hurricanes. Although past their best as fighters, they all carried bombs. We saw a flight of three of them suddenly peel off to attack something on the road ahead. "Watch out lads!"

I heard weapons being cocked. The Canadians behind us could not be seen because of the twists in the road. I heard the sound of machine guns and then an explosion. A column of smoke rose. It became apparent that the Hurricanes had hit something in Saint-Sylvain. The road passed through some houses and then took a sharp right. As Emerson took the corner I heard Hay's machine gun open up. Ahead of us was a burning Rad Sd.Kfz. 231 armoured car. We had met them before. Hay finished off the soldiers racing towards it. I saw two surprised machine gunners almost next to me and I sprayed them with my Thompson. As we passed, Sergeant Poulson threw a grenade. We were thirty yards away when it exploded. I heard the shrapnel ping off our armoured sides. There might have been survivors but they would pose no threat to the Shermans. This had been their outpost to warn them of our advance.

We had two miles to Soignolles. I had a feeling that the Germans were putting their own scouts out as early warning. The air cover had briefly disappeared. "Slow down Fred." I turned and said to the others, in the back, "I think there will be a half-track or an armoured car in the next village. We hit it hard and we hit it fast. Gordy be ready with that grenade launcher. Corporal Fletcher, tell the column what to expect. There is no armour as yet." I saw the village ahead. This one was even smaller. "Right Emerson, floor it!"

We leapt ahead. By the standards of an ordinary car it was not very fast but for an armoured vehicle it was spectacular. I put the Thompson over the folded down windscreen. As Bill Hay opened fire I caught a glimpse of grey and felt the machine gun bullets strike the door. I sprayed blindly. Emerson was right; we were fast and the men were finished off by Poulson. One advantage of the men in the back was that they had height. They could see further ahead than we could and I heard the sound of the grenade launcher being fired. A moment later it fired again. Ahead of us there were two explosions. It was a German half-track and it was facing us. The two grenades sent shrapnel towards them and allowed Bill and the men in the back to pour bullets into the cab and gun position. The grenades had made their own machine gunner take cover from the deadly shrapnel. I had run out of bullets and needed to reload. I took a grenade and, when we were thirty feet away, lobbed it high in the air. We were travelling fast and

I had to judge the throw perfectly. "Grenade!" I watched it head for the open back of the German half-track.

The men in the back ducked and Emerson swung the wheel to the left so that any metal would hit the sides. The grenade had fallen into the back of the half-track so that the explosion was contained. I knew that the back would be like a charnel house.

"Stop!" I jumped out of the cab and pulled my Colt. A German sergeant was staggering from the cab of the half-track. I fired at point blank range and his head disappeared. I jumped in the back but they were all dead.

I turned back, "Any injuries?"

Scouse shook his head, "No sir but it is a good job I am wearing brown trousers! Emerson drives like a loony sir!"

"Let's go. Corporal Fletcher tell them there is a half-track they will have to shift out of the way. It is half blocking the road."

We had to take a sharp left to reach our next way point. Once we were at the river, Le Laizon, we would be within touching distance of the German front lines. As we passed through the first village, which consisted of just three houses, I began to wonder about this village and river we were approaching. Lieutenant Ross had said they knew we were coming. The rivers were a perfect place to stop us.

"Corporal Fletcher, where is the main column?"

A moment or two later he said, "Five miles back, sir."

"Right Emerson, go as fast as you can but stop two hundred yards before the village. Private Beaumont you and Davis with me when we stop. Davis bring our sniper rifles."

Private Emerson stopped just eighty yards from where the river road to our right joined us. "Sergeant Poulson, take charge." I chucked my helmet on to the seat and grabbed the Mauser. I had taken a few practice shots with it. I was confident. You could always tell a good gun from the first few shots. The dead sniper had looked after his weapon well and I would reap the benefit. The two privates followed me as I crossed the second road and headed down to the river. We used the cover from the river to move east. We had gone barely thirty yards when I saw the Panther's barrel across the river. Once I knew where it was I was able to spot the hidden panzer grenadiers and the anti-tank gun. Looking to my left and the north bank I saw more panzer grenadiers armed with Panzerfausts. I saw explosives beneath the bridge.

I said quietly, "Private Beaumont go back and tell Fletcher to warn the column that there is an anti-tank ambush waiting for them at the river. They plan on a flank attack from across the river. We will get closer and distract them with the rifles."

"Sir."

"Right Davis. I hope you aren't rusty."

"Me too sir."

We crept along the bank. Sometimes we waded, where it was shallow, and at other times we kept to the bushes. We stopped just a hundred and fifty yards from the northern ambush and two hundred or so from the tank and the panzer grenadiers. The river hid us from view but we were between the two sets of Germans. I reached down into the river and picked up a handful of mud. I smeared it on my face and the backs of my hands. Davis did the same. He took off his helmet. We lay down and readied our guns. I pointed to the Germans with the Panzerfausts and Davis nodded. I took a bead on the S.S. officer who was half out of the turret of the tank scanning the road behind us through binoculars. If he had lowered them he might have seen us.

We were now in the hands of the Major and his Shermans. We waited. If we fired too soon then the Germans would know that we had been alerted. Waiting helped to disguise us for the Germans would not know how close we were. Suddenly there was an explosion in the middle of the road close to the Panzerfausts. It was a grenade. Even as I prepared to fire I knew that had to have been a grenade launcher. The range was too great for a hand thrown one. I squeezed the trigger and the tank commander fell. Davis' gun barked and the German with the Panzerfaust closest to us fell. I switched to one of the anti-tank gunners. I saw someone pointing. I squeezed the trigger and he fell. Davis had another shot before the trees above us were sprayed with machine gun bullets. They were firing too high.

I heard the triple crack as three seventeen pounders fired. The rest of the tanks in the column had a smaller gun but the front three were capable of hurting a Panther. The Panther returned fire. A second and third grenade hit the ambush and suddenly the Germans on the north bank were gone. The last grenade had wiped them out. Davis and I both began to fire at the machine gunners. I saw the flash of the muzzle. I aimed just above it and fired three shots in quick succession. When the gun stopped I knew I had had some success. The Panther continued to fire and the Shermans sent their own shells in reply. I then joined Davis in peppering the anti-tank guns. We did not hit anyone but so long as they were sheltering they could not fire back.

Then there was a huge explosion as the bridge was blown. The wave of concussion deafened us and we were showered with debris. When I looked up the Germans had gone. They had pulled back. Grabbing our guns we ran back to the road. I saw that the Kangaroos had disembarked their men and they were rushing down the road. I saw the half-track pulled off to the side.

When I reached it I dropped my Mauser in the back and took my beret. "Well done lads. Was it you, Sergeant, with the grenade launcher?"

"It was sir. Took a bomb or two for me to get my eye in."

"I'll go and have a look see. You be ready to move."

"But sir, the bridge has been blown."

"I know Davis but we will see."

One of the Canadian tanks had been hit. The turret had been blown completely off. It looked like a Kangaroo with half a roof. I could see the handles they used to steer it. The medics were already seeing to the two wounded. There was no sign of the men who would have been in the turret. The Major had a cigar in his mouth. "Could have been worse. If you hadn't taken out those rocket launchers we might have been in trouble. But what do we do about that?" He waved a hand at the bridge.

"Actually sir they have done a poor job of demolition. If you notice they have only blown the central section."

"It might as well be the whole damned bridge. We will have to wait for a bridging unit."

"Not if we make our own bridge, sir."

"Our own bridge?"

"Your brewed up tank. We either push or drive it over the bridge. It will fall into the river we should be able to drive over it and the parts which remain."

I saw him looking at the damaged section and, in his head, working out if my plan was feasible. "That might just work." He banged on the side of his tank," Kowalski."

A head popped up, "Sir!"

"See if you can get number six started."

"There's no turret sir!"

"I didn't ask that. See if it will drive." He shook his head. "Three hits on the Panther and it still drove off. The Germans have good tanks!"

"And their eighty eights are deadly, sir. As you have discovered."

We heard the sound of the Sherman's engines as it started. Kowalski's head popped up. "It goes sir!"

"Good now drive it over the bridge and into the river."

"Into the river, sir?"

"Yes, Sergeant, we are going to make a bridge. I want you to take it and bridge the broken ends of the bridge."

I said, "If I might suggest, Sergeant. Get up as much speed as you can otherwise you will land nose down."

"Is this your idea sir?"

"Yes Sergeant."

"Then do you want to come with me? This is a cockamamie idea!"

"Sergeant!"

"Sorry Major but..."

"No he is quite right. I'll join you Sergeant."

"You don't' need to Captain. The Sergeant will obey orders."

"He might need help, sir."

I climbed into the co-driver's seat. The handles were slick with blood. The sergeant handed me a cloth. "A bit messy." He pointed, "That blood was Joe Grant the gunner's."

"Thanks."

"You think this will work Captain?"

"In theory. What do you need me to do?"

I'll shout left or right, forward or back. If you know your left from your right then we should be fine."

I smiled, "We have right and left in England Sergeant."

He grinned, "Yeah you guys drive on the left don't you? Crazy! Well let's try this. Left forward right back and then keep them together." We lurched forward and I saw that he had lined us up with the narrow bridge. There would be just enough space for us but no more. He shook his head, "Full speed and into a space no wider than a garage! Crazy! Geronimo!"

I did not think we would be going fast enough. I had forgotten that the bridge had a slight slope but perhaps the loss of the turret gave us more speed for the sergeant said, "We might just make this. Hold on Captain!"

I wouldn't say we leapt but we were travelling faster than I had thought. After rising when we approached the bridge the front suddenly dipped alarmingly. The tracks scraped the broken abutments and then we fell. I put my hands on the handles to protect myself. I saw the water looming up and then we hit. Holding the handles partly saved me but I still smacked my head on what remained of the tank chassis. The engines were still going and I saw that the Sergeant was unconscious. I pushed him from the controls and we stopped. I stood and, putting my hands under his armpits began to lift. The tank was filling with water as the river level rose. We were like a steel dam in the river.

"Get them out of there!" I turned and saw that the remains of the bridge were just three feet above my feet when I stood. Two more of the Major's crew jumped down to help me. One grinned, "You sure have guts, Captain!"

I shrugged, "It comes with the red flash!"

We managed to manhandle Kowalski on to the bridge where medics were ready. I walked over to the Major. He pointed to the tank which was now almost underwater. "That is going to flood eventually."

I nodded. "But not until we have got across. We have lost one crossing but there are a lot more." I whistled and circled my arm, "My vehicle is lighter than yours. I will try it first and we can check for booby traps on the other side."

"Booby traps?"

"We would certainly leave them and the S.S. are even sneakier than we are."

I turned and saw Kowalski being helped to his feet. He looked at the bridge and said, smiling, "You are all right, Captain!"

Emerson pulled up next to me, "Sir?"

"I want us to drive over that."

"Over what sir? That bloody big hole in the bridge?"

I climbed into the cab and stood, "Exactly. Take it steady but keep the power on. You will drop a couple of feet and then you will be on the tank. We are narrow. You will have about eight or nine inches on each side. Once the tracks hit the tank they will grip. You watch ahead and I will keep you straight."

"If you say so sir." I saw him cross himself.

He did as I asked. The rubble on the bridge had already been crushed by the Sherman and we drove smoothly until we dropped on to the tank. It was now completely submerged but the water only came half way up the wheels. "Your way a tadge and keep the power on!" Emerson corrected. "Spot on!" Had we just had wheels then we would not have made it but the tracks had purchase on the bridge and they pushed us over.

Getting up the other side was harder. We did not seem to be moving and Gordy shouted, "Put your foot down! I hate swimming!"

The tracks suddenly found their grip and they pushed us up the other side. We slewed a little and the rear end slammed into the parapet and knocked stones into the river. "We have a puncture!"

"Just get us on the road and off to the side! Well done Freddie!" As we drove along the road so recently occupied by the Germans he beamed, "Nowt to it sir."

"Shepherd, Davis, help Emerson change the tyre. The rest of you spread out and look for booby traps."

The Major cupped his hands, "How is it Captain?"

"When we have checked for booby traps you can come over. We will have to be quick. The river is rising."

Private Beaumont found the first ones. They were the kind we used with a potato masher grenade and some trip wire. If you knew what to look for then it was easy to disarm them. At night it would have been harder. Corporal Fletcher found the second. It soon became apparent that they had not had much time.

"Sergeant Poulson check out the house."

"Sir!"

"Major, all clear!"

I heard the sound of the Shermans as they started their engines. I walked over to the half-track. "Well?"

"We have a spare but this one needs an inner."

Davis said, "We should have taken the spare from the half-track we destroyed."

I nodded, "We'll remember the next time. How long?"

"Five minutes. I made sure we had air in the spare before we left. I had a kit to repair the inner tube but a stone gashed the rubber in the tyre. We won't get far if we lose another tyre sir."

I turned as the Major, with Kowalski's bandaged head sticking out of the driver's hatch, slewed to a halt next to me. "We can expect more of this eh, Captain?"

"I think so. Sir, if you want my opinion I don't think we want to push on at night. These ambushes would have been deadly in the dark."

"I agree Captain. Find us somewhere safe to stay eh?"

I nodded, "Five star with English breakfast eh sir?"

"Good to go, Captain."

"Sergeant Poulson, all aboard!"

"Coming sir." My men emerged from the house and their arms were laden. We had food!

As they clambered aboard the Major said, "I can see we have much to learn from our British cousins Kowalski!"

"Ain't that the truth Major. And I guess those guys will be eating better than us tonight."

I heard no more as Emerson set off down the road to Sassy. The afternoon was fading fast.

Chapter 12

As we passed Sassy, Emerson said, "Sir, isn't that the Château we found the other day?"

I looked ahead and saw that it was. "We will stop at the bridge and the tanks can laager up at the Château. That should be five star enough for them eh?"

We halted at the bridge. It was, mercifully, free from Germans. "Sergeant Poulson, go and check the bridge for explosives. Lance Sergeant Hay direct the Major to the Château."

Private Emerson said, "I'll get this puncture repaired. Can't be driving around without a spare!"

I was left alone at the half-track. I looked to the south and saw flashes in the evening sky and the sound of explosions. Small arms fire could be heard in the distance to the north and south. We had an apparent haven of peace in our corridor and that worried me. I was about to head for the bridge when Private Beaumont shouted, "Sir, the bridge is wired to explode and it is on a timer!"

Conflicting thoughts raced through my mind. I did not want my men to die and yet we needed the bridge.

"Can we defuse it safely?"

"There doesn't look to be any booby traps... hang on sir. They have used our trick." Private Beaumont shouted, "They have grenades attached to the wires. We need to disarm the grenades first."

I joined my men under the bridge. John Hewitt was very agile and I saw that he had swung to the middle of the bridge and was using his snips to cut the wires. "No grenade here sir."

I found a spot where no one else was working. I saw the wires and the explosive. I could not see a grenade and I was about to cut the wires when my eye caught sight of a piece of metal. It was beneath the water and jammed between rocks. I reached down and felt the familiar and deadly shape of a German grenade. My hand found the cord attached to the detonator and then the wire which joined it to the fuse. I lifted the grenade, keeping hold of the cord. I took out my snips and cut the wire holding the cord. "Lay the grenades gently on the bank. They are still live and dangerous. We will explode them when the bridge is clear."

We worked carefully and methodically. I heard Sherman engines and then the Major's voice, "Where is Captain Harsker?"

"Under the bridge sir getting rid of the demolitions."

Private Beaumont shouted, "Clear!"

The call was repeated. I had a last look around and shouted, "Clear!"

I took the grenade and the explosives to the bank. The others joined me. The major whistled, "That is some ordnance. When was it due to explode?"

Private Beaumont held up the timer. "In about five minutes, sir, just about the time you and your tanks would have been crossing."

"Sneaky bastards."

"It would be a shame to disappoint them."

"What do you mean, Captain?"

"They will have observers down the road waiting for the explosion. Take the explosives over the river and make a pile in the undergrowth over there. Private Beaumont..."

"I will use an electrical charge to blow them up sir. It will be safer."

I left Sergeant Poulson and Private Beaumont to organise the demolitions. "The Château is empty, sir. There is plenty of room to park your tanks. I would just make sure you have sentries by the river. It can be crossed easily."

"You have been here too?"

"Yes sir but we didn't get to enjoy the Château. The Germans left in a hurry. You never know what you might find."

"And you guys?"

"Oh we are happy enough here. We will need to watch the bridge. I should warn your chaps about the explosives. They will make a bit of a bang."

My men hurried back and, five minutes later Private Beaumont and Fletcher followed with the wires and the plunger. While Private Beaumont attached the cables Corporal Fletcher primed it. Private Beaumont looked at me and I nodded, "Fire in the hole!" We all put our hands over our ears.

I was sheltered by the half-track but the force of the explosion seemed to suck the air from around us. The air cleared and we opened and closed our mouths to clear our ears. The Major laughed. "Well that should make them think the road is clear." He turned to me. "I would like to make a start at 0430. That way we can be close to Trun by the time they have the air umbrella up."

"I am guessing sir, that they will have a few surprises for us before Trun. There are a couple of crossroads and small villages where they can hold us up. We will leave at 0400. Corporal Fletcher will keep you informed of any danger along the way."

"Good luck and thanks for today. I wasn't certain how useful such a small unit could be. I know now!"

We ate well that night. There was an abandoned house a little way from the bridge. The French family must have evacuated in a hurry for there was fresh milk, day old bread, ham, home grown tomatoes, cheese and some wine. We even used their stove to brew up too. A constantly bubbling kettle was always a must for soldiers. There was no hardship in camping alone. Sergeant Poulson arranged the rota for sentry duty. Although he did not use me I woke at about two and joined Lance Sergeant Hewitt and Private Shepherd. I wanted to get the lie of the land before we left. All was silent. Fighting had finished for the day. It was too early to know how the offensive was going but we seemed to have made better gains. The night sky was clear and there were no sounds of battle. Peace had come, albeit briefly, to this part of Normandy. When daylight came it would resume.

With hot tea inside us and the last of the stale bread toasted we left well before dawn. I was cautious as we headed down the road towards the hamlet of Morteaux-Coulibeouf. We approached gingerly but I saw no grey. We stopped at the crossroads. I stepped out of the cab and people began to emerge.

An old man said, "Is this the liberation?"

I nodded, "There are tanks behind us. Where are the Germans?"

"They pulled out after the bridge was blown. They headed down the road to Falaise. Is it true? Is the war over?"

"No, my friend but that day is coming closer." I turned and said, "Corporal Fletcher, tell the Major the Germans pulled out last night. He is safe up to here. We will head for Trun." Despite their requests to stay we drove off. The Germans had only pulled back because they had thought they had stopped us crossing the river. They would be waiting. The question was where?

As we drove Emerson asked, "Where to then sir?"

"Let's go to Trun and the bridge where we were supposed to get to on day one."

"You are the boss, sir."

We never reached Trun. We didn't even make the river. We reached Beaumais. The houses had been ransacked but, worse than that, there were bodies lying all over. With guns in hand we went inside. The handiwork of the S.S. was clearly visible. We moved the bodies from the street. We had no time to bury them but we mounted our half-track in a more sombre mood. The calibre of our enemy could be seen. We killed but we did not kill civilians. We had travelled just a mile or so when Bill Hay, standing above the cab, shouted, "Get off the road! I can see German tanks and they are across the river!"

As soon as we stopped I clambered up next to Bill. He pointed south. I took out my field glasses. The Germans were dug in close to the woods on the La Filiane river. Eventually it joined La Dives. I turned to the men in the rear of the half-track, "Corporal Fletcher tell the Major that there are

Germans in force across the river. There is German armour and they are dug in. Emerson, take the road to Le Marais-le-Chapelle. Looking at the map, it is hidden from the tanks and will bring us out at Mandeville. That is on the Dives. Corporal Fletcher tell the Major to halt at Beaumais until we can check out the road." Emerson turned away from the river and took the small road which headed north and then joined another road heading east. The roads were too small for a tank but we fitted; just.

There were no Germans at Le Marais but we did hear firing to our left and right. It was in the distance. Overhead we saw more flights of fighter bombers as they raced to the aid of the two columns which flanked us. We seemed to be having our own private war. I saw a tiny road heading south. "Head down that road but go carefully."

We did not have to drive far to find Mandeville which was little more than a pair of houses. It was very close to Trun. When we reached it I said, "Stop. Sergeant Poulson, take charge. Davis, bring your sniper rifle." The two houses were deserted. We stopped behind them so that we could not be seen and we made our way to the river. We stayed in the woods and I scanned the river and the opposite bank. It was a ford. I saw Germans in the woods. You had to look carefully but they were there.

Davis used his sniper scope and he said, "Eighty eights sir. A pair of them upstream towards Trun. They are well camouflaged and look to be a hundred yards inside the woods. Clever buggers. You won't see them from the air. It looks like they are covering the ford from that side."

I turned the glasses downstream, to the right, and saw that were two guns there too. They would enfilade anything trying to cross the ford and could easily penetrate the side armour of a Sherman. It was the perfect angle for an ambush. "Right let's get back without showing ourselves."

We only had a hundred or so yards to travel before we reached the half-track. "Jerries and they are dug in. Corporal Fletcher tell the Major that we have found a ford. We can't see German armour but they have anti-tank guns. Give him the map coordinates."

"Sir."

"Emerson you stay here with the half-track. Wait for the major and tell him where we are. The rest of you, arm yourselves and don't forget your tin lids. Stay under cover and let's go Al Jolson eh?"

We took out our sticks of burnt cork and blacked up. I took pieces of twigs and jammed them in the netting on my helmet. Finally I grabbed two of our camouflage nets and handed one of them to Davis.

"All sorted sir. The Major is bringing the column down that little road. I hope they fit!" I knew they would not but a Sherman could demolish the small wall and tear up the hedges. New paintwork was cheaper than men's lives and they would be hidden from view.

When we were ready I led them down towards the river. We crawled the last fifty yards on our bellies. The Germans had not moved. I had my sniper rifle. We needed accuracy if we were to take out the gunners. I pointed to Sergeant Poulson and tapped my pips. He was in command. He nodded and I led Davis up the bank, keeping to the cover of the undergrowth so that we could use our rifles against the anti-tank guns' gunners. We covered ourselves in our netting and went on all fours.

It was when we neared the anti-tank guns that I saw a dark hidden shape some forty yards inside the woods on the southern bank. It was a Tiger. Davis saw it too. He whispered, "What do we do, sir?"

"Sit tight. The tanks will be crossing the ford to our right." My heart sank, however, as I knew there would be a second tank on that side too. The Germans were clever. They had used just four guns and two tanks. They would, however, be able to stop a whole column of Shermans.

I sensed a movement to my rear. If I moved quickly then I might alert the gunners. I rolled slowly on to my back. I saw a blacked up Private Beaumont crawling towards me. "Sir, there is a Tiger downstream."

"And there is one upstream. Tell the Major and have Sergeant Barker try to take out the anti-tank guns with his grenade launcher."

"Sir," He disappeared crawling backwards.

I rolled back on to my front and waited.

An hour passed. I heard the sound of Sherman tanks as they closed with the bank. I guessed that the Major had been preparing his plan. The ground beneath us began to shake as they approached. I aimed at the sergeant who commanded one of the anti-tank guns. He had heard the sound of the tanks and he ordered his men to action. I risked looking over my shoulder. At first I saw nothing and then I saw a Sherman. I guessed the others were close by. It looked to me as though they had been lined up a hundred yards behind the woods on the road. It made sense. They would have firmer ground. When I saw the sergeant open his mouth I fired and my bullet smacked into the side of his head. Davis hit the officer in the other gun emplacement and he spun around.

Then all hell broke loose. The other two eighty eights, downstream, fired and then I heard the crump of a grenade. Even as I switched targets and fired at another gunner the Shermans opened fire. The air above my head was filled with cordite, shells and shredded trees. I fired as fast as I could reload. Our luck could not last and soon I saw German panzer grenadiers rushing to the river bank to eliminate us. I switched targets and hit a German setting up a machine gun. Then I heard the chatter of an MG 42. It was not in front of us but behind us. Bill Hay had brought up that most powerful of machine guns.

I watched as a Sherman drove down to the ford. It began to cross, the water lapping three quarters of the way up the tracks. I fired at another German and hit his gun. Then the Tiger fired. The shell slammed into the side of the Sherman and it burst into flames. The crew who survived leapt out but were wreathed in flames. When their charred bodies fell into the water and didn't move it was a mercy.

I fired again at the anti-tank guns. So far they had done no damage. The tanks behind us had now seen the danger of the Tiger and four of them fired at it. The trees, the fact that it was hull down, and the superior armour meant that the shells bounced off. The Tiger fired one shell and a Sherman's turret was blasted off. I saw the remaining Shermans withdraw.

We kept sniping. Thanks to Lance Sergeant Hay's machine gun the panzer grenadiers were being kept back from the edge of the woods. It went quiet. We had no more targets. I took out my binoculars but could see nothing that was moving. I looked at my watch. It was after noon! I heard Sergeant Poulson, "Sir, can you come?"

"Davis stay here and keep an eye on them." I handed him my spare clips. We had more in the half-track. I crawled backwards so as not to attract any fire. After forty yards I stood. "What is it Sergeant?"

"The Major needs you." He pointed to the east. "There is German armour heading from Trun along the road."

"Tigers?"

"No, sir, we got the message from a Mosquito pilot flying reconnaissance. He said they were a hotch potch of Mark IVs, self-propelled guns and armoured cars. There are about twelve of them with infantry support."

I was going to ask Poulson what the Major expected of me but I knew that was unfair. I saw that the Major had pulled six tanks around across the road and on either side of it. The Kangaroos had disgorged their crews. "Captain, you have been up the road aways. What is there?"

"Trun. There were two bridges to the south but we destroyed them. The Germans were supposed to be repairing them but I doubt that they will support tanks if they have begun to rebuild them. That means the ford is our only way across and the only way for the Germans to escape."

He nodded and threw away the stub of his cigar. "We have elements in the outskirts of Falaise and the Poles have taken Hill 262. That means that the Germans are surrounded. The Americans are at Chambois. We have to hold them here. I have left two tanks at the ford."

"I don't think either of those German Panzers are going anywhere. The one closest to us is hull down. They are using it as a defensive position."

"A shame there is no damn cover here. "

"There are trees sir. Put your Shermans behind them."

"And leave the road wide open?"

"Just taking a page out of the German's book. Your tanks will get a shot at their side armour. "If you want a road block sir then use a Kangaroo."

Just then the Tiger fired from the woods on the other side of the river. The Sherman on the right hand side of the road was hit in its tracks.

"Damn! Lieutenant pull that Sherman off the road. Get the others in the woods and cover them. Captain Maxwell put a Kangaroo across the road." He smiled, "Thanks Captain. I don't know where we would be without your know how. Now if you could do something about those Tigers..."

"I have an idea or two."

"I was joking!"

"When it comes to the S.S. sir, you do not joke. With your permission I will pull my men back and let them have some rest."

"Of course. Captain Maxwell I want a platoon on the river keeping down the heads of those Krauts!"

Once back at the half-track I saw that the Canadians had set up a camp around the hamlet of Mandeville. "Emerson get some food on the go. Sergeant Poulson, go and round up the men."

I took off my helmet and rolled up my camouflage netting. I put the sniper rifle in the back of the half-track. I had a feeling I would need it again. I checked that I had plenty of magazines for the Colt. I didn't. I only had five clips left. However, the job I had in mind needed the silenced Colt. I would have to use my precious ammunition up. I took out my dagger and my whet stone and sharpened it. That I would need.

The men arrived. All looked intact and reasonably happy. "Thanks for the MG, Hay. It was getting a bit hairy."

"No bother, sir."

"Private Beaumont what kind of charge would you need to destroy a Tiger tank?"

"From the outside, sir, a lorry load, from the inside nowhere near as much. The strength of the armour would work against it you see. It would contain the explosion. If we use some petrol and just some TNT and a grenade then, with the hatch closed, everything inside would be destroyed. If you are thinking about the ones over the river then half the job is done for us already. They are hull down. I'll go and get something ready." Beaumont would make a good chess player; he always thought three moves ahead.

"No, eat first and demolitions later. We won't leave until dark. You and Shepherd prepare the charges. We will have two teams. I will go with Private Beaumont and Fletcher. We will take the upstream tank. Bill Hay will take Shepherd and Davis, they will take the downstream one. Sergeant Poulson and Emerson will guard my team and Sergeant Barker and Corporal Hewitt the other."

They nodded. "What about the anti-tank guns?"

I looked at Private Beaumont. He shrugged, "Put some shells in the emplacements and chuck in a couple of grenades. Simple."

Often it was the simplest ideas which were the best. After we had eaten we reapplied the blacking. The hard part would be getting across the river. Gordy came up with a solution to that. "We'll distract them sir. I'll lob a few grenades over the ford and then Polly can fire the MG 42. They will think we are attacking there and you lads can swim over the river. It is not that wide and looks to be fairly shallow."

"That will do. 2200 hundred hours for the off."

Private Beaumont supervised the charges we would be using. He filled two empty wine bottles with petrol. If we doused the inside of the tanks then we would have instant fire. The real problem would be the crew. This was the 1st SS. They would die hard! While Barker and Poulson were getting in position I said, "Take no chances with these S.S. They are all ruthless killers. We have two Colts between us, Fletcher, and our job is to watch Private Beaumont's back!"

"Sir!"

We were wearing our rubber soled shoes. They would not weigh us down. We crept closer to the river and waited. One of the German sentries was careless. I saw the glow of his cigarette. I marked his position. The sound of the grenade landing and exploding was our signal and we slipped into the water. I guessed it would not be very deep and so it proved. There was the sound of alarm in the German camp. Then the heavy MG 42 started up. It sounded like a chain saw as it ripped through the undergrowth. It must have confused the Germans. A second grenade landed and the machine guns fired again. We were on the other bank when it stopped. There was silence. Then I heard Germans shouting orders and there was movement deep in the woods as men were rushed to defend the ford. I drew my Colt and held it before me as I emerged from the water. I saw a white face appear from my right and I fired. At a range of twenty feet I could not miss. I heard the sound of Fletcher's silenced gun and then a German asked, "What is that Dieter?"

I mumbled, "Something I ate," and made a vomiting noise. When he laughed there was a second phut and Fletcher shot him. We moved down the bank towards the anti-tank guns. There were sandbags around them and two sentries sat atop them smoking and talking. They were darker lumps against the blackness of the night. Fletcher and I crept forward. As I neared them, moving silently, I heard them speaking.

"What do you think that firing was before?"

"The damned British and Americans just want to keep us awake. Don't worry the men we sent there will send them back to their beds. They do not attack in the night." He laughed, "At least not without artillery! They are fools. You know when they are coming! Look on the bright side. We now have this magnificent sandbagged hotel all to ourselves. Hans left that half sausage he stole from the farmhouse. When we have our coffee we will have some."

There was silence. It was so quiet now that the firing had stopped that I could hear them breathing.

"The Engineer sergeant says we pull out tomorrow."

"And where would we go? Across this puddle? Their Sherman tanks might be death traps but there are still enough of them to stop us."

"Seth told me that he heard there are poles to the north of us. I wouldn't want to go there. The Poles have long memories."

"The Fuhrer was right; they are not humans. We did not kill enough when we were there. But how does Seth know? He listens to the radio that is all. We know that their chatter is just that, chatter. We have been in worse than this and survived. The sergeant does not know us. Let him make the tank traps and then he can scurry back to Dusseldorf. We are S.S. and we stay and fight."

We were less than four feet from them. I raised my gun and, after nodding to Fletcher, fired two bullets into the back of the one on the right. They both pitched forward. In one movement the three of us leapt into the first emplacement. Private Beaumont quickly grabbed shells and began to lay them around the gun. Fletcher went to the second one while I scanned the woods. I could see, some way in, a glow. They had a fire going. Although I could not see it I knew that the Tiger was deeper in the woods. I did not think the next part would be as easy.

I found the path which led into the woods. I went to scout it out. I could neither see nor hear anyone close by. It made sense. Our machine gun and rifles had made the bank untenable. They would not risk us firing at night. The sentries had told me where the rest of the watch was. They had gone to the ford. Private Beaumont and Fletcher joined me and we walked cautiously down the path. With the bodies littering the riverbank we now had to work quickly but too much speed meant noise. We would not be careless.

There were five men near the tank. In their black uniforms they were almost invisible. I only knew where they were from their conversation. These were playing cards and gambling. The fact that there were five meant it was the full crew. I saw the long snout of the barrel and the huge turret. It was a blacker shadow against a black night. This would be a harder kill than the last one. The backs of three were to us. That meant that two faced us. They had to die first.

Lying prone I held my Colt in two hands. The range was just fifty feet but it was dark. I did not want to risk going closer for the Germans who faced us might see us. They had some sort of dim light to enable them to see their cards and it gave a slight glow to the faces of the two men on the far side. I aimed at the one on the right. Annoyingly one of those with his back to us kept moving. I hissed, "One, two, three."

On three I fired. My first bullet must have clipped the arm of one of those with their backs to us before hitting the man at whom I had aimed. I shifted to the right and fired again. The man I had clipped had cried out but my second bullet silenced him. Fletcher had hit one but the other two had risen. One shouted, "Alarm!" as they hurtled towards the danger. I saw they had pulled S.S. daggers from their belts. I shot the one, who had shouted, with two bullets. I heard the click of a jam from my left and Fletcher mumbled, "Shit!" The German dived on to Fletcher. I put my Colt to the side of the German's head and fired. The head disappeared, showering Fletcher in blood, bones and brains.

Just then one of the Germans I thought was dead reached out and grabbed me. My gun was empty and, as I fell I let it fall and drew my dagger. I saw a flash of metal in his right hand and I grabbed it with my left. My right hand darted in and stabbed him in the throat. His right arm went limp and he gurgled his life away.

I stood, "Private Beaumont, you have minutes, if that!"

"Sir."

In the distance I could hear shouts. At night sound can be misleading. They had heard the shout but would not know the direction. Then I heard firing. It was the other team. It was all going badly wrong.

"You alright Fletcher?"

"No sir. Bastard stuck me." He held his hand to his shoulder.

I took a dressing from my webbing and jammed it under his battledress. "Get back to the eight eights and we will follow. Go!" As he lurched away, clutching his shoulder I reloaded my Colt. I saw the dagger in the German's hand. I stuck it in my battledress. It was the least I could do for Fletcher.

I heard footsteps coming through the woods. I ran towards them and knelt. I saw white faces. Holding the Colt in two hands I fired steadily. There was a cry and a German voice said, "Take cover, they are by the tank."

I took out a grenade and hurled it high into the air. I turned and ran back to the tank. "Private Beaumont! Now would be a good time!"

He emerged from the top of the tank. I could smell the petrol. He slammed shut the hatch. "It is a five minute timer sir but they are not that accurate....."The sound of his voice was drowned by the exploding grenade I had thrown. There were cries and then a machine gun chattered.

"Run! Fletcher is injured by the eighty eights. I will cover you." As he ran I turned and fired four shots in an arc. Then I followed him. Bullets shredded the trees above my head. I was just a hundred feet away when the tank exploded. It did not make as much noise as I had expected. Private Beaumont had been right; the hull had contained most of it. Then I heard the ammunition as it exploded inside. It sounded like a fire fight. As I neared the gun emplacement I heard a second explosion from the other side of the ford. This one was not as loud. Fletcher was slumped on the ground.

"Private Beaumont, get him across the river."

"But the guns sir!"

"Leave that with me!" As he helped Fletcher to his feet and headed to the river I holstered my Colt and picked up the sentry's sub machine gun. I emptied the magazine into the darkness and threw it into a gun pit. Then I took out two grenades. I took out the pins of both of them. I dropped them into the two sandbagged gun emplacements and then ran towards the river. The Germans were closer than I had expected and they were firing lower.

As bullets zipped through the air I heard Sergeant Poulson shout, "Get down sir!" I took a flat dive and hit the water. Our guns began to fire back. I stayed beneath the water. I felt a wave of concussion pass over the water above my head. I was safe from stray bullets and shrapnel there. I kicked hard. My hands touched the bank and I allowed my head to break surface. I turned and saw two fires where the guns were.

Fred Emerson reached down and held his hand out for me, "Come on sir. I think you have overstayed your welcome at this particular party!"

As I stood on the bank I looked back. The fire from the burning Tiger could be seen as a glow in the dark. "I think you are right, Freddie."

Chapter 13

"We'll stay here and keep an eye on them, sir. Private Beaumont took Fletcher to the doc."

"Thanks Sergeant Poulson. I hope that the others had a little more luck than we did."

Polly shook his head, "You came back alive, sir. I reckon you did have luck."

"What about the others?"

"Not back yet, sir."

I followed my men to the camp. The sound of the explosions had woken the Major. He wandered over, "What the hell happened, Captain? Did the Germans attack?"

"Not quite, sir. We nipped over and blew up the Tiger and the guns. One of my men was wounded."

He clapped me around the shoulder. "Dammit, I thought you were joking about doing something! You are full of surprises."

Just then Gordy Barker and John Hewitt appeared carrying Private Davis. "Davis was hit sir. I am not certain how bad it is. Shepherd has a flesh wound, Hay is bringing him."

The Major roared, "Medic!" Four men appeared, "Get this man to the doc and you two go and help the other Commando."

"Did they get the job done, Sergeant?"

"Half done sir. They got the tank but not the guns."

I turned to the Major. "Sorry sir."

"Don't apologise son. We just keep the tanks away from the ford. Our boys can cross and take out the eighty eights. Damned fine job! Go to the mess tent. There will be food on the go." He looked to the east. "Dawn is not very far away and I guess we will have to face those tanks they brought up."

Just then a sergeant came up, "Major, we have just heard from Headquarters. They are beginning their attack on Falaise. They want us to attack at 0700."

He nodded, "Thanks for the wakeup call, Captain. I guess you can be a spectator here. This will be tank against tank."

I went to the mess tent. I was not hungry but the coffee was more than welcome. I smiled as I saw Sergeant Poulson wrinkle his forehead. He was a tea man! My men were all seated around a table. "What happened to Scouse, Captain?"

"His Colt jammed and he was stabbed." They nodded. "Davis?"

"He took a bullet sir. Shepherd too but Ken was lucky it hit his gun first. He will need a new rifle and the doc will have a forest of splinters to remove but he will be right as rain. Davis? Not so certain. It was a big hole." Lance Sergeant Hewitt was a realist. If he said it was serious then you could take that to the bank.

"We may not be needed today. But I want everyone ready in case we are."

"Not likely is it, sir?"

"No Gordy. The Major was right. We will see how the Shermans do against the self-propelled guns and the Mark IVs. At least those two Tigers can't make flanking shots."

I went along to the sick bay. It was the back of a lorry. The doctor had a makeshift operating room under a large piece of canvas. Fletcher and Shepherd were sat up. I saw that Fletcher's side was bandaged. It was Shepherd's upper arm. They made to rise. "No, lads. You recuperate. They won't need us today."

"How is Davis sir? He was next to me. That could have been me."

"The doc is working on him, Shepherd. I guess he will do what he can and then send him back to Caen."

"Sorry about the gun sir. I clean it every day..."

"Don't worry about it, Scouse. These things happen and here is a souvenir." I handed him the S.S. dagger. "It is the knife that cut you. Might be something to show to the kids... if you live long enough to have them!"

"Don't you worry sir. I have plans. This war has shown me that I can move and do great things."

"Such as?"

He grinned and shrugged, "At the moment, sir, I haven't got the faintest idea but after the war." He tapped his nose, "I shall keep my eyes open!"

We had heard the sound of fighting. It was just a few miles away in Falaise but there seemed to be even more coming from the north of us. After I left the sick bay I wandered over to the headquarters' tent. The Regimental Sergeant Major, Angus Watson, looked up when I entered, "Captain Harsker. That was a nice piece of work last night."

"It is what we do. When the enemy threatens to hang you for wearing a Commando uniform it sort of throws out the rule book."

"Aye, you are right there. What can I do for you sir? The Major and the lads are getting ready to go into action."

"I know. What is going on to the north of us? I have heard firing there since the early hours."

"That would be the Poles sir, Koszutski's battle group, the 1st Armoured Division. They are part of the First Canadian Army sir. They took Hill 462 and Jerry wants it back. They are blocking his way home."

"They are pulling out?"

"Between you and me sir, I reckon so. Intelligence reckons that is why they threw together the armour to face us. It is there to allow their big boys to escape." He held up his hands. "I may be wrong but I have been reading reports and listening to radio chatter."

"You could be right Sergeant Major. Why else dig in a pair of Tigers? They had no intention of crossing the river. They just didn't want us advancing into their flanks."

I headed to the half-track and stood watching the Shermans as they prepared to advance. The sun was up now and the battlefield bathed in the cold blue light of morning. We had a good piece of high ground and I could see down the valley of the La Dives to Trun. The bombers and the battles thus far had thinned the trees considerably. I watched as the Major raised his arm and Kowalski took his Sherman forward. The foot soldiers marched behind having left their Kangaroos. I did not blame them. This way they could take advantage of all the cover they had. The bombing had made it easier for men to find somewhere to shelter. The German self-propelled guns fired first. I could not see them but I recognised the sound of their shells. A direct hit could take out a Sherman but they missed more than they hit. The danger was to the infantry who could be struck by flying shrapnel.

Behind me I heard a roar as a flight of Typhoons flew in so low that I could see the pilots! The sound of the Sherman's guns firing drowned out the sound of the rockets as they all converged on the German armour. I doubted that anything would survive such a barrage but amazingly a self-propelled gun and one Mark IV continued to fire and a Sherman burst into flames. Every tank turned to fire at the Mark IV. It erupted into a fire ball as three shells hit it. The self-propelled gun tried to retreat but the Shermans were fast and they closed with it. That, too, was destroyed. The infantry cheered and raced through the trees dispersing the Germans who, when they could, ran. The diehards, the S.S., stayed to fight to the death. I put down my binoculars and wandered back to the half-track.

"Emerson, get everything packed. I think we will be heading for Trun soon."

"Sir!"

"Hewitt, go and find out if we can have our wounded. If not then they will have to go to hospital with Private Davis."

"Private Davis was taken an hour since sir. He was in a bad way."

"Right. Look after his things for him eh? I shall get my head down for half an hour. Sergeant Poulson, wake me when we are needed."

"Yes sir."

A Commando could almost fall asleep at will. I curled up in a foetal ball and was soon asleep. I woke just as quickly when I was shaken by Sergeant Poulson. "It's time sir."

"What time is it?"

"Two o'clock in the afternoon sir. The Canadians have taken Falaise and they have mopped up the last of those who were at the road block."

"And the Major wants us to sniff out trouble again?"

"That's about the size of it, sir. I had Lance Sergeant Hay take the lads out and pick up ammo and guns. We have another MG 42. That'll come in handy. We have more grenades and plenty of ammo for the Mauser and your Luger."

I felt more cheerful already. "Thanks. Let's go then."

Just then Emerson appeared with a large steaming mug. "Here y'are sir. We found some tea and we put on a brew. You can't go to war with just coffee inside you. It's not British!"

It was after dark that we were summoned. The column had halted and the Canadians were assessing the situation. We drove down the road passing the dead Germans. I noticed that many of these were not the S.S. They had been sacrificed to save the elite. Then we passed the burnt out armour. Charred bodies lay alongside them. I saw that the Shermans had not escaped unscathed. At least five had been knocked out. Two of them had their crews working on them, cannibalising the ones with more damage. We found the Major with his officers just a mile from Trun.

He smiled as he lit the stub of a cigar. "Sorry to call on you again, Captain, but we have been ordered to take Trun. I am reluctant to go charging in. I am running out of tanks. We have heard that the S.S. are banging on the door of Hill 462 and the Poles are having a tough time of it. Can you get in and tell me what we might find? If you like I can give you some of my men to help you."

I nodded, "It is what we do. We will go in first and if we need your men we will send for them. Have some ready eh sir?" I turned and said, "Al Jolson time. Mount up."

The Major said, "Just like that?"

"No point in wasting time chatting is there, sir?" I pointed to the blackened area of forest to the south of us. "We were there not long ago, at night. We had to fight our way back to our lines. At least this time, if we have to run, you guys are close!"

He nodded, "Good luck!"

114

I jumped in the cab and began to black up. "Emerson drive up to the outskirts. Take it slowly and no lights."

Trun was tiny. The bombers had devastated it and I suspected that the civilians had fled long ago. In theory the Major should have been able to drive in but there was something not quite right. From the map there appeared to be one road which ran north to south and one which ran east west. We stopped at the pile of rubble which had been the first house. "Fletcher you and Shepherd stay here and man the machine gun. Sergeant Poulson, I want you and Sergeant Barker to take Emerson. Go down the south side of the town. I will take Lance Sergeant Hewitt and Private Beaumont. We will do the north side. I don't think there are any civilians so shoot first and ask questions later. It doesn't matter if they know we are here."

"Sir."

I took my Thompson. I still had five magazines. After that I would be using my Luger. "Beaumont, Tail End Charlie!" I climbed over the rubble and headed for the next half wrecked building. Some of the ones I could see looked to have half a roof and, perhaps, one or two walls. Others had none. I stared ahead and looked from left to right. I was looking for things which shouldn't be there. I hurried to the solid looking wall of what looked to have been a boulangerie. I peered around the corner. I was about to step forward when I glanced down and saw a wire. There was a booby trap. I whistled to attract Sergeant Poulson's attention. He glanced over. I knelt and pointed to the wire. He nodded. He would check his side for such booby traps.

I whispered, "Booby trap. Beaumont, disarm it and then follow."

"Right sir but just check ahead eh? If this was us we would lay two."

He was right and I looked around. I didn't see any wire but I did see a man made pile of stones. Kneeling down I put my hands inside and felt a potato masher. "You are right, there is another one here under these stones." I stepped out into the street. I was taking a risk but it was less risky than a booby trap. I knew there could be a sniper with his gun trained on me. It was ironic because I had done the same more than twenty four hours earlier. I suddenly stepped to the left and then crouched. I knew that Hewitt would do the same. It would throw off any sniper who had a telescopic sight.

We had almost reached the crossroads and I had begun to think that Trun had been abandoned when I saw, across from the ruined buildings and road, the camouflaged barrel of an eighty eight. I pretended that I hadn't seen it. I turned and said, "There is an anti-tank gun behind me. Beaumont, you have good eyes. Can you see it?"

He just moved his eyes and not his head. Keeping his voice level he said, "Yes sir, and there is a machine gun to its right."

"Let's have a bit of play acting eh?" I shouted, "Sergeant Poulson. It looks clear. We are heading back. Just check the far side of the buildings over there will you?"

"What sir? We aren't far from the crossroads."

"I know but Private Davis here has good eyes and he can see nothing directly ahead."

Sergeant Poulson caught on and he nodded, "You are right sir. Dead eyed Davis, eh? Right lads over the rubble."

I began to walk back. When I reached the place where Beaumont had disarmed the booby traps I quickly clambered over the stones. Hewitt and Beaumont had barely managed it when the machine gun opened up. The Germans had realised they had been seen and their ambush spotted. They were using tracer and I saw the arc of bullets strike where we had stood. Sergeant Poulson and his team had already taken up a defensive position and their machine guns returned fire. I kept going. I knew that the Canadians would now realise that there were Germans in Trun. Part of our job was done but I needed to see the extent of their defence. Was it just a last ditch defence at the crossroads? While my other section fired at the ambush I crawled over the rubble towards the north south road. Hewitt and Beaumont followed me. Another machine gun fired but it was firing blind. We were in dead ground but it did tell me where a second defensive position was. It was north of the first one. We took shelter behind a chimney. It had once been inside a house but the house had now gone leaving it like a skeletal finger pointing to the sky.

Hewitt hissed, "There is a tower sir. It looks like the remains of a church. I think I saw someone up there."

I did not peer around the chimney. A tower would be a perfect place for a sniper. "How far away would you say it was?"

"A hundred yards sir, no more."

"Right. I am going to make a move. When I do the two of you see if you can make his position untenable!"

"Sir."

I crouched and readied myself. I risked a glance ahead. There were broken chairs and a sofa before me. I had a plan. "Ready! Go!"

I jumped up and dived on to the wrecked sofa. A bullet pinged off the chimney. I had heard no report. He was using a silencer. Then the two Thompsons sent sparks flying from the tower. I jumped up and ran towards the edge of the road. I could not be seen from the tower. Wriggling through a tunnel of stones and rocks I glanced across the road. I was hidden from view but there, less than forty yards from me were Germans. I saw the barrels of their guns. I spotted the eighty eight. They had at least three of them. Then I realised where they might have got them from. The petrol dump had been ringed with anti aircraft guns. With the dump destroyed they had been given another use. I backed out. When I could see the sofa again I whistled.

"Sir?"

"I am on my way back. Give him a burst and I will join you."

I could see the chimney. It was just feet away but with a sniper on the loose that was a lifetime. The two Thompsons rattled away. I ran. I did not go in a straight line. As I threw myself behind the chimney a bullet struck the brickwork just above Hewitt's head.

"I have seen enough. Let's get back to the Major." We crawled until we hit the dead ground and then we stood. Reaching the first booby trap we ran as fast as we could back to the Shermans. As we passed the half-track I said, "Fletcher, get my sniper rifle ready and find the rocket launcher!"

"You guys found something huh?"

"They have anti-tanks guns and machine guns along the Vimoutiers to Argentan road. They are camouflaged. You should wait until you can have some air support."

He shook his head, "Headquarters say that the Poles are running out of ammo. We have to get to that road so that they can relieve them. They are trapping the whole of the Seventh Army. We have to do it tonight." He turned, "Start the engines."

"Major before you do that think, please. You have lost too many tanks. You go down that road and I guarantee that you will lose another three or four. Use your infantry. If they move in small groups with one group covering and the other moving they can get close. If you have grenade launchers or mortars then you can make it too hard for them." He did not look convinced. "What have you got to lose, sir? It will take an hour to find out if this will work and if the infantry can destroy a gun or two then you might have a better chance of success. It would be a slim one but better than this."

He nodded, "Very well and what will you be doing?"

"There is sniper and an observation post. We are going to get rid of it." I turned and headed back to the half-track. I turned to Beaumont and Hewitt, "You two, I want you to take the rocket launcher we acquired. I will try to take out the sniper. You take out the tower."

"Sir."

Fletcher was waiting for us. "How's it going sir?"

"The same as always, Fletcher, trying to stay alive when every German on the planet seems intent on killing us!" While the other two prepared the launcher and rockets I made sure I had spare Mauser clips. I looked through the sight. It was not perfect. It was too dark to be that but it would have to do.

I turned as a company of Canadian soldiers appeared, "Captain Harsker?"

"Yes sir."

"I am Major Grogan. I have been told you know where Jerry is?"

"I know where some are. They have the crossroads covered with at least one anti-tank gun and machine guns. There are more to the north of the crossroads and, I am guessing to the south. There is a church tower with a sniper and an OP. We will take that out. It should make your task easier." I pointed across the road. "I have three men dug in over there. They can give covering fire. If you can get men across then I am certain they will give you information on the southern road."

"If?"

"They have a machine gun and it is aimed at the middle of the road."

"Thanks."

"You will know if we succeed."

"How?"

"You won't be able to see a church tower!"

We ran back to the booby trap sight and then crawled to the chimney. The fire from the other side was more sporadic now. I guessed the Germans were saving their ammunition. I had a problem. I had to expose myself in order to get into position.

"Beaumont, give me your Thompson. I will give you cover. If you make the sofa I used then you can't be seen by the sniper but you can see the tower. I will then use the Mauser."

"Right sir."

"Ready?"

"Ready."

I took a step to the right and emptied the magazine at the church tower. I saw the bullets chipping stone from it and then, as I dived back in I felt a tug on my right sleeve. I laid down the Thompson and picked up the Mauser. Hewitt and Beaumont had gone. They now needed me to keep the sniper and OP crew occupied. I dropped to my knees and then laid full length. I rolled to my left. A pair of stones formed a V and I laid the barrel between it. Two bullets in quick succession struck the stones. A splinter of stone struck my cheek. I peered through the sight. I could not see the sniper but I could see where he was firing from. I kept my right finger on the trigger and reached over to find a rock. I wanted to make a movement and attract his attention. I hurled the rock high. A bullet smacked into the stone close to where my left hand had been. I had seen the flash from his muzzle. I fired two shots then moved my rifle marginally to the right and fired another two. I sent the last one to the left. I jammed another clip in.

118

I heard a whoosh from in front of me and watched the trail of the rocket head towards the tower. Although intended for tanks a damaged church tower was as good a target. The effect was spectacular. It hit slightly above where they intended but the flash showed those within and I snapped off another clip. I hit two. I could not tell if one was the sniper or not. I reloaded and then the second rocket hit. This time there was no mistake and the top of the tower tumbled and crashed to the ground. The sniper was dead now!

Chapter 14

I crawled over the rubble to join the other two. I took the Tommy gun with me. I could hear increased gunfire from the south side of the road. The wall of rubble which hid us from the Germans also meant that we could not see them.

I carefully laid the rifle down. We would need that again soon. "Well done you two. That was a fine shot. How many rockets do you have left?"

"Two sir. Hey, your face! It is bleeding."

Hewitt dived into his bag for his kit. I put my hand up to my face and it came away wet. Beaumont said, "Sir, you have been shot too! In the arm. It is bleeding!"

I looked and saw that my battle dress was bloody. I remembered something hitting my right arm but thought it had been a rock.

Lance Sergeant Hewitt took charge, "Beaumont, get his battle dress off." He held a dressing to my face as Beaumont stripped my battle dress off. "We'll have to get you back, sir."

"This is a scratch and you know it. We will stay."

Beaumont tore the shirt at the shoulder. "Keep this dressing pressed tightly against his face, Rog." My medic began to examine the wound. How he could I had no idea for it was still dark. "The bullet went through and if you aren't in pain then it missed the bone. You have been lucky." He poured water from his canteen over it and then used my torn shirt to dry it. He shook sulphanilamide powder on it and then applied a dressing. He fastened the bandage tightly.

"Your face is a mess sir. We should get back and get it seen to. Your young lady won't be happy if you go back like Scarface."

"Just do your best. I am not going to die am I?"

"No sir."

"Then just get it done. Time is wasting."

He used a small dressing. I felt like a fool with what felt like an enormous dressing stuck to the side of my face but Hewitt seemed happier when it was done. I put my battle dress back on and then picked up my rifle. All this time we had heard fighting behind us and now we turned as we heard footsteps on the rocks. A dozen Canadians, led by the sergeant arrived.

"Jeez sir, are you alright?"

"Fine sergeant. I am just auditioning for the next Boris Karloff film, *'The Mummy Returns'*." He laughed. "Keep your heads down. This is dead ground here but once you get over this next pile of rubble you will be within range of their machine guns."

"Right." He turned. "You heard him boys. Spread out and crawl. You get killed and you are in trouble with me!"

They were good. They used the cover of the dead ground and the damaged buildings. Even so a machine gun chattered and a soldier fell back with a line of bullet holes in his chest. One moment of carelessness had cost him. The angry Canadians began to fire back. Their Bren gun was the only machine gun they had.

"Come on, let's give them some help here."

"Sir, that dressing will make you stand out like a sore thumb!"

I put my hand up and wiped it along the sooty wood from the fire which had destroyed this house. I smeared it on the dressing. "There. That good enough?"

Hewitt shook his head and grinned, "Yes sir!"

We made our way down to the end of the line of Canadians. This was the furthest north that we had been and the one we knew the least about. There was a broken house front. The remains of the window frame and the door broke up the outline. Smoke from guns and grenades now drifted over the town. It was all light arms. The sound of mortars from both sides and the crump of grenades was punctuated by rifle and machine gun fire. I glanced at my watch as we neared it. There was less than an hour until dawn. We had until then to clear the anti-tank gun so that the armour could complete their mission. I raised myself slowly so that I could see over the edge of what had been the window frame. As I did so a mortar shell landed forty feet in front of me. I was protected from the blast by the remains of the wall but, by its flash, I saw that we were sixty yards from the Germans. The open road lay between us. It was a sixty yards killing zone. I could see the anti-tank gun down the street. Opposite us was a German machine gun behind sand bags.

I lowered my head. "Sixty yards away is a machine gun post. If we take that then the Canadians have a chance. See if you can get in the wrecked door. I will try to cover you from the window. Take out the machine gun and then see what you can do about the anti-tank gun."

"Sir."

I made sure I had a fresh clip in the rifle and then slowly raised my head. The machine gun and the German defenders were firing at the Canadian gun flashes. The firing was sporadic from both sides. Ammunition had to be tight. The Canadians had cover as did the Germans. It was the machine gun which made the difference. If they had not been husbanding their ammunition it might have been a different story. However they were firing in short bursts when the Canadians fired in reply. I brought up the rifle and aimed at the gunner. In the sight, even at night, he looked close enough to touch. I fired one shot and then moved the rifle a touch to the left and fired at the loader. I dropped my head and pressed it against the wall as rifle bullets smacked into the bricks. I felt them as they struck. There was a whoosh from my right as the rocket was launched. I heard it strike and raised my head. They had hit the gun and it was broken beyond repair. Those around it had been laid low by the effect. I brought up the rifle and shot three dazed Germans before they had time to recover.

As I ducked to reload I shouted, "Hit the anti-tank gun while they are still disorientated."

"Sir!"

I heard a German officer shout for his men to bring up a spare machine gun. I also heard the Canadian sergeant shout, "Come on boys!"

I half stood and aimed my rifle. I saw the officer pointing at the Canadians. He had a pistol out. I shot him in the chest and switched to his sergeant. He saw me and was ducking when my bullet hit his shoulder. There was a whoosh close by as the rocket sped towards the anti-tank gun. I spun around to the next broken window and dropped to my knee. It was not before time. Where I had just stood was hit by rifles and automatic gun fire. I heard an explosion further down the street and then heard the cheer as the Canadians charged. They were lucky. The attention of the Germans was on the rocket launcher and me. They made it to the edge of the road before the Germans saw their problem. I stood and fired my last three bullets from my magazine at the Germans. They were snap shots but they kept the heads of the Germans down.

Slinging my rifle over my shoulder I drew my Luger. Firing I clambered through the broken window frame and joined the Canadians. Glancing down the street I saw the anti-tank gun. They were trying to repair it. The rocket had damaged it. As we crossed the road the Germans began to fall back. I emptied my pistol at their backs.

I dropped close by the sandbags of the wrecked machine gun post. My men joined me. I saw that the Sergeant and six men had survived. He grinned, "An officer who leads from the front! I like it, sir!"

"I think we have pushed our luck enough eh Sergeant? Send a runner back to the Major and tell him that we have the north end of the road heading north. We need support."

"Right sir. Hargreaves, you heard the officer. Now get back and keep your head down. The rest of you take cover and reload."

I was already reloading my Luger. That done I crawled to the top of the sandbags. I saw that there were five dead Germans inside. Now that dawn was breaking I could see that they had another defensive line on the far side of the village. It was a hundred and fifty yards away behind the wrecked church tower. There was still fighting going on to the south of us by the crossroads. The village was not taken but we had the main road and that had been our primary objective.

The sergeant crawled over to me, "What will they do next sir?"

"It depends how badly they want this road. Have your men find any German guns and grenades. Until we are relieved this could get hot. They will have glasses on us and now that it is almost daylight they will see how few we are."

My men had already started to gather equipment, They did not need to be told. Beaumont grinned as he held up an S.S. dagger. "Scouse is not the only one with one now eh sir?"

We began to pile stones up in front of us. I knew they would soon try to dislodge us and it would take time to bring up the tanks and reinforcements. I had no idea how Sergeant Poulson and the others were doing south of us. Lance Corporal Hewitt put his arm across me to stop me working. "It is bad enough you staying here sir without undoing my work. If you start this bleeding again then I will have to look at it and that means I can't fight can I sir?"

He was right and I smiled, "Point taken."

I lifted the rifle and rested it on the stones in front of me. He had been right to chastise me for I felt blood seeping from my wound. My face felt like a balloon and it was beginning to hurt. To take my mind off the pain I peered through the telescopic sight. I saw that the Germans were keeping their heads down. To encourage them I fired at a helmet. I saw the helmet fall to the side when my bullet clanked into it and then every head disappeared. They had no high ground for their own sniper. We had that in our favour, at least. We had just finished our makeshift repairs when Hargreaves ran back. "They are on their way, sergeant."

"Sir, Hargreaves, there is an officer present. Sorry sir. The Major is on his way. Company E are right behind me. They haven't taken the crossroads yet and there is still an anti-tank gun. The Major is sending F and G to eliminate it."

I turned to the sergeant, "If they are holding at the crossroads then they will come here next. If they can get rid of us then they hold their line and the S.S. can escape the trap."

"Right sir, you are the expert, what do we do?"

"They will come in pairs; one firing while the other runs. Have your men fire in pairs themselves. Until Company E gets here then the handful we have will have to do."

"We have a couple of the German submachine guns."

"Good, they are handy. Beaumont show them how to use the German grenades."

"Right sir."

I had four grenades ready; two of each. I could hear the firing to the south of us but there was ominously little movement ahead. It meant they were preparing. "Sergeant, stand to!"

"Right lads, stand to! Jerry is on his way. Make the bastards bleed eh?"

They began with mortars. Ironically their own defences worked in our favour. We had the sandbags they had used to protect our fore. Even so it was an effective barrage for we had to keep our heads down and they advanced while we sheltered. I shouted, "The second it stops up and fire at them. Their infantry will be coming behind the mortars." I laid down my rifle and took out my Luger and Colt.

When the mortars began to fall behind us I knew they were coming. I raised my head and using the two automatics began firing. The sergeant shouted, "Right lads, let's join Billy the Kid here!" I heard both guns click empty.

They rose and laid down a withering fire. The Germans took cover but not before I heard two shouts. "Sarge, Wyatt has been hit and Jorgenson!"

"Hewitt!"

"On it sir."

I picked up my rifle and raised my head. "Here they come!" As I had expected they now fired and ran. I was glad that I had my helmet as a bullet ricocheted off a stone and struck the top of my tin lid. I fired at a German who was firing. Beaumont shot the one who was running. They were now within forty yards of us. "Beaumont, get a grenade ready." I smashed the porcelain top of the German grenade. The advantage they had was that you could get more distance with them. I pulled the cord and hurled it. I watched as it spun end over end. It travelled further that way. "Grenade!"

"Grenade!" Beaumont's went a moment after mine. The two explosions were almost simultaneous.

I peered through the sights of my rifle. I saw a hand rise and I fired at it. I saw the grenade it had been holding, drop and then there was an explosion. I saw a German with half his face missing fall forward. They stopped coming. I saw guns appear over stones as they fired blind to keep our heads down.

"Watch for grenades and mortars!"

A chorus of, "Sir!" came from my right.

I scanned the enemy line with my scope. I saw the hint of a helmet and fired. I was so close that I almost hit it. I did hit the brick next to it. Shards flew off. Then the mortars began to track towards us. It was a creeping barrage as they increased the range. I tried to bury myself in the rubble. Lying with my back to the wall I saw the advancing Canadians. The mortars had thinned out Company E but I saw, with them, Private

Fletcher. He ran faster than the Canadians. He was used to this and they were not. I heard Lance Sergeant Hewitt groan, "If he tears his stitches I will have him. I swear I will."

He almost leapt over the road and showed how lucky he was by arriving between two mortar shells. He slumped next to me. "I'll have to give up the ciggies!" I had heard that before. Before I could say anything he handed me two smoke grenades. "Sir, Headquarters have been on the radio. They are sending some Hurries with bombs. They will make one pass and on the second they want you to pop smoke. They will bomb on the far side of the smoke."

"Thanks Fletcher but why you?"

"I was there when it came in. I had to do my bit."

"You have done your bit and then some. Right, take cover. These mortars are getting damned close."

I heard Beaumont shout, "Grenade!"

I pushed myself on top of Fletcher. It was only when I heard an explosion behind me I realised that he had thrown one. I turned and peered into the telescopic sight. I saw a German half-track making its way across the rubble. It didn't look to be as uneven on the German side.

"Any more rockets, Beaumont?" I handed him the two smoke grenades. He had a good arm. He had played cricket for his school before the war.

"All gone sir."

Fletcher said, "There are some back at camp sir."

Hewitt snarled, "Stay there Scouse. It will be too late by the time anyone got there and back."

I aimed my rifle at the half-track. They had the windscreen and metal visor up. However there was a slit through which the driver could look. I took aim and fired five bullets in quick succession. When the vehicle slewed to the left I knew I had hit something or worried the driver at the very least. I put a fresh clip in and, as the half-track lumbered obliquely from us, took a couple of shots at the gunner. One must have wounded him for he disappeared.

"Good shot sir."

"Thank you Beaumont but I fear I have only sent it in the direction of the crossroads."

We now had another forty men from Company E. They began to fill in along the line. Then I heard the familiar sound of Hawker Hurricanes. The flight of three came over. They waggled their wings as they did so.

"Cover fire! Beaumont, smoke!"

I reloaded my pistols as he did so. He stood, as we all opened fire, and hurled the two grenades. The red smoke drifted with the wind as the three fighter bombers came so low that you felt you could touch them. Dad had told me that was the sign of a very skilful and confident pilot.

"Take cover!"

The three fighter bombers had incendiary bombs and HE. The combination was lethal. One bomb must have hit the half-track while the rest took out the mortar crews. When the ringing had stopped in my ears, I stood. I saw the wrecked half-track and spied two Germans, wreathed in fire.

"Right lads! At them!" I said to Fletcher. "Stay here and watch my rifle." I took my reloaded Colt and Luger and ran towards the German lines. There were the grisly, writhing bodies of dying Germans as well as the dismembered bodies of those struck by HE. As we neared the rear of their lines dazed Germans stood. I had quick reactions and two automatic weapons. They fell before me. When we reached the mortar pits we stopped. The Germans had fled. To the south I could still hear fighting at the crossroads but we had a perimeter. Then I heard the sound of a Sherman seventeen pounder. The armour had arrived.

I heard the Captain of Company E say, "Form a perimeter!"

Then as I felt the blood dripping from my arm I found myself blacking out. It was though night had fallen again.

Chapter 15

I woke and looked up at a doctor. He shook his head, "What is it about you Commandos? I have had to stitch your Corporal again! And now you have undone all the good work of your Lance Sergeant!"

I said, weakly, "Sorry Doc but no one told the Germans."

"Well you can lie there and rest for at least six hours as can Corporal Fletcher."

"I need to..."

"You need to sleep and this," I felt a prick in my arm, "will ensure that you do."

Blackness followed. When I awoke again I was no longer in a sick bay but in a cot and under one of our tents. Gordy Barker sat by me, "At last, Sleeping Beauty awakes! Morning sir!"

"Morning? What day is this?"

"You were brought back yesterday afternoon just after the Major took the crossroads." He grinned, "We were completely out of ammunition sir! If the Major hadn't arrived we would have had to resort to hoying bricks at them! Trun is in our hands now but the Poles are still having a hard time at Hill 462. I reckon that we have not seen the end of those S.S. yet. Word is that there are still thousands trapped to the south and west of us. The only way home is through here and Hill 462. This isn't over yet sir."

"Did all of your team survive?"

"Freddie and Polly both have flesh wounds but nothing as spectacular as yours. The doc worked for hours stitching your face back together so that you wouldn't look like Frankenstein's Creature!"

"And the rest of the lads?"

"Outside making a brew. We are short of ammo, grenades and food but Fletcher managed to find a couple of bottles of wine! You know sir, that Scouser could fall in a pile of shit and find a ten bob note!"

My arm was bandaged and I struggled to rise.

"Here y'are sir. Give us your good hand. "I reckon you need to walk about a bit and get that anaesthetic out of your head. It took days for me to smell proper after my op."

I emerged from the tent and saw that it was bright sunshine. My men gave me a cheer as I did so.

"Thank you one and all." I tried to give a mock bow but as I nearly fell over I stopped.

Hewitt pulled over an old ammunition box. "Sit down sir. You did too much yesterday. We need to build you up again."

They handed me Sergeant Major's medicine, a huge mug full of hot, over sweetened and incredibly strong tea. As I drank it they told me of the half of the battle I had not seen. "We were hard pushed, sir, on the south side of the road. When the Canadians came it was easier but we had nowt to knock out their machine gun and eighty eight. The Canadians are brave buggers. They lost half their strength. When you lads knocked out the tower then we were able to get closer and we started lobbing grenades. The Canadians had the old Boys rifle. That did the job. It didn't knock out the eighty eight but they made sure it couldn't move and traverse. When the Hurries came the Major was right behind them and the Shermans finished it. We now have a perimeter a couple of miles the other side of Trun."

"But the Germans are still in the hole?"

Sergeant Poulson nodded, "Exactly sir. Their choice is surrender or fight their way out."

"And these are S.S. so we know exactly what they will choose."

"Then we had better be prepared to fight in the line again. I know we are short of ammo and guns. There must be a ton of stuff in Trun."

"That is where Beaumont and Shepherd are right now sir. They went with Bill Hay at first light. If there is anything out there then they will find it."

I relaxed a little, "Good. This is excellent tea. Any food?"

Emerson handed me some cardboard like bread around a huge chunk of mustard covered corned beef. "Sorry sir. The bread is God knows how many days old but we opened the tin fresh this morning!"

I ate it mechanically. The heavy dose of mustard killed any other taste and I knew I needed something inside me.

"Oh by the way sir, the Major asked if you could pop to his headquarters when you have a minute. I'll take you in Bertha if you like." I had not realised that we were still by the river close to the ford.

"Right. When I have finished this feast we will nip down."

I was keen to speak with the Major; not least because I want to know the bigger picture. If we had, indeed, trapped the Seventh Army and the S.S. Panzer divisions then we had the chance to end the war. My wounds and the prospect of losing Susan were a powerful incitement to survive the war.

Already the crossroads in Trun looked different. The road had been cleared of rubble. I could see the road blocks which had been erected on the north south road. The Shermans were all lined up facing the East. This was a bottleneck. The Major had just eight tanks in working order. As we had left our camp I had seen mechanics and engineers working furiously to repair three damaged tanks. They represented more than thirty three percent of our force.

The Major heard the half-track and came out to see us. He had the inevitable cigar. He grasped my hand. "My guys have not stopped talking about you! Another Sergeant York! God dammit, Captain, you are a hero. I have put you in for the Military Cross."

"Thank you, sir, but I was just doing what we do."

He shook his head, "Why is it you Brits have to be so modest? You did a damned fine job. You did everything that was asked of and more."

I shrugged, "It is just our nature. Your chaps were splendid. They held the line magnificently. They deserve any credit which is going."

He shook his head, "It looks like it is almost over. We have nearly closed the gap. The Americans and the French are racing for Paris and the Seine! The war is almost over!"

I spoke quietly, "Sir, we are facing the S.S. They do not surrender."

"We have destroyed more than fifty percent of their armour. They have no fuel! They can't hold out."

"They will fight you with everything they have. If they have no fuel they will dig in their Tigers and fight until they have no shells left. Then they will come out and fight until they have no bullets. If they are still alive then they will use their S.S. daggers, their teeth and their claws. When they are dead, that is the time they will stop fighting and they will kill many young men who should live. Do not take your foot off, what is it you say? The gas! They are not finished."

He looked deflated like a balloon from a carnival. He shook his head, "I thought you would have been excited!"

"Major, I joined in September nineteen thirty nine. I was at Dunkirk, Dieppe and St. Nazaire. I landed in Italy and Normandy. I have learned one thing: Germans do not give in. They do not surrender. When we are in Berlin you will see the hint of a smile. When I am walking the down the aisle, back in England, with my fiancée you will see a grin as big as all the world. Until then you will see caution."

He smiled, "I am glad I met you ,Captain. I had no idea what need we had of a handful of Commandos. Now I know. So you think we should dig in?"

I nodded, "Just like the Germans. If they are going to get home they have to come through here. The Poles, from what I have heard, are doing a great job. The more men and tanks we stop here the less we fight in Germany and if you think they are fighting hard for France then just imagine how hard they will fight for Germany!"

"You are right. Thanks for the advice but I am still putting you in for a medal."

When I got back to the camp our foragers had returned. We were now better equipped as Germans. They had more MG 42 and MG 34 as well as belt loads of ammunition. They were festooned with grenades. Beaumont shook his head. "It was like wandering through Father Christmas' grotto.

All the Canadians wanted were S.S. badges, daggers and hats. We could have brought back a ton more."

"Tomorrow we go back in line. The Germans have to break through here if they are to get home. How many rockets do we have left Beaumont?"

"Eight."

"We use them well. Grenades for the grenade launcher?"

Bill Hay said, "Ten."

"Then we use them wisely. The Canadians are brave lads but you are all fighters and you are killers. That is what we will need tomorrow. Fighters and killers."

They understood and they nodded. Sergeant Poulson asked, "And where will we be sir?"

"Where it is hottest. These lads need us. We won't let them down."

Word was passed to us that Pete Davis was on the mend. He would need a fortnight but we would get him back, eventually. The news raised the spirits of everyone. That night, as I went to the latrine I looked at my face in the mirror. I could not afford for the war to end soon. I looked hideous. The doctor had done a good job but I had a scar running from my eye to my chin. Susan would not want to know me and yet I had tried to protect myself. Sometimes things happened and you had no control over them. It was fate. If she accepted me with a scarred face, then it was meant to be.

We left before dawn for the new front line. We were not asked to go. We did so because the fight was not over and none of us were the sort to back off from bullies. The half-track was laden and we were better armed than we had been for some time. We were placed close by the La Dives river and on the road to Magny. The spot we were asked to hold was a little marshy and soft. The Shermans were in danger of bogging down had they used it. Our half-track could cope. As soon as we arrived I had the men cut down trees and undergrowth to give us protection and to clear a killing ground. By the time we had finished there was a jumble of wood and bushes before us. An enemy would have to find a way through them before they could get passed. To our left were Company G. They were dug in with machine guns and Bren guns. I did not think there were enough of them for the nearest tank was fifty yards to their left. It too had been dug in. The Canadians were learning how to fight the German way.

We left Bill Hay and John Hewitt in the half-track with the MG 42. Sergeant Poulson took the second MG 42 and Emerson with Ken Shepherd. They were by the river. Beaumont and Fletcher took the rocket launcher and their Thompsons. They were to the left of the half-track while Sergeant Gordy Barker had the grenade launcher behind the half-track. We would direct Gordy from the half-track. We had no one spare. There was no reserve. I had the two sniper rifles and I was in the half-track. We were committed. The river was to our south and Company A was to our left. The nearest Sherman was sixty yards to our left. I hoped it was close enough.

It was ten when we heard the rumble of armour. In the time we had had left we had placed many booby traps before us. We had plenty of Mills Bombs. We had learned the value of a thrown German grenade. We would use them well. They had no artillery. They had to use their tanks. They were, however, the 1st S.S. Panzer.

They used H.E. first. Luckily for us it was to our left. The Canadians had heeded our advice and dug in. I scanned the advancing troops with my binoculars. I saw few Panthers and Tigers left. They appeared to have a mixed bag of tanks but I did see Paratroopers. I recognised them from their distinctive helmets. From the intelligence we had they were the Sixth Parachute division. They were better than the S.S. for they were good soldiers as well as being fanatical. They would not be easy to kill.

"Watch it lads. These are paratroopers!"

My men needed no further information. I lifted my Mauser. I had two which meant I could fire ten shots before I needed to reload. My arm ached but the doctor had done a good job. I would not be able to indulge in any hand to hand combat but I could still squeeze a trigger. I also had the luxury of the metal of the half-track upon which to rest the gun. I would not tire as easily. The paratroopers moved quickly and, like Commandos, used cover well. I sought their officers and sergeants. These were paratroopers and that was not easy. Every paratrooper could make decisions for himself. I chose a close target first. I would then move my aim to the rear of the advancing enemy. I squeezed the trigger as the German soldier darted to take cover behind a tree some four hundred yards from us. He pitched into the river and the others took cover.

I switched to a line of grey a hundred yards further away. It would be harder to make a kill but I just needed to hit them and make them worry about me. These men were zig zagging. I led one and squeezed my trigger again. He fell clutching his shoulder and they went to ground. Lance Sergeant Hay chuckled, "That has them worried now, sir."

I risked looking to my left for I saw their tanks advancing. There were S.S. troops and paratroopers following. The huge Tigers and Panthers afforded good shelter and both types of panzer were hard to kill. I turned my head to look at the advancing paratroopers. They were within two hundred yards of us now. I saw a mortar crew setting up a mortar. They were using a stunted tree for cover. I squeezed off three bullets and both men fell. One was dead but the other was only wounded. I had time to change clips.

"They will be within range soon."

131

"Yes sir."

To our left the Tigers and Shermans had begun to fire at each other. The Germans were conserving their ammunition and the Major had waited until his shells had the chance of penetrating the thicker German armour.

"Beaumont you might get a side shot at that lead Tiger soon."

"Yes sir but I only have eight rockets left."

If they get too close it will be too late. Use them!"

I fired as he answered me for I had seen another two paratroopers trying to set up the mortar. They were trying to take us out. The half-track was our strong point and these were good soldiers. They had identified the danger and would eliminate it. I shot three men before they gave up with that particular mortar.

Next to me the MG 42 ripped away as a line of paratroopers broke cover to get closer to us. Sergeant Poulson's gun joined in. Hewitt shouted, "They were trying to use the river sir!"

I fired another two bullets and then picked up my second Mauser. I heard a whoosh and Beaumont fired a rocket at the Tiger which was now two hundred yards from us. It had already brewed up a Sherman. Private Beaumont had a sharp mind. His rocket could do nothing against the armour of the tank but he could against the track. His rocket exploded against the leading sprocket. The track was irrevocably damaged.

I turned my attention back to the paratroopers as bullets pinged off the half-track. I hit one who was raising his sub machine gun. They were not accurate at the range they were using them but they could get a lucky shot. As I glanced to my left I saw the Tiger's barrel turning ominously towards us. Beaumont's rocket had identified a problem. The gun would eliminate it.

"Beaumont!"

"Seen it sir!"

Fletcher banged him on the shoulder after reloading and I saw the flash of the rocket. This time he aimed between the turret and the chassis. He hit and the barrel stopped turning. It was stuck. It could still fire but obliquely. I saw a shell from a seventeen pounder smack into the turret and blow it off. The threat from that damaged Tiger was gone but the bullets which hit our half-track showed that we had a closer danger.

I looked over the top. They were now a hundred yards from us. It was the flashes from their guns which identified their position. I shouted, "It is time Gordy. One hundred yards directly in line with us. Try one for effect!"

"Sir!"

I saw the grenade soar high. It exploded ninety yards from us. It must have hit someone for I heard a shout.

"Short!"

"Right sir!"

The second landed thirty yards further on and this time it did hit them. "Bob on! A pattern left and right. When you are empty come up here!"

"Sir!"

The eight grenades were used to great effect. The two MG 42 machine guns were able to take advantage of paratroopers who were trying to avoid the grenades and the bullets. I found that the fire against the half-track had lessened and I sought more targets. I saw a huddle of men behind the damaged Tiger. They were hidden from the Canadians but not us. I fired all five bullets in quick succession. Two fell before they knew where the bullets were coming from and I felled a third before they took cover. An exploding grenade just in front of the half-track showered us with shrapnel and Bill Hay fell.

"Gordy, up here now!"

Hewitt pulled Hay to the rear of the half-track so that he could tend to his wounds. I grabbed the MG 42. The paratroopers were getting desperate now. I pulled the trigger. It was hard to fire the gun and feed the belt. I only managed a couple of shots at a time. Then Gordy appeared. "Sorry sir."

Once he was on the belt we were able to fire almost continuously. "How is he Hewitt?"

"Left shoulder has splinters and he is another one who now has a face only a mother could love! But he will live!"

I heard Bill say, "Less of the cheek, Hewitt. I call it ruggedly handsome!"

As Gordy changed the belt on the gun I took a potato masher and, using my left hand, threw it high in the air. "Grenade!"

My men were already in cover but they hunkered down a little more as the grenade exploded in the air spraying metal at head height. Then there were no Germans before us. They had gone to ground. As we could not see them and we had no more grenades for the grenade launcher it was stalemate.

Hewitt and a freshly bandaged Hay returned, "Lance Sergeant Hay you rest for a while. Sergeant Barker can feed the gun."

I took out my glasses and looked to the left. Two more Shermans were brewed up and the S.S. were advancing ever closer. I realised that Beaumont did not have line of sight to the tanks. "Beaumont, get up here. You will have a better line of sight to the tanks."

"Sir!"

I knew he only had six rockets left but as the tanks approached his angle of fire would become better.

"You lads keep your eyes on the paratroopers. I will see what I can do about those advancing to our left."

133

I reloaded both guns and took aim at an officer urging his men forward. He spun around when I hit him. The men with him dropped to the ground and began firing back at us. Some had rifles and their bullets hit the half-track. I saw that there were at least four tanks heading for the remaining Shermans. Just then I heard the sound of aeroplanes. I looked to the west and saw tank busting Typhoons, three of them, roaring in. When some of the Germans looked up I took advantage and shot at them. I saw two fall.

Beaumont arrived and he placed the rocket launcher on the side of the half-track, "This is better sir." As one Panther was hit by the rockets from the leading Typhoon Beaumont fired at the one following. Once again he hit the leading sprocket. As it stopped the second Typhoon hit it and the tank became a raging inferno. The last Typhoon hit a self-propelled gun which was lumbering towards the Shermans. Our line held.

"Sir, they are pulling back!"

The attack by the Typhoons had been the last straw. The paratroopers moved back as the remaining tanks did. Fletcher asked, "Is that it, sir? Is it over?"

"No, Fletcher, it means they will risk a night attack. We can't use the Typhoons then and they will have cover." I stood, "Anyone else hurt?"

My men stood and waved. They were all alive.

"Hay, get some food on the go. Fletcher, get on the radio and find out what is going on. Tell the Canadians we have held. Beaumont, Hewitt, come with me and bring grenades."

We left the safety of the half-track. I took out my Luger and held it in my left hand. "Sergeant Poulson, bring your men. They will come again tonight. We need to make some booby traps."

We reached the first of the bodies just eighty yards from our half-track. The ones who had been hit by the grenades were a mess. "Take their grenades and ammunition." While my men worked their way south I went ahead. As Beaumont searched a dead Sergeant I saw a corpse rise and raise his pistol to shoot at him. I fired half a magazine into him. When I reached his body I saw that he had already been badly wounded. He had a stump for a foot and yet he had fought to the end. These were fanatics.

"Thanks sir." He held up some parachute cord. "It looks like they hold on to this stuff too, sir."

"When you have finished join me."

I found the dead ground in which they had sheltered. It was two hundred yards from our position. There were no bodies to be seen. I walked to the river and looked back to the half-track. I could only see the top corner. As my men arrived I said, "We start here and we make a line of booby traps. Offset them. I do not want them in a line. I want a front of a hundred and fifty yards covering. It does not need to be continuous. It is early warning. I will go and find our secondary position. Join me when you are done."

I walked back a hundred yards. I could see the half-track from here. We needed to make this into a killing zone. If we did not then we would be overwhelmed.

As I was inspecting the ground a captain from the Canadian company joined me. "What are you doing, Captain Harsker? My men have been watching and they are curious."

"This is not over. Jerry has to get through this gap before it is closed. They will come back tonight. We have no aeroplanes then. We will have limited line of sight and the men we are fighting are ruthless with nothing to lose. We are making this somewhere they will avoid." I pointed to our half-track. "I am going to have my two machine guns fixed to fire here. We will have them in a cross fire. I have eight men left. There could be two hundred paratroopers coming for us. I have to make them decide that you are the easier target!"

He looked offended, "Thanks a lot!"

I shrugged, "Would you rather we were killed and you were outflanked?"

"But we thought it was over."

"It is never over until you take the guns from their cold dead hands." To make the point I reached down and pick up the sub machine gun from the dead paratrooper whose sightless eyes stared up at the sky. "I would suggest you have your men clear the ground in front of you and set booby traps. When you hear ours going off then you can bet there will be men approaching you."

"Very lights?"

I nodded, "I would use them. You will hear their armour so I am guessing they will send infantry in first. The Major is down to a handful of tanks. I have not seen any Panzerfausts yet. If they have them they will use them tonight. If they eliminate your armour then they can waltz back to Germany!"

Chapter 16

Bill Hay had been resourceful. He had rigged up a trap in the river and we ate fresh fish for our meal. Cooked over an open fire they augmented our dull rations well. With a dixie of tea inside us we would be ready for the night. Leaving just myself and Sergeant Poulson on watch I let the rest of the men sleep.

"What did the Major say sir?"

"That the Poles had almost run out of ammunition but they still held and the gap was almost closed. Headquarters are sending reinforcements to us and the Americans are already racing for the Seine. If this was anyone but the S.S. they would have surrendered already. I think that tonight will be hard. I just hope that those to our left are on the ball."

"How is the arm sir?"

"It aches but I have yet to spring a leak!"

He nodded to the men who were sleeping in the half-track and on the ground around it. "The lads have done well."

"They always do. I feel guilty that they are still at the same rank. They should all be promoted. You should be too. You deserve it."

"None of them are bothered, sir. They are not professional soldiers."

I nodded, "Warriors for the working day."

"That Shakespeare sir?"

"Yes, Sergeant, Henry Vth."

"That's us then. Just working soldiers. We all want to finish the war together. It is more like a family. We know we can rely on each other. Joe Wilkinson found that and he was only with us for a short time. The other lads told me how much he wanted to stay. He wasn't bothered that he had been promoted. If the Yanks are heading for Paris then we will soon have France recaptured. I know what you are saying about the Germans defending Germany but I reckon that there will be peace when we get to the German border."

"I am not so sure, Polly. The border goes from Belgium all the way to the Alps. It is mountainous country and unless we get a foothold by winter it will be hard. I just want to get through this night."

A couple of hours into the watch Gordy woke and insisted that Sergeant Poulson and I get our heads down for an hour at least. Reluctantly we complied. Fearful of my wrath they woke me an hour before night fell. We had more fish from Bill Hay's trap augmented by some ridiculously early blackberries. After a mug of tea we were ready for the onslaught which we knew would be coming.

Fletcher had been on the radio and when I was woken he reported, "Germans are still escaping, sir. Headquarters has ordered every unit on full alert. Some of our lads are coming to plug the gap."

"Our lads? Commandos?"

"No, sir, 'fraid not. Regulars. They'll be alright though. They have six pounders."

That was what we needed, anti-tank guns. We now had a couple of rockets left and no grenades for the rocket launcher. We had very little ammunition for the Colts and the Thompsons. If we had not looted the dead we would be out of ammunition as were the Poles. It was ironic but if we threw back the Germans then it would be by using their own bullets and weapons against them.

We were probably more relaxed than the other units for we had our own early warning system. I hoped that the Canadian company next to us had heeded our warning or we could be outflanked and with the river to our right we had nowhere to run! An hour after dark we heard firing far to our left. There had not been the sound of tanks and so I deduced that it had to be infantry. Then the night was lit up as a tank exploded. From the size of the fireball I knew that it was a Sherman and that meant they had Panzerfausts.

"Stand to lads. They are out there." I had my Mauser in my hand. I would not be using the telescopic sight but it had a longer range than the submachine guns. We had measured the range to our booby traps. As soon as the second set was triggered they would be a hundred yards away and I would just fire blind at waist height. I had a small pile of Mauser clips. Every German with a rifle who had been killed carried four. Not much for a single German but plenty for me. We also had the grenades we had not used for the booby traps. The two machines were also set to fire at the second set of booby traps. We had suffered from them in the Low Countries back in forty and we had learned our lessons well. We knew how to make a killing ground.

The firing grew in intensity to our left and then we heard the sound of armour. The Germans were bringing up their tanks. Perhaps they were not trying to get through on a broad front. That theory was blown out of the water when a booby trap in front of the Canadians was triggered. The Canadians opened fire. It was nerves. We would have waited.

Then the first of our booby traps was triggered. Expecting it, we had been looking for the enemy. The flash from the grenade illuminated the Germans. It was tempting to fire but the range was still a little long for the submachine guns. The closer they were the more devastating the effect of our firepower. We wanted them walking into a wall of bullets. Another three explosions showed that they were coming in force. To our left we could hear the sound of heavy ordinance. The tanks were engaging each other. A night battle was always dramatic. There were sudden flashes of light against the night sky and huge explosions and with the ground vibrating under the fifty four tones of Krupp's steel the effect was even more heightened. There was silence from our front or at least they had stopped triggering the booby traps. They were either disarming them or moving more cautiously. After the first set there was a hundred yards before they were within range of our guns.

Alarmingly the sound of the tank battle was moving north. It sounded to me as though the Germans had broken through. Panic would be the worst thing for us to do. We had to stay where we were and tough it out. We had a half-track and we could move quickly. We would do our job and hold on. If we were outflanked we would fight our way out. When the next booby trap was set off just a hundred yards from us we knew where the enemy were. I began to fire. I made small adjustments as I traversed my gun. I had no idea of the effect but by keeping the gun level I hoped to hit as many as possible. Then the two MG 42 machine guns opened fire followed by the MG 34s. I heard cries as men were hit and then more explosions as they triggered more booby traps. I changed rifles and kept firing. I had no idea if I was hitting anything or not and I kept firing. I reloaded and fired again. Four clips later my barrel was almost too hot to touch.

"Cease fire!" The sound of the fighting to our left had diminished for it had passed further north and allowed us to hear the moans and cries from the Germans before us. Shepherd and Beaumont both had good arms. I shouted, "Ken, Roger, chuck a few German grenades just in case anyone has got close to us or are playing dead."

It was the sort of thing we would do. The paratroopers were as good as we were. In the dark it was impossible to see someone wriggling close to us. "Grenade!"

We ducked down as the two grenades exploded and we heard cries of pain. "Two more!"

They threw another two and then we waited. There was silence. Ominously the Shermans to our left were silent too. "Fletcher, get on the radio. Find out what has happened. Lance Sergeant Hay, nip along to the Canadian Company see if they are all right."

"Sir!"

I heard Fletcher as he spoke on the radio. Of course the battle was still underway and confusion reigned but any news would be welcome.

When he returned his face was grim. "Sir, the Germans have broken through. They went between the Major's tanks and the next battalion. We have been told to sit tight and wait it out."

Billy Hay returned half an hour later. "It is a bit grim sir but they held out too. Jerry got into their front lines and there was hand to hand and close in fighting but they held on. Major Hamilton was wounded and he has one tank left. The Germans are streaming towards hill 462."

I shook my head. The Poles had had a hard enough time before now. How would they cope with the remnants of the S.S. Panzers descending upon them? What was certain was that we could do little about it. As far as we knew the next attack could walk over our tiny unit. The firing to our left gradually died down and we waited for dawn. Alert for the whole night we were tired as the sun broke in the east.

"Sergeant Poulson and Sergeant Barker man the machine guns. Beaumont and Emerson, come with me. Bring your hand guns. Let's see who we fought. Sergeant Poulson, I will wave if it is safe."

As we made our way through the stiffening corpses it became obvious that it was not the paratroopers we had fought. These were line infantry and grenadiers cobbled together from at least six different units. We even found a couple from a pioneer battalion. We reached the first line of booby traps and saw that we had hurt them badly there. Our machine guns at the second line had decimated them These were regular infantry. I lost count of the dead. As we went I took papers from the tunics of the dead German officers I found. It might provide useful intelligence. I put them in my battledress.. It was no wonder the attack had failed. We had expected the best and destroyed the ordinary. It left a sour taste in my mouth. They had been sacrificed to allow the S.S. and the paratroopers to escape.

I waved and the others joined us. "Fletcher, radio Headquarters and tell them that our sector is clear. Ask them, what are our orders?"

"Right sir. Rog if you find any daggers keep them for me will ya?"

Beaumont shook his head but I knew he would do as his friend had asked.

"The rest of you, let's see what we can get. Pick up any grenades and clips. Who knows when we will get more ammo!"

It was late morning when we had finished collecting ammo. The Germans had taken their wounded with them. Our orders were clear. We were to head back towards Trun and await instructions. I could not leave Major Hamilton and the Canadians without saying goodbye. I left the section loading the half-track and walked across the battlefield to the lone Sherman. It had battle damage but it still functioned as a tank. The men of the Canadian Company who had been our neighbours waved and shouted as I passed. We had shared a battle. We might never meet again but we all knew that without the other we would have died. We had protected each other's flanks and we had not flinched. That made brothers of soldiers.

Major Hamilton had a heavy bandage over the right side of his head. He still had the inevitable cigar in his mouth, "You and me, Captain, could get a part in the next Lon Chaney film!"

I laughed and held out my hand, "I'll take the money and the adulation, sir. What is the prognosis?"

"They think I have lost the eye." He shrugged, "Hell I can make do with one! They always said, when I was young, that if I kept on doing that I would go blind! I guess this is just retribution."

I laughed. He could still joke about a disability. The Major was a gutsy guy. I remembered Dad's old gunner, Lumpy, "Dad always said that it didn't matter how you survived a war, just so long as you survived!"

"He is right." He came closer, "I just want to thank you. The advice you gave my men saved their butts! And you nine men did the job of a company. I shall be sorry to see you go. I guess they have plans for you."

"You never know. It is has been an honour to serve with you and your men, Major. I shall have to visit Canada when all this is over."

"You do that and come see me. I live in Guelph, it is a little place in Ontario."

"I will." I shook his hand and then saluted. As I left I reflected that was war in a microcosm. You briefly met other warriors you fought and men died and then you left. I headed back across a battlefield littered with dead men. We had fought over a tiny piece of France. We had held but Germans had achieved a victory of sorts. They had escaped to fight another day. Such was life. I discovered that the breakthrough had been made by the paratroopers who had fought us. They had spearheaded the attack and the captain who spoke to me said that over two thousand had escaped. I knew then, as I headed back to my men, that we had been lucky.

Private Emerson had the engine fired up when I arrived. I sat in the cab feeling weary. My arm was aching and my face itched. "Take us back to Trun, Emerson." I closed my eyes as we headed back to the road which would take us to Trun. When we reached it I could not believe the change which had taken place. All of the roads had been cleared of rubble and there were neat ranks of tents all around. It was now a jumping off point. There were tanks and self-propelled guns. There were lorries with anti-tank guns. All of them appeared to be heading north west. We seemed to be a salmon swimming against the tide.

"Where should I go sir?"

"If in doubt, Emerson, head for the flag."

He turned towards the flag which was above a tent on the northern avenue. "I'll go and see what the S.P. is."

A sentry saluted as I walked towards it. "Yes sir?"

"Captain Harsker reporting as ordered."

He put his head inside the tent and shouted, " Captain Harsker reporting as ordered."

A familiar voice shouted, "Tell him to come in."

I entered and saw Major Foster and a smiling Lieutenant Ross. The Major stood, "Well done, Tom! You did just what we expected of you... the unexpected!"

I smiled, "And now, of course, you are sending us home."

He shook his head, "Of course not. We wouldn't want Susan to see you with that scar. We need a few weeks to let it heal. No, we need you to join the chaps racing towards the Seine and Paris."

He said it so calmly and casually that I thought I had misheard him, "What?"

"You and your chaps have shown that you are resilient. You speak French and German." He waved me closer. "The thing is we had some chaps ready to do this job but the S.S. caught them behind enemy lines close to Paris. They were all shot. We need you to join the vanguard in case we have to go behind the lines. You are the best qualified chaps we have and with the other team captured I am afraid that you are it."

"There must be more to it than that, sir!"

"There is. Look, the French Second Armoured Division is racing towards Paris. They will be the ones to capture it. It is seen as symbolic but we need eyes on the ground. Because you went in with the French Commandos your name is respected as are you. You need not fight but you will be attached to the French when they advance on Paris. The Americans are sending their Fourth Infantry Division to show that it is the allies who are liberating France. You will be the British representative.

"We are spies on our allies."

He sat back and looked down at the desk and map. "Crudely put but yes. Your radio man Private Fletcher will report in the progress and it will help us to gauge what decisions should be made. When it is over, Tom, you and your chaps will be sent home. You deserve a leave."

"This does not sit well, sir."

"I know but it comes from the top." I nodded. I knew when I was beaten. "Good man! You need to get to Lisieux as soon as you can. The American Fourth Division is there. They have been in action and are refitting. We have petrol and ammunition for you as well as supplies. You will have to motor." I nodded. "Report to Major Connor. He is expecting you."

"What does he think our purpose is?"

"You are Commandos who can go behind the enemy lines."

"So we will be fighting?"

He shrugged, "I doubt it but...."

"Right sir. I had better get started. The supplies?"

"Lieutenant Ross."

"I'll show you sir." Once outside the tent he said, "Sir, this isn't the Major's doing. Field Marshal Montgomery himself gave the order. When Monty found out the Americans were going he wanted to send a whole division too. You are a compromise. The Major was not happy."

"Would you like to spy on the men you fight alongside?"

"Captain, I couldn't even begin to think about doing one tenth of what you and the lads do so I am the wrong person to ask."

"Sorry, John. That was unfair. Where are these supplies?"

"Over here." We had parked next to a lorry and I saw that we had chosen the perfect location.

"Sergeant Poulson, the supplies in that lorry are for us. Private Emerson there are cans of fuel in there too. They are your department."

They nodded and got on with it. Fletcher said, "Where we off to this time sir?"

I smiled, "You will soon discover that young Fletcher!"

It took some time to unload the lorry and then pack everything in our half-track. We distributed the ammunition. I saw that they had even provided us with new uniforms. We had to look good. It was late afternoon when we had finished. Lieutenant Ross gave me a manila envelope with my orders and papers to show Major Connor.

"When your mission is completed, sir, then you can head for Caen. Transport will be waiting to take you back to England."

The section heard that and cheered. "That's great sir. Where to then? Let's get this over and then get home. I have a Nazi dagger or two to sell!"

"Get on board and I will tell you." I shook hands with Lieutenant Ross. "See you around John. Sorry for my bad temper."

"Don't worry about it, sir. In your position I would be even worse." He turned and headed for the command tent.

"Where to, sir?"

"First we head to Lisieux, Private Emerson, and then Paris. We are going to liberate the French capital."

It took a great deal to silence my men but my words succeeded. We drove slowly as we headed north not because we wanted to but because the roads were choked with vehicles and men going in opposite directions. We did not reach Lisieux until the early hours of the morning. Then we discovered that the Fourth Infantry Division was not there. They were further south on the Argentan road. We had wasted a whole night and we were further away from our allies than when we had started! All that we found were a handful of Canadian and British troops who had pursued the fleeing Germans. There was little evidence of armour. This was the front line!

"That's it then, sir. We can't do what we have to do. It looks like we are stuck here now."

"So what do you suggest, Sergeant Barker? We sit on our backsides here and do nothing? Sergeant Poulson get a camp set up. We all need some sleep and Fletcher get on to Major Foster and tell him about the SNAFU."

Scouse grinned, "Right sir!"

Chapter 17

While Fletcher was on the radio I studied the maps. The roads we had just passed were too crowded with traffic for us to reach the Americans or indeed the French. We would be playing catch up on roads which would be choked with traffic. Dreux looked to be somewhere we could intercept them.

"Sir, I have Major Foster on the radio."

He handed me the microphone and headphones. It was not a good signal. "Sorry, Tom. Eisenhower decided to send the Fourth with the Second. We weren't told. Monty is not a happy man. You will have to come south and join them."

"That is not on, sir. The roads are a nightmare. It would take us all day, at least, to reach them. I am going to head for Dreux."

"That would be madness! We have yet to liberate that area. If is filled with Germans heading back to the Seine."

"And we are a German half-track, sir. It is the quickest route. The only way we can make the Argentan road is if they wait for us."

"That is impossible, Tom. Paris has risen. De Gaulle is insisting that we go to the aid of his city before the Germans destroy it. Hitler has promised to leave it a wasteland. It will be another Stalingrad or Warsaw."

"Then the only way we can be part of it is to do as I have suggested."

The silence on the other end made me wonder if we had lost the signal. Then a weary voice came in my ears. "Very well. Put Fletcher back on and I will get Lieutenant Ross to give him the passwords you will need. Good luck, Tom. I think you will need it."

Sergeant Poulson had done as I had ordered. I gathered my four NCOs around me. Laying the map on the ground I showed them my plan. "We will head for Dreux. We have yet to capture this so technically it will be enemy territory. The shortest route will be here through Thiberville, Bernay, Ajou and Damville. As near as I reckon that will be just sixty nine miles."

"Through enemy territory, sir?"

"Pretty much Sergeant Barker. The armoured column and the mechanized infantry will, I think, be slower. Jerry will know they are coming and will try to slow them up. That is why I intend to leave after dark. We will sneak though their lines. I want us in the German greatcoats."

"Sir, we only have four left. We just kept them for blankets!"

"Then Emerson and I will have two. Beaumont's German is good he can have one and Bill, you are better at German than the other two, you have the fourth. If we meet any Germans then the rest just play dead in the back.

144

We tool up with German weapons. I took some papers from the dead Germans from Trun. It should work."

They nodded, "Well sir, it's a plan and that is a start. I'll get some food on the go. You had better get your head down. I will tell Freddie to get some kip too!"

I lay down and closed my eyes. I had sounded confident to my men but I knew the risks we took. We had to travel at night to avoid the Allied aeroplanes. Soldiers we met would be more nervous at night and more likely to fire first and ask questions later. I knew why I was doing this. It was nothing to do with my ego but all to do with duty. My orders were to join the Americans. I would do all in my power to obey those orders even if that meant not doing them the way I had been advised. The safety of my men came first. A sudden dash at night might succeed where a longer, slower trek through congested roads might end in disaster. I had cast the die. Now I would live with the consequences.

Bill Hay shook me awake. "Not far off dark sir. We have made a brew. Shepherd cooked something hot for you."

"Thanks Lance Sergeant. Did everyone get their heads down for an hour?"

He shook his head, "Polly and Gordy reckoned they could sleep when we were driving. I think Gordy is a bit miffed about your comments sir." He smiled, "He thinks he speaks German like a native."

I laughed, "Aye, a native of Grimsby perhaps!"

"For what it is worth sir I think the plan is a good one. There is so much confusion and travelling in the direction we are we have the best chance of avoiding anybody!"

The sentries were surprised to see us heading east. The Sergeant on duty said, "Sir, there's nothing but Germans out there. I know they are heading east but even so..."

"Don't worry, Sergeant, we will be careful. Off you go Emerson and remember they drive on the right over here!"

Thiberville was not far down the road. As I had expected it was deserted. The people had their doors and shutters closed and we passed through what felt like a ghost town. We began to head south east. The further down the road we travelled the more likely we would be to find Germans. Beaumont stood on the MG 42 with my binoculars scanning the darkness ahead. We did not expect to see Germans but if they were careless enough to light a cigarette or a fire then we would see evidence of them. Tanks would not be a problem. The ones which had escaped Falaise had had a whole two days to reach the Seine. They would be there and perhaps beyond. If the Fuhrer had had an attempt on his life then he would want his beloved S.S. as close to him as he could.

We met little on the road until we reached the narrow bridge at Ajou. Sharp eyed Beaumont spotted it as we turned out of the woods on the Bernay road and paralleled the Risle river. "Sir! There is a road block at the bridge. It looks like German field police, Feldgendarmerie."

Feldgendarmerie were nasty! They were just failed Gestapo recruits.

"Right, silenced Colts. Stick your German field caps on. We will try to talk our way through it but if not then we shoot our way through. What is the road block made of?"

"Just a couple of poles sir. They look like they are lifting it to let men through. There seems to be about twenty Germans waiting to cross."

"Emerson, take it steady. Rest your arm on the window and smoke one of those German cigarettes we liberated."

"Do I have to sir? They are horrible."

"Just look natural eh? When I say go then floor it." He did as I asked and the cab was filled with the foul smelling tobacco.

We pulled up behind the last of the German soldiers waiting to cross. One of them, a corporal, shouted up, "Give us a lift, friend. We have walked from Trun!"

"We are full. We have wounded we have picked up. If you can walk then you are better off than they are."

He nodded, "You are right." He saw Emerson's cigarette. "Have you got a smoke? I am gasping."

I took a packet from my greatcoat pocket. "Here, we can't give you a lift but we can give you these."

"You are a life saver. Where are you from?"

"Lisieux."

He lowered his voice, "Soon we will have peace eh? The S.S. were slaughtered at Trun."

I held my finger to my lips, "Do not say that too loudly, my friend. You never know who is listening. These are Kettenhunde." That was the derogatory name for the field police.

"You are right there."

"Next!" The German field police waved the corporal and his four companions forward. Emerson followed with the half-track so that we were close enough to hear their conversation. I slid my Colt out from under my greatcoat and held it beneath the door.

"Where are you from?"

"Trun, Lieutenant. The 353rd Engineers."

"And where are your orders. Who gave you permission to retreat?"

The Corporal flourished a paper, "Here Lieutenant. We are ordered to the Seine." I realised that we had missed a trick. If we had offered them a lift then when they were allowed through we would have had our passage guaranteed.

"Very well. Move along!" The corporal waved and he and his men trudged across the narrow bridge. It looked just wide enough for our half-track. A tank would not fit. "Next!"

I waved Emerson forward and he nudged it closer to the Lieutenant and the four policemen. They were well armed and well dressed. These had not fought in the battle for Normandy.

"Papers!"

I handed him the bloodstained papers I had taken from the corpse. They gave me the rank of captain. The lieutenant stiffened when he saw them. It was as close to a salute as I would get.

"These have blood on them."

I pointed to my bandaged face, "War."

He nodded, "And where are your orders to retreat?"

I growled, "Where are my orders to retreat, Captain?"

"You are right, sir. Sorry. Where are your orders to retreat, Captain?"

I smiled, "It is funny, when we followed the S.S. out of the trap at Trun, no one thought to give us any. We were all too busy avoiding death."

"And where are the S.S. who fled with you, sir?"

"They would have crushed this bridge. They took the road north of Thiberville."

He nodded and kept hold of my papers. "I am afraid I cannot let you pass. This vehicle could be used to defend the bridge from the enemies of the Reich."

"I have wounded men on board." I saw that three of his men, including his sergeant were behind him. The fourth was on the other side, close to Emerson.

"Then they can fight and die for the Fatherland."

I smiled, "You first!"

I pulled up my Colt and shot him in the head at point blank range. The sergeant next to him looked in shock and disbelief as blood, brains and bone showered him. I shot him. Fletcher and Beaumont shot the others.

"Go!"

Emerson hurled his German cigarette into the river as he jammed his foot down on the accelerator. The bridge was empty as we hurtled across. The silenced bullets had not attracted any attention but the sound of our engine made the Corporal and his companions turn. They got off the road and waved. As we passed them Emerson said, "The soldiers behind us saw what happened. I hope they haven't got a radio."

I hadn't seen one but it didn't matter. The narrow bridge at Ajou was our last bottleneck. We now had options of side roads. The engine strained as we climbed up the steep sides of the valley. This would have been a good place to hold off our pursuit. The size of the German tanks had worked against them. Once we reached the top we were plunged into the darkness of a forest on both sides of us. As we drove I used the torch to check out the route ahead. Our next problem might be Conches-en-Ouche. When I looked at map I saw that it was roughly the same size as Ajou but there was no bridge. We were making good time. I would turn off the road at Damville and take the smaller D45 road. Nonancourt was on the main road. It was big and there was a river with a bridge. We were now getting close to Paris and the Seine. The closer we got the more chance we had of running into Germans. I turned off the torch. "Emerson we go through the next place as though we have every right to do so."

"Right sir. Just so long as I don't have to smoke another German fag!"

I took the opportunity of reloading. I knew my men would do the same.

"That town is coming up sir. The roads look a bit narrow."

"See anything Beaumont?"

"Quiet as sir. It is the middle of the night." We rumbled through and the inhabitants of Conches-en-Ouche stayed hidden. The rumble of tracks meant danger.

As we turned left after Damville I saw dawn breaking in the east. "Go slowly Emerson. I don't want to miss the turn off. It is not a big road."

"Right sir."

"Fletcher get on the radio and see if you can pick anything up."

"Sir."

Suddenly I spied the gap. It was just a lighter shade of black. "There it is. Take the turn off, Emerson."

We entered a dark tunnel through a forest as we headed south and east. Any sign of dawn was now hidden from us.

"All I am getting sir is German chatter. I can understand a bit of it but not enough. No American voices that is for sure."

When the forest finished we were bathed in early morning sunlight from our left. There were fields stretching out on both sides. "Beaumont, scan the horizon."

After a few minutes he said, "All clear sir."

I was aware that if he could see nothing then it meant that we were early and the column had not reached Dreux yet. I took out the map again. There looked to be a farm at La Bremien. It was just five miles from Dreux but the road passed through a forest. We would wait out the arrival of the American and French column there. As we passed the farm we saw our first Frenchman. The farmer came out and stood looking at us. We still wore our German greatcoats and hats but he did not seem put out by it. I waved to him. He ignored the wave.

We were almost at Muzy before we found a track which would take us into the forest. According to the map we were just three miles from the outskirts of Dreux and on the eastern side. "There, Emerson, take the track to the south. We will be well hidden from the road there."

As soon as we found a clearing we stopped.

"Fletcher, radio to find out what is happening and tell them where we are. Shepherd, get some food sorted out. Emerson, refill the tank." I turned to Sergeant Poulson. "I will leave you in charge. I am going to take Beaumont and Hay to scout out Dreux. " He looked ready to object. "Three words, Sergeant, French and German." He nodded. "It is only three miles or so. Let's say three hours. See if Fletcher can find out where the column is and we will scout of the lie of the land."

I took my Luger and left the Colt in the half-track. Beaumont and Lance Sergeant Hay took the two MG 34s. Our greatcoats would cover our brown battledress. We reached the edge of the forest and ran across the road. We took to the fields passing the village of Muzy to our right. The fields dropped to the river. It was only waist deep and we jumped in. I wanted to be out of sight for as long as we could be. We crossed more fields and passed Flonville. It was then we saw the Germans. There were an eclectic mix of tanks and Germans who were digging in. There was neither river nor bridge at Dreux. The Germans would slow down the allied advance.

We took cover behind a stand of trees. While Beaumont and Hay kept watch I used my binoculars. It was a rag tag army before us. The S.S. and paratroopers were mercifully missing but there were anti-tank guns, Mark IV tanks as well as self-propelled artillery pieces. Even as we watched I saw them piling sand bags around mortars and machine guns. On the other side of Dreux I saw aeroplanes landing. There was an airfield. They were FW 190s. I had to see more and so I began to climb the tree. My wounded arm made it difficult although not impossible. When I was thirty feet up I leaned against a solid looking branch and peered across the town. I could see more tanks and grey uniforms by the airfield. I did not have a good view in the town but I guessed that they would have the main roads blocked too.

I clambered slowly down, "It looks like they are making a strongpoint of Dreux. We will need to warn our allies. Time to get back."

We were just heading across the open field towards the road when disaster struck. A pair of Kübelwagens came down the same road we had taken from Bernay. They stopped and it became obvious that they had seen us. We were walking away from a defended town and it would look suspicious. If we ran it would look even more suspicious. They were a hundred yards away and watching us. I said, quietly, "Get ready with your guns but make it look casual. I will try to talk our way out of it. If you two keep behind me they won't notice your hands are on your guns."

"What about you, sir?"

"I have a Mills bomb in my greatcoat pocket."

I saw that one MG 42 was aimed in our direction as we neared them. I decided to play the officer card. When we were ten yards away and before they could speak I snapped, in my best Teutonic German, "What are you doing here? Don't you know that we need every vehicle to defend the town against the Amis?"

The sergeant said, "I was going to ask you the same thing."

I used my left hand to tap my collar and pips, "Sir!"

All of them clicked their heels and said, "Sir!"

Even as I said, "That's better!" I had taken out the Mills bomb, pulled the pin and thrown it into the Kübelwagen with the machine gunner. Then I ran at the sergeant, drawing my Luger as I did so. Behind me Hay and Beaumont sprayed the two Kübelwagen with the MG 34s. As I fell on the German Sergeant he head butted me. As luck would have it I had landed with my Luger against his stomach and I squeezed the trigger. His body convulsed and his hand came up . I pulled my hand back a little and emptied half the magazine into him. His body jumped as though he was having a fit. I leapt to my feet but the rest were all dead.

I took the sergeant's Luger and ammunition. "Let's move. Someone will investigate."

"Should we booby trap them sir?"

"We haven't got time. Run!"

We hurried across the road and made the shelter of the trees. We kept going to put as much daylight between us as we could. We were almost at the camp when I heard the sound of an aero engine. I could not see the aircraft but it sounded like a fighter. They should have used a slower Storch. It passed overhead in a heartbeat. We were safe... for a while.

Everyone had taken cover. When they recognised us they showed themselves. "We heard the firing and expected the worst." Sergeant Poulson looked at my head, "In the wars again sir?"

I nodded, "A sergeant head butted me."

Scouse grinned, "The old Scotty Road kiss eh sir?"

"There were two Kübelwagen. We tried to talk our way out of it but they were suspicious. Have you contacted the column?"

Fletcher nodded, "Yes sir. They expect to reach Dreux in the morning. They seem to think they can walk through."

I said, "Then get in touch and tell them that there are tanks, anti-tank guns, infantry and aeroplanes waiting for them. Ask them if they have orders for us."

"Do we leave then, sir?"

"No. We eat. We check our weapons and we turn the half-track around. Then we wait. There is nowhere better than this for us to wait. When they find their Kübelwagen and dead men they might search but I think that they will be more worried about an armoured division supported by a motorized one heading this way but we will be ready."

After ten minutes Fletcher returned, "Sir, they are going to go for an air strike first thing in the morning. They want us to pop smoke on their positions at 0900."

My heart sank to my boots. I shook my head, "Tell them that if they can't spot an airfield then they need glasses and the ones in the town are hidden. We will use red smoke and we will place it to the north of their position close to us."

Scouse grinned, "Right sir. You tell 'em!"

As he went off I said, "We will take the half-track to the road. It is about two miles to their positions. I daresay we could get the half-track closer but we would be spotted. Gordy we will leave you, Emerson and Fletcher with the half-track. Bill, you can take Beaumont and Shepherd to the east and I will take the rest to the west. We take submachine guns. It only takes one to throw the smoke grenade and the others can provide cover. We can ditch the Jerry uniforms. Tomorrow we fight as Commandos."

They nodded and Sergeant Poulson asked, "And after the air strike sir?"

"Yes sir. Jerry will either be after us or heading east. You may not have noticed it but we are smack bang in their line of retreat."

"You are right. We head up the Bernay road and come back here. This is as good a spot as any. In fact let's booby trap it now. We leave one way in and one way out." Pleased that they had something to do they set about with a will.

Fletcher came towards me, grinning, "What is so funny Fletcher?"

"Your dad, sir! After I passed the message on he spoke to me. He said, *'Tell my son I am pleased he knows how to question a damn fool order!'* He sounds like a good bloke sir."

"He is, Scouse, he is." I knew I had done the right thing but it felt good to have it confirmed by my father.

As darkness fell the men returned. We did not risk a fire. We had heard vehicles travelling up and down the road but none ventured close to us. We ate cold rations with no tea and we kept watch. No one minded the poor fare and lack of sleep. We had ridden our luck of late and fate had a habit of jumping up and biting you on the bum when you least expected it.

I had taken the midnight shift. Bill Hay woke me at five thirty with a cup of tea. "You lit a fire, Bill?" I was not criticising but it had been risky.

"It was quiet as the grave sir and we shielded the fire. It seemed safe enough. Anyway the lads fight better with a brew inside them and we will be fighting today won't we sir?"

"I think so." I sipped the hot sweet tea and felt immediately better.

"What do you reckon they would have done if we hadn't warned them sir? I mean it was pure luck we found them."

I could have taken offence at his words. I had always planned on scouting out the area but I knew what he meant. "In the long run it wouldn't have made a difference, Bill, the Germans could not have held out for long but it would have slowed up the advance and the people of Paris have risen. We need speed. The airstrikes should achieve success. It will be a double victory for if they knock out the airfield then we will have dented the German's ability to attack our fighters."

Just then I heard a dull rumble in the distance. A civilian would have said it was thunder. We knew better. This was a heavy bomber raid. Although we could see nothing when I heard the twin Merlin engines my heart soared. They were using a Mosquito fighter bomber as a pathfinder. Dad had told me about them. Incredibly fast and light, they would drop an incendiary to mark the target for the Handley Page bombers which followed. Sure enough when the Merlin engines began to fade the sky was lit up by a fireball as it dropped an incendiary right in the middle of the airfield and then the bombers arrived. We were a couple of miles away and the bombs all must have fallen on the airfield but we felt the wall of concussion as the airfield was destroyed. No one slept. We all looked west and south as the raid demolished any airpower the Germans had in the area..

Afterwards there was silence until I said, "Right lads. Time for us to do our bit. Let's go."

It took some time to travel slowly through the woods, in the dark and without lights. We had time. When we reached the ambush site I saw that they had removed both the bodies and the Kübelwagens. All that remained was a charred patch of tarmac.

"Emerson, turn the half-track around. We may need a speedy retreat. Fletcher, when you see the smoke tell the column."

"Good luck sir."

"Good luck lads!"

"We'll be waiting here for you."

We separated and I led Hewitt and Poulson towards the western side of the German defences. It was light by the time we neared them and I used my glasses to see how much work they had done. The tanks and self-propelled guns were hull down. They were going nowhere. The sandbags around the mortars would stop small arms fire. If the air strike did not do its job then a lot of French and American mothers would be wearing black in the near future. I pointed to the ground and Poulson and Hewitt set up the MG 42. I had insisted that I be the one to deploy the smoke. It was not heroics. I knew that I had to get it just right or the whole effort would have been a waste.

I crawled on all fours. I had my comforter on and only carried my two automatics. I had four smoke grenades while Bill Hay had another four. We would take no chances. They had few sentries on this side. They were all facing west but there were small camps with Germans soldiers cooking breakfast and brewing coffee made from acorns. I stopped fifty yards from them. I was confident that I could remain hidden. There were folds in the ground and I had chosen a hollow, a piece of dead ground below their eye line, if they turned around. We had all mastered the technique of lying still and not moving. I suspected that it was too close but I wanted to be sure that the air strike was effective. I took out the grenades and laid them before me. I checked my watch. It was 0845. Bill and the other team should have had an easier task. I was closest to the tanks. They were closer to the ammunition and the transport. If the Germans had to flee they had the means to do so. We needed the aeroplanes to destroy their escape route.

It was 0855 when I heard the sound of small arms fire to my left. That had to be Hay's team and they had been spotted. The men camped before me looked east. Luckily they did not look north and I held my nerve and kept to my position. I turned my head left and saw the red smoke. They had popped it early. If they had been discovered then it was understandable. It might still be there when the air strike came in but I could not hear any aeroplanes. I had to wait. An officer shouted for a squad to investigate and the men closest to me stood, grabbed their rifles and headed east. I prayed that Sergeant Poulson would hold his nerve. The second hand edged around really slowly. There was a great temptation to just throw the smoke bombs but that would have been a mistake. Finally it was 0900. I pulled the pins on two of the grenades and threw them. While they were in the air I pulled the pins on the other two and threw them. Even as the smoke began to climb to the skies I heard the sound of Typhoons as a squadron roared in.

As I ran up the hill I had my Luger out ready. The Germans fired bullets blindly into the smoke. I was lucky; they missed. I did not return fire for that would have identified my position. I ran for my two men. Sergeant Poulson shouted, "To your left sir and drop!"

I did as ordered and the chain saw of a machine gun spat death above my head. I heard shouts, cries and screams as men were hit.

"Up, sir, and run. We have your back!"

I ran and threw myself into the forest. I rose and turned. Raising my
Luger I fired at the half dozen Germans who had survived the machine gun.
Sergeant Poulson's burst ended their chase as the first Typhoon rockets
slammed into the tanks and artillery. They might have been hull down and
dug in but a pair of rockets could do serious damage to them. The camp
erupted into huge explosions and we were forgotten as a great threat
brought death from the skies.

"Right Sergeant! Time to go home!"

Chapter 18

We reached the half-track but there was no sign of Bill Hay's section. "Get the MG 42 up in the half-track. Emerson, be ready to move as soon as they get aboard. Fletcher, tell them we have set the smoke." I watched the Typhoons as they peeled off, their attack finished, to head west. Palls of smoke rose from the camp. The airfield in the distance was also wreathed in flames. In the distance I heard the crack of tanks guns as the French and American columns began their advance into Dreux.

Lance Sergeant Hewitt shouted, "I can see them, sir. Ken Shepherd is hurt." He grabbed his bag and, jumping down from the half-track ran towards the three men who were hastening towards us.

I climbed up to join Sergeant Poulson. The road below us disappeared around a corner and behind some trees. We were close to the junction with the main Paris road. I pointed. "There will be Germans coming up that road soon enough. I will act as loader."

"Right sir." The MG 42 just rested on the rear of the half-track but it would allow Poulson to traverse if he needed to.

While Hay and Beaumont carried Shepherd to the half-track I saw Hewitt working on his leg. Gordy Barker opened the rear doors of the half-track and, as the wounded man was dragged on board, Gordy shouted, "Right Fred, drive!"

Just then a German lorry appeared at the bottom of the road some hundred and fifty yards from us. Sergeant Poulson gave a burst. He hit the truck without doing too much damage and then Emerson gunned the engine and we were climbing the hill. As we twisted around the bend the Germans disappeared from sight.

"Sir."

"Yes Fletcher."

"The Yanks say to keep our heads down. They are in the outskirts of Dreux."

We made the bend and Emerson turned down the track towards our camp. We had made the ground into a deadly trap for any Germans who tried to pass through it. The Germans were all around us. "Turn it around, Fred so that we are facing the right direction. We stay inside this and make it our fort. With any luck Jerry will just take the road east to Paris and we will be safe here."

Bill Hay joined me and Sergeant Poulson. "I'll take over as loader sir. Sorry about that."

"What happened, Bill?"

"A couple of Germans came to have a pee I guess. Anyway they saw us and we had to shoot them. Then all hell broke loose. I knew that we were close to the time for the smoke and I popped mine. Then Shepherd was hit. We lost a machine gun. Sorry, sir."

"It can't be helped and, apart from Shepherd's leg, no damage was done."

We looked up as the Lightnings of the 370th fighter group swooped down. They disappeared behind the trees and I heard their four Brownings as they opened fire. I presumed they were strafing the road. Dad had told me that these twin boomed aircraft were almost as good as the Mosquito. As smoke rose to the south of us this seemed to be confirmed. Our camouflage netting hid us from our friends who would just see a German half-track.

"How is Shepherd?"

"He will live sir but he won't be moving so well for a while."

"Right, well see that he is comfortable. This could be a long day." Driving a German vehicle meant that we had to stay put until dark. There would be an air umbrella up to ensure that the Germans did not dig in and any German vehicle would be seen as fair game. The P-38s stayed just twenty minutes and then disappeared west. I knew that more aircraft would be sent over. If Eisenhower and De Gaulle had sanctioned this race for Paris then it was important. For the French this was not just a military target, it was a symbolic target. It was their capital. Hitler had made much of its conquest when it had been captured intact. Would we find it intact now or would the Germans destroy it? That was the reason for the urgency.

An hour after the aeroplanes had left one of the booby traps was triggered, it was more than two hundred yards from our camp. My men had made a deadly circle around us. With weapons cocked we were ready to sell our lives dearly.

"Stand to!"

I picked up my Mauser and peered through the sights. Moving in the trees were German soldiers. They did not appear to be in skirmish order. It looked to me as though they were the survivors of the P-38 attack and were taking a way home that avoided the road.

"Hold your fire. If they avoid us then we don't open fire. They are just trying to get home." I daresay I might be criticised for this but the men who were in the woods were not S.S. They were ordinary soldiers. Little would be gained in their death. If they were old soldiers then they would find a different route. If they meant us harm then they would come for the half-track.

A second and a third booby trap were triggered. These were not old soldiers. I decided to warn them off. I aimed at an officer who was standing next to a tree. I fired a bullet at the tree and he was showered in splinters. If they had any sense they would now avoid the danger which was patently to their front. The way home lay east. I saw, through the sights, a sergeant, who waved his men in that direction. I thanked God for the man's intelligence.

Then there were explosions to our right and bullets clanged off the half-track. "Sir, there are men in the woods. They are wearing black!"

That meant they were either S.S. or tank crew. "Open fire!"

I scanned the ground to the south. I could see grey uniforms, in the distance, hurrying east. As our machine guns opened fire I turned and placed my Mauser between Beaumont's machine gun and Hewitt's rifle. I saw that they were the crews of damaged or destroyed tanks. An officer raised his pistol and my bullet smacked into his head. I switched to the man on his left and my bullet hit him in the shoulder and he spun around. It was the MG 42 which ended the attack. Two of the Germans managed to get to within thirty yards of the half-track before they fell. Then there was silence. One or two of the wounded in the forest moaned for a while. When there was the sound of a booby trap exploding we knew that men still lived.

By afternoon we had heard no more from the forest and the Typhoons returned. They flew overhead and disappeared east. We heard their guns a little later.

"Beaumont, come with me. The rest of you prepare the half-track. We will leave when we return. I think this will be the last sortie of the day. We should be safe."

I took Beaumont in case there were any more booby traps. He had set most of them. When we turned over the first of the dead I saw that although they were tank men they were the 1st S.S. They were the ones we had fought at Trun. They were fanatical until the end. I found an officer and took the papers from his tunic. Beaumont picked up a couple more S.S. daggers. "Not you too Beaumont!"

"It's for Scouse. He has an idea that they might be worth a few bob after the war."

He was probably right.

None were alive and we headed back to the half-track. I climbed into the cab with Emerson. "Let's see if we can get into Dreux. I haven't heard any tank guns for a while. Fletcher, get on the radio and tell them that we will be the German half-track coming from the east. Don't hit us!"

"Right sir."

It took some time to negotiate the track but once we were on the road we made better time. As we neared the Paris road we saw the burned out vehicles and corpses. Many were blackened and burned. It was a grisly sight.

As we turned on to the main road I said, "Take it steady, Fred. We don't want to give these Americans a shock."

"Righto sir."

As the road turned right, after some trees we found ourselves facing the business end of an American half-track and a fifty calibre machine gun manned by the 22nd Infantry regiment. As Emerson stopped I opened the door and stepped out, "Captain Tom Harsker of Number 4 Commando."

A grey haired Colonel in a leather jacket climbed down from the half-track. He had a big grin on his face. "Colonel Buck Lanham!" He pumped my hand. "I have heard of you guys but until I saw the half-track I thought you were some sort of myth!"

"No sir. We would have been down sooner but we thought that the fly boys might see us as a soft target."

"You are right. We are the spearhead. We are camping here tonight. If you and your boys make camp in the woods I will take you to meet the French General. He is keen to meet you too."

"Sir, do you have a doctor? We have a wounded man."

"Of course. Lieutenant Higgins fetch the doctor to the half-track will you?"

A civilian, who had been standing close to the American half-track, stepped forward, "Can I come too, Colonel? This might need recording for posterity."

The Colonel gave a wry smile, "Why not. I think you two might get on. Captain, this is the war correspondent and writer, Ernest Hemingway."

He shook my hand, "Pleased to meet you, Captain."

"And you Mr. Hemingway."

The Colonel whistled and an American jeep raced up and spun around. We climbed on board and we sped off down the road. The noise from the engine and the speed at which we travelled made conversation impossible. I saw tanks with the French tricolour as well as American half-tracks and trucks. This was a fast moving column.

The flamboyant driver spun the jeep around to stop in front of the command tent. The French officers wrinkled their noses at the smell of burned rubber and the noise. The American colonel grinned, "Davis here fancies himself as a racing driver. Isn't that right Davis?"

"Darned tooting Colonel! There are no Sheriffs out here!"

The Colonel stood to attention and saluted. I did the same, "General, this is Captain Harsker. He is the Commando we were told to watch out for. "

The General did not smile but held out his hand. He spoke in French, "I am General Philippe Leclerc de Hauteclocque. I have heard much about you."

I answered in French. "It is an honour to serve with you sir. You and your men were legends in North Africa."

Then he smiled, "Commander Kieffer spoke highly of you. He was right, you do not butcher our language!"

"That is kind of you to say so, sir. I spent many summers here in France."

"Ah yes, your father, he was an ace in the Great War was he not?"

"Yes sir. He is in command of the airfield in Caen."

"Good. Now I hear that you have a German half-track and are not afraid of going behind the enemy lines."

"Correct sir."

"Then I want you ahead of us tomorrow. I will send one of my aides to act as liaison with you. Our countrymen are dying in the Paris streets yet we trundle down this road while old men wonder if it is safe!" He shook his head. "Thank you for your intelligence. It would have been bloody had we walked into their defences. We would have won but it would have cost too many of my men." He nodded, "Perhaps with the three allies working together we might achieve something eh? Nice to have met you."

"And you sir." I saluted and turned.

Colonel Lanham grinned, "I guess you and Hemingway here can chatter away in French. I didn't get any of that."

As we walked back to the jeep I said, "He wants us as point. He is sending me an officer to act as liaison."

"Then let's get up the road. Davis, get us there in one piece eh?"

"Right sir!"

He pulled up next to the Colonel's vehicle. "If you come with me to my tent we can examine the map and you can tell me what you have seen. We both know that aerial photographs don't give the whole picture."

The reporter tried to follow us. The colonel shook his head, "Now you know you can't come in here, Bumby. You are a correspondent and this is not your remit."

"But Buck, how the hell will I be able to give the full flavour of the excitement of the chase if I don't know the full picture."

"Go and talk to the Captain's men! They must have tales to tell!"

"Good idea."

As we went into the tent he said, "Hemingway is a good guy really but he pushes the boundaries. I had to take a carbine from him. If the Germans caught a correspondent with a gun he would be shot!"

There was a large map laid out on a portable table. "There are two routes into Paris. There is this northern one but that goes through too many places where we can be held up. The General wants us to go this way, in the south through this forest, by Rambouillet. We can bypass their towns and get to Paris without fighting a major battle. We like that. It suits my guys.

159

There are three armies following us. They can mop up the pockets of resistance. What do you think?"

"At the moment the German armour is scattered. We found some of the crews from the 1st S.S. in the forest east of here. The tanks that were waiting for you were just the ones which couldn't escape."

He nodded, "The Air Force say that they are preparing to gather at the Seine."

"And that helps you, sir."

"How so?"

I swept my hand in a line below the Seine. "That means there will be no armour here. If the General sends his Shermans in they should be able to sweep through the suburbs."

"That's what he says. My guys wanted to be the first into Paris but I guess it makes sense to allow the French to do it. So, you will run interference for us?"

"Interference?"

"A football term. You stop the Krauts getting close to us."

"Yes sir, I guess that is what we will do. The German half-track gives us the slightest of edges. The Germans hesitate. Battles are won and lost by such margins."

"Well good luck, Captain. I will have my adjutant bring over the passwords and frequencies. I hope you have a good man on the radio?"

"We do sir. Sometimes hard to understand but he is good. I think I was supposed to liaise with a Major Connor."

"Sorry, son, Mike was killed this morning in the attack. You two would have got along real well."

When I reached my camp the men were sat around the correspondent and he was scribbling away. My men looked up when I approached, "Don't stand for me. We have an early start so when Mr Hemingway is finished get some food on the go."

The writer shook his head, "It's Ernie, Papa or Bumby! Mr Hemingway was my father! You Brits are always so damned formal."

I smiled, "It's just the way we are."

"And so understated. Your guys just told me about your V.C. and your old man's too. I never would have guessed. You seemed so quiet. I have to get to know you a little more. I could use you in one of my books."

"I am afraid that we will be ahead of the main column. We don't fight a conventional war..." I hesitated, "Ernie. We are more like guerrillas."

"That would be for me too." He turned, "So, Scouse, isn't' it?"

"Yes sir."

"Tell me how you acquired so many S.S. daggers."

I saw Fletcher shrug. He would spin a yarn. I waved Sergeant Poulson over. "We are heading through the forests. See if you can get some camouflage netting and use some of the undergrowth to disguise the half-track. We will be at the sharp end tomorrow."

"Right sir."

"And how is Shepherd?"

"He is fine. The American doctor wanted him evacuating but Shepherd said he was just sitting in the half-track and so it would not hurt his wound." That was my men all over. Some soldiers would have taken the opportunity of getting out of the war. Commandos were different.

I heard a vehicle pull up and turned. A young French officer walked over to us. He was short enough to be a jockey. He had, under his left arm, a clip board. He snapped to attention and saluted, "I am Lieutenant Julian Lemay of the Fusiliers-Marins Commandos. I am your liaison officer."

I saluted, "I am Captain Tom Harsker. You can speak French, Lieutenant. It might make life easier."

He answered in French. "I am keen to speak English though, sir."

"Then speak English to my men. Their French is appalling!"

Beaumont looked at me indignantly. He had been listening and he spoke in French. "Sir, I object!"

"I apologise Private. This, Lieutenant Lemay, is the exception." He nodded and smiled. "Is that the information we need?"

"Yes sir. I have the details of where the Resistance is fighting and we will, hopefully, liberate them soon."

"Good, well if you let me have a look at them you can go and meet the chaps. Beaumont, if you would do the honours."

While they were away I sat with my back against the front wheel and looked at the plan. Once we left the relative safety of the forest then, it seemed to me, that the Germans would have many places where they could slow us down. I knew that there was a war going on in Paris. The Resistance had risen but there was only so long that they could hold out. Speed was of the essence. The American motorized infantry could make headway and then it would be down to the French armour to blast a way through. They had been lucky hitherto. I could not see their luck lasting.

When the lieutenant returned it was amusing seeing Beaumont translate Fletcher's Liverpudlian into English which the Frenchman could understand. However they seemed to get on and that was more important. We set him up in the half-track so that he was close to Fletcher and I made sure that Beaumont was also nearby. His engineering skills might not be needed. We also rigged the second MG 42 at the front so that we had two machine guns there. The battlefield yielded even more ammunition. We amused the Americans. They only searched the battlefield for souvenirs and not usable weapons.

The Colonel invited me to eat with his officers. I noticed that Ernest Hemingway was not present. I asked about it and the Colonel frowned. "It seems the war correspondent has decided to find some resistance himself. We won't let him fight and so he hopes the Resistance will! He can't do that. It is against the Geneva convention."

"So far, Colonel, I have seen little evidence that the Germans pay much attention to the convention."

"Really?"

"Have you not seen the Hitler Commando order?" He shook his head. "I tapped the flashed on my shoulder. "If we are caught then German soldiers are ordered to shoot us. They don't take Commandos prisoner."

"A different enemy then, Captain."

"It certainly is. What time is the kick off tomorrow?"

"Kick off?"

"When do we start?"

"0500."

"Then we will be on the road by 0400. We will push on to Montfort. It is a long drive but as it is mainly through the forest there should not be a problem. If we hit trouble we will get on the radio to you."

One of his Captains, Captain Miller, said, "You like going out on a limb, Captain Harsker?"

"I am afraid that your motorized battalion makes a lot more noise than we do. Jerry will know you are coming. If there is an ambush they will hear a half-track and they will wait. That gives us an edge. Sometimes we can bluff our way through and at other times we fight but the element of surprise is worth being on our own. My chaps are good at what they do and they don't panic."

I declined the offer of French brandy and cigars. I needed my wits about me and I left for our bivouac. After checking and loading my weapons I added a little more to my ongoing letter to Susan and then curled up under the stars.

Chapter 19

It was dark when we set out. We ate cold rations. We had plenty of fuel and ammunition but we were heading into the unknown. We passed a large Château at Grandchamp. It had been deserted but the sandbags outside told us that it had been recently occupied. I wondered if the Germans had abandoned all the land before Paris. It seemed unlikely. Fletcher kept a dialogue going with both Colonel Buck and General Leclerc. After the first transmission to the French command vehicle Lieutenant Lemay took over. It made for better understanding!

Sharp eyed Hewitt spotted the guns up ahead before we reached them. They were just beyond the small village of Le Hallier and they were close to the forest. They were well camouflaged. We stopped half a mile from where Hewitt said he had seen them. The houses disguised us. I took out my glasses. Hewitt was right. There were two anti-tank guns; I saw their barrels. The German infantry on either side had machine guns but I had no idea of their number.

"Scouse, get on to the Americans. We have an anti-tank ambush ahead."

"Sir."

"We could take them out, sir."

"I don't want to risk being hit by those anti-tank guns. The beauty of the half-track is that it is German. We won't get another."

"That's right sir! We don't want Bertha damaging!"

Gordy said, "You do know Emerson that you can't take this thing back to England with you!"

"You don't know that, Sarge!"

Lieutenant Lemay said, "I am not sure I understand this. He wants to take this German vehicle back to England?"

I shrugged, "He has grown attached to it."

After Fletcher had spoken with the Americans he said, "They are on their way sir."

"We can give them a hand. Gordy, bring the grenade launcher. Bill, you and Beaumont bring your sub machine guns. Lieutenant Lemay, you are in charge." I grabbed my rifle and we slipped out of the back and headed along the buildings which lined the road. I was not worried that they would fire at us. They did not have a clear shot. The road bent a little. They would be alerted but so long as their attention was on the half-track then we had a chance.

As we trotted along the backs of the houses and outbuildings of the farms Gordy asked, "What have you got in mind sir?"

"Find somewhere you can lob grenades into the gun emplacements. We are just here to protect you."

He grinned, "That's nice of you." He pointed ahead, "There's a nice wall and by my estimate that would be about a hundred and fifty yards from the guns. Someone will have to check."

We crawled the last fifty yards. We could see the forest but the Germans had not used the trees to observe. They were just intent on stopping armour coming down the road. I slowly pulled myself up the stone wall which was at the top of a bank. It looked to be ancient as though some other structure had stood here in days gone by. Gordy was right. We were about a hundred and sixty yards from the intersection and the gun emplacements. I saw that they were debating what to do about the half-track.

I slid back down. "One hundred and sixty yards, Gordy. You two come up with me and we will open fire on the machine gunners when the first grenade explodes. We will direct your fire."

"Right sir."

When the three of us reached the top of the remains of the wall we slowly moved our guns to rest on the ancient stones. With just our arms and head exposed we would be presenting the smallest of targets. I knew that machine guns tended to fire high at first. I aimed my rifle at the nearest machine gunner. I heard the sound of the grenade being launched. It exploded twenty yards in front of the guns. As I fired I shouted. "Short twenty yards!"

The machine gunner fell and then I was deafened by the sound of the two sub machine guns next to me. The next grenade exploded between the two guns. The far machine gun fired and, as I had expected was high. Leaving the nearest one to the other two I fired five bullets at the far crew. I must have hit something for it stopped firing. I heard orders being shouted as Gordy's next grenade had a direct hit on one of the anti-tank guns. Then the infantry burst from the woods firing. I saw Bill's cheek laid open by a stone splinter as Beaumont dropped two Germans, one of whom had a grenade. "Grenade!"

We dropped to the ground as the grenade exploded.

"Right lads we have done enough. Throw grenades over the wall and then leg it!"

The four of us pulled pins, hurled our grenades and then rolled down the bank before running back to the half-track. The four explosions sounded almost simultaneous. We did not stop to look we kept running. When we reached the half-track we saw the motorized infantry arriving.

The Colonel leaned out of the cab. "We saw the smoke. What happened?"

"We thought we would buy time sir, we lobbed a few grenades. There is just one anti-tank gun now and the crew have been hit by shrapnel."

He shook his head, "Leave us some of the war, eh Captain!"

The half-track moved off and I saw that they had a PIAT on the top next to the machine gun. It made the half-track into a small tank.

"Hewitt, Hay needs some work."

"Another one going back like Frankenstein's creature."

"Emerson when this is cleared we will head off again."

The Americans went in fast. A second M2 was echeloned just behind the Colonel and the two PIATS sent rockets towards the guns. With every machine gun firing they were like whirling Dervishes! The Germans who survived surrendered.

"Right Emerson. Into the woods!"

Gordy chuckled, "Be gentle with him sir, it is his first time!"

All of my men laughed at the crude joke. Lieutenant Lemay looked puzzled. Beaumont leaned over and explained it to him. He coloured and then laughed. He turned to me, "Your men are like the Fusiliers-Marins. They make such jokes with each other."

"I think it is fighting men all over, Lieutenant. We have to do some fairly horrible things. This is just one way to cope with them."

As we passed the Colonel he shouted, "We are a good team Captain!"

"So far so good, so far so good!"

We entered the Stygian darkness of the forest. If the Germans had had enough tanks left then this would have been a good place for an ambush. They did not. We had to turn north east at Saint-Léger-en-Yvelines. It was a tiny hamlet. The Germans had not been there recently for the villagers came out to wave and cheer us when they saw our uniforms. I began to think that we would make Paris in the next twelve hours. As I looked at the map I saw some potential trouble spots. After we passed Méré things might become difficult.

Fletcher shouted, as we approached the village, "Sir, they want Lieutenant Lemay."

He took the microphone. I was staring at the road. The trees had thinned considerably. Méré was much bigger than Léger-en-Yvelines. One or two of the houses looked to be substantial.

Lieutenant Lemay said, "I am sorry sir but the General thinks we go too fast. The tanks are spread out over a large distance and he worries about air attacks. He asks that we make camp."

I nodded and shouted, "Fletcher, tell the Colonel that we will camp here at Méré."

"Right sir."

It looked a good place to stop. We parked at the northern end of the village and the Lieutenant and I went to speak with the men of the village. There were no young men. All looked to be my father's age or older. I let the Lieutenant ask the questions. This was his country and I was a foreigner. Their news disturbed me. We spoke with eight of them just to confirm that what they said was right. When we heard the 22nd Infantry Regiment arrive, we walked back to speak with the Colonel.

He looked pleased with himself. "We should be in Paris by dawn!"

I shook my head, "We have just received intelligence, sir, that Germans troops have been building defences north of us. We will have to fight our way through them."

"Damn! How certain are you of the information?"

"The farmers have been watching Germans disappearing into the land north of here. They report anti-tank guns and Panzerfausts as wells as tanks."

He looked at the Lieutenant, "Does the General know?"

"No sir, we only just found out."

"Perhaps it is a good thing that we have to bivouac here then. We might be able to plan something."

By the time we reached the half-track my resourceful team had managed to barter some food from the farmers and we had a stew with a couple of scrawny chickens as well as fresh bread. Lieutenant Lemay tutted and shook his head when he saw the fare. He and Beaumont disappeared. An hour later they returned. They had wine and they had some fresh goat's cheese.

"I can live with poor stew but at least let us have some decent wine and a fine cheese to leave a pleasant taste in our mouths."

It was dark when we finished. A sergeant came to fetch us, "Gentlemen, the General wishes a word. If you would follow me."

I saw that the Colonel had joined him and they were around a table lit by oil lamps. There was a map on the table. "Thank you for coming so promptly. Your news has been confirmed. The Germans are trying to stop us reaching Paris. Here at St Cyr they have fortified the military school!" The General sounded outraged. "And here, at Neauphle-le-Château they have a few tanks with a mined road and anti-tank guns. We will be delayed by at least two days!"

Everyone went silent and I wondered why we were there. Was it to share their misery?

The Colonel said, quietly, "We have a plan but it involves you and your half-track, Captain." I nodded. "The air force will bomb the mined road tomorrow at dawn. We will then use the French tanks to smash through their defences but we need a diversion. We want you and my B Company

166

to go across country and attack their flank. We need you to make them think that it is a division attacking them. Then they will move the tanks to counter your attack."

"As soon as we are through then the General intends to send a flying column under the command of Captain Dronne. They will be the first to reach Paris and we will follow."

I nodded, "It should work but why not use two companies? That would be even more believable."

The Colonel glanced at the General and I guessed that had already been suggested by the Colonel and dismissed by the General. The General said, "We must ensure that we break through to allow Captain Dronne to reach Paris. That, Captain Harsker, is imperative."

"Then we need rocket launchers and as many grenade launchers as we can get. Who is the officer commanding Company B?"

"Lieutenant Cooper. His captain was wounded in the last attack. I am going to make him a brevet captain but we want you to command."

This was not an honour. If it went wrong then it would be me who would shoulder the blame. "Very well sir. I take it we will be attacking at dawn?"

"That is right."

"Then I will go and organise my men. If you send this Lieutenant Cooper and his sergeants to our half-track we can work out the details."

"Just like that?"

"Just like that Colonel. You are right it has to be done and my team are, probably, expendable. It must be a French unit which liberates Paris, we all know that. We will get the job done."

Lieutenant Cooper was older than I expected. He had the hint of grey about his temples. He and his men arrived with four M2 half-tracks, four M3 half-tracks and two jeeps. "Sergeant, have the men set up camp here and then you and the other non-coms come and join us." He grinned and saluted, "Lieutenant Cooper, sir. I hear we are going to be a diversion eh?"

"That's right. We are going to make Jerry think that a division is attacking his flank. Did Colonel Lanham send the grenade launchers?"

"Yes sir but I am curious why?"

"What have you noticed about the land around here, Lieutenant Cooper?"

"It's Coop, sir." I nodded. "Roads I wouldn't drive my Oldsmobile down if it was at home. Lots of little woods and damned hedges all over the place."

"And we use them to our advantage. They allow us to get close without observation. Oh by the way this is Lieutenant Lemay. This is his country!" The American sergeants arrived. None of mine were present. They knew what we were doing and they were preparing for the attack. I just had Lieutenant Lemay.

I took out the map I had sketched and placed it on the ground.

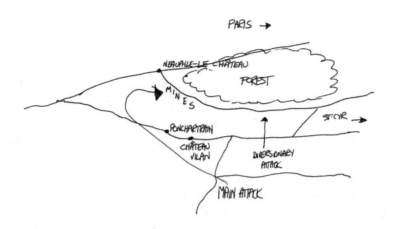

I used my dagger to point out the features as I mentioned them. "Jerry is ten miles to the north east of us. They have fortified St. Cyr, here." I pointed on the map to the old Military School. "That will be a hard nut to crack. It is stone and defensible. The other strong point is astride the main road to Paris and protected by these woods to the left. We will drive to within a mile of their left flank. I will lead twenty of your men with a mixture of rocket launchers and grenade launchers. We will attack before dawn. There are stone walls with hedges on both sides of the road. The field in front of their defences is no more than a hundred yards or so. Our weapons will have the range."

The Lieutenant said, "But the air attack will be in daylight!"

I nodded, "Exactly which is why they will think that we are the main attack. Your half-tracks can be driven in low gear can't they?"

"Yes sir."

"Then you will approach the battle in low gear. Make them think we are tanks. I saw how you use your rocket launchers. In the dark they can have the same effect as a tank. All we need to do is to draw the armour and anti-tank guns from the road so that General Leclerc and his tanks can punch through."

"Sir, what about the tanks which are dug in?"

I shrugged, "Your General, Lieutenant Lemay, will have to deal with them himself. There is a limit to what a company can do." I turned to the Americans. "The men who are coming with me need to be here in ten minutes. We leave in thirty."

One of the sergeants asked, "I thought you Limeys stopped for tea."

I kept a straight face as I said, "That is why we are leaving in thirty minutes and not twenty. We need to let it brew."

They looked at me with surprised expressions until the Lieutenant laughed, "He is pulling your leg, Sergeant Lee. Go and sort out the men." As they went he said, "Sorry about that sir. This is the first time we have worked alongside you guys."

"Don't worry, Lieutenant, I came up through the ranks. I know how it works. How come there are no other officers?"

"We have been at the sharp end since Omaha. We take it as a compliment but we are the smallest company in the regiment. These are good guys."

"You don't need to convince me. Let's see if we can keep most of them alive eh?"

The twenty men arrived with their weapons. They were led by Sergeant Lee. I had my sergeants with me. "There are less than thirty of us but we are going to make the Germans think we are a regiment. I hope you can move quietly because I intend to get to within fifty yards of their lines. We will find cover and, on my command, we will used the grenade launchers on their defences."

"Sir how can we get that close? Surely their sentries will see us?"

"No Sergeant. I will take four of my men and we will kill their sentries. That will be the key to our success. When the grenades start to fall they will think we are using either artillery or tanks. The sound of your M3 and M2 half-tracks rumbling in low gear towards them will make them think that it is a major tank attack. By the time our aeroplanes are bombing the minefield they should be committed to attacking us. They will see the half-tracks and try to destroy them. We will be hidden less than fifty yards from them. If we have cleared the sentries then you will have time to camouflage your weapons in the hedges. The Germans won't even see them. That is when you men with the rocket launchers can do the damage. You can stop even a Tiger at fifty yards with a PIAT."

One of the corporals said, "That is close range sir."

I nodded, "And they will not be looking that closely." I tapped the map. "This is where we will be. There is a road and hedgerow here just fifty yards from the woods where they have their sentries. The half-tracks will be a mile away here." I smiled, "So any questions?"

Sergeant Lee shook his head wryly and asked, "Just one sir. What the hell do you guys put in your tea? Pennsylvanian steel?"

Sergeant Poulson said, "Two sugars and a drop of milk. But the secret is to make it so strong that you can stand a teaspoon in it!"

"Right, let's go." I found Coop. He had the maps and the coordinates. "We do this by timing. You will lead the vehicles in to the attack at 0430. A few minutes early will not hurt but if you hear firing then you know they are aware of us. We will begin our barrage with the grenades at 0445. You will halt at the hedge line and wait until they begin to attack."

"And you guys?"

"We will pull out as soon as the air attack has destroyed the minefield. The General plans on attacking at 0900."

Chapter 20

I was counting on the thick woods to help us. We reached our drop off point unseen. To the west, some half a mile distant, was the Château de Ponchartrain, Vilan. I was just grateful that the Germans had not fortified it. I had begun to realise that the German military had taken over the fine homes of France as luxurious quarters for their senior officers. That, I believe, saved them from becoming strong points. I left Shepherd and Fletcher in the half-track. Emerson was reluctant to leave Bertha but I needed my men to be fit and the two I left still nursed wounds.

I led the Americans the mile from the drop off point to the first road and the hedgerow. The woods could be seen to the north of us but they were a dark mass only. We left our rifles, grenade launchers and machine guns with Lieutenant Lemay and the Americans. Sergeant Lee had been amused to see us black up. We headed through the gate into the field. I could see the woods a little clearer now. We had eighty yards until the next hedge and after that we would be within sight of their sentries. I had my silenced Colt ready. We crawled across the field. When we reached the next hedge I peered through the broken gate. The road appeared clear and I waved my men through. The wall alongside the road gave us some protection and I lifted my head to peer through the hedge. I could see the woods just fifty yards from us. The glow of a cigarette butt identified at least one sentry. I also heard the murmur of conversation.

I waved Sergeant Poulson and his team to the east while I took my men to the west. I found a broken section of the wall and we slipped over. I crawled towards the tree line. I used my hands to feel the ground. I prayed that they had not mined it although the proximity of their sentries suggested they had not. My men spread out on either side of me. We crawled across the fifty yards. We had time and, so long as we made no sound, it was unlikely the Germans sentries would see our subtle movements.

I saw two shadows which appeared to be moving and I headed towards them. I heard the two Germans talking. I could not make out their words. They were obviously avoiding the wrath of a superior officer by whispering. I worked out that they were less than ten yards from me. I slowly raised my Colt and, kneeling, held it in two hands. I fired twice. The two men fell. I heard a grunt from further down the field. I stood and hurried to the trees. I scanned the interior of this forest. The trees were more open than I had expected. They had done some clearance. The lumber had been used to make the defences stronger. You could drive a tank between the remaining trees. Glancing down I saw that the two men were dead. I saw, fifty yards further in, the faint glow of a fire. It was the camp of the men who would man the machine guns and anti-tank guns which lay to the left and right of us.

I took out the stick grenade I had brought with me and another from one of the dead Germans. I made a booby trap. As soon as they moved the machine gun then the grenades would explode. I covered them in a belt of ammunition. It was as I looked up that I saw the anti-tank gun. It was tantalisingly close to me. As I approached the sandbagged emplacement, the German, who had been asleep inside the sandbags, sat up and stared at me from less than six feet. I fired two snap shots and he fell back. I did not need to check if he was dead. I could see the black patch in the sandbags opposite where his blood had spattered. This was a better target to booby trap and, after I had set the dead German's grenades, I spent a couple of minutes hiding my handiwork. Satisfied I gave a low whistle and moved back across the field. My team joined me. I saw shadows moving to our left and knew that Sergeant Poulson's team had done their job too. As we clambered back over the wall I could not help but feel guilty. The Germans we had killed were not the S.S. but there had been no way to neutralize them without killing them. That was war.

We headed back to the wall and hedgerow and watched. I sent my men back for Sergeant Lee and our equipment back with the half-track. The danger was now that the sentries would be relieved and their deaths discovered. There was little we could do about that but it was now 0400. Even if they were discovered the attack would begin in thirty minutes. I spent the minutes they were away poking my Mauser through the hedge and adding branches and twigs to disguise it. I left enough space for the sight.

As my men returned Sergeant Poulson directed the Americans to their positions. My section would be on the extreme left of the line. With just one rocket launcher and one grenade rifle we had less hardware than the Americans but we had brought the MG 42 and that would not only bring confusion to the Germans but death too. At 0415 I heard the shout of alarm. The bodies had been found. There was a whistle and then much louder noises from inside the camp as they prepared for action.

"Be ready but don't fire until I give the word." Just then I heard the sound of the half-tracks' engines. Lieutenant Cooper had kept to the timetable. I heard a German shout, "Panzer!"

Before I could order the men to fire there was an explosion as one of the booby traps was triggered. All of them went off in a rippling line as the crews went to man the guns. The largest explosion came from the anti-tank gun for I had piled ammunition around it. I could see men racing through the trees, illuminated by the light of the explosions.

"Grenades! Fire!"

I peered through my telescopic sight. Although it was dark I could make out the lighter faces of the soldiers. I was tempted to fire but I did not want them to see my muzzle flash. We had eight grenade rifles. We had taken not only Company B's but the rifles from another two companies. The Americans did not rate them. We had had to persuade them of their worth. They would now see it first-hand. The eight explosions were behind the front line, as we had planned. They caught men running to join those at the edge of the wood. We had loaders for them and the eight rifles kept up a barrage. We had not disabled all the guns and I saw the muzzle flash of an anti-tank gun. I said, "Sergeant Lee, have your PIATs take out the anti-tank gun."

It would give away our position but it could not be helped. I did not want the half-tracks damaging, not, at least, until the tanks had arrived. Then our job would be done. I took a bead on the officer at the anti-tank gun. I squeezed the trigger just a heartbeat before the rocket smashed into the side of the gun. It would not fire again. The rocket, however, had alerted the Germans to our position.

"Open fire!"

My men let rip with their machine guns as I shot at the vital men, the actual gunners and the officers. I heard shouts from my right as machine guns took out the PIAT crew. Then more grenades landed close to the machine guns as our men shortened the range. The fire diminished. The half-tracks were now behind the road at our rear. Men disgorged to join us. Lieutenant Lemay had been given Private Beaumont's Thompson and he was using it well. Despite his apparent youth he was using the short bursts of a veteran and moving between each burst.

The fifty calibre machine guns on the half-tracks opened up. Their extra fire power shredded the front lines. The booby traps had destroyed the defences of the guns and the extra height allowed the half-track gunners to fire down into the them. I heard a German officer shout, "Fall back! Fall back!"

I glanced at my watch. It was 0530 and dawn would break in a matter of moments. "Lieutenant, take over. Keep the grenades falling."

I ran across the road and jumped over the broken section of wall. I ran to the Lieutenant's M3. "We have them, Lieutenant. They are falling back. Get on the radio to the Colonel and find out when the air force is coming in."

"Yes sir. Have we been hurt?"

I nodded, "A machine gun took out a rocket crew. I don't know how badly yet but they have no anti-tank guns left and they are falling back. Even if the air force doesn't get here for a while as soon as the tanks come then we pull out. The wood is not a dense one. They can get through."

Leaving him to pass the message on I went back to my men. Sergeant Lee was with Sergeant Poulson, "Sir, they have fallen back! We could capture their positions!"

I shook my head, "That is not our mission, sergeant. We have to draw their tanks here to allow the General to drive on. How are your men?"

"They were just wounded sir. I sent them back to the Lieutenant."

"Good. Your chaps are doing well. They will reinforce soon. I am guessing we can expect mortars soon enough."

"Don't worry sir, the Lieutenant will be setting our own up over the wall." He tapped the stone wall with the butt of his rifle. "This is a good defensive position sir!"

Polly said, "This isn't the first time we have done this."

"I can see that."

We watched the woods and fired at any grey we saw. They were having to move up slowly and, until their tanks arrived, we would have the advantage.

A short time after 0630 a runner came towards us. "Sir, the bombers will be over us at seven. They are going to bomb the woods and the mined area. The Lieutenant said you should move back behind the road."

I shook my head. "Tell him we will stay here until the bombers come over."

He nodded and ran.

"Isn't that a risk, sir?"

"Not really, Sergeant Lee. You said yourself we have two walls, one on either side. We would have to be incredibly unlucky to be hit. Besides, have faith in the air force!"

"I heard they killed Poles and Canucks at Falaise."

"They did but they will have learned their lesson."

Private Beaumont shouted, "Sir I can hear armour. Sounds like a Mark IV!"

"Get your rocket launchers ready, Sergeant! This is the big one!"

I looked through the telescopic sight. The lightening of the sky made it easier to see into the woods. The fact that it was an open wood made life easier for me. The mortars from B Company began to rain down, deeper into the undergrowth. I saw one German mortar team blown up as they set up their own mortar. I aimed at a German officer who was rallying and organising his men. I squeezed the trigger and hit him in the shoulder as he turned. I moved a foot to my right. The ones around him dropped. Bullets cracked into the wall before me but they were blind shots aimed at the muzzle flash. I would need to move between each shot to confuse the enemy.

The American mortars stopped the fire from the Germans, briefly. Then I heard the sound of a French 75. The Germans had captured many in 1940 and they still gave good service. They were dependable artillery pieces. There was an explosion behind us and shouts. They had the range. I hoped that Lieutenant Cooper would use his mobility. I knew that Fletcher and Shepherd would. The Germans had no spotter to direct their fire and so they were just trying to disrupt what they thought were tanks. The M3 half-track was a similar size to the old Lee Grant, M3 tank. The Germans reused old vehicles and they might think the Americans had done so too. The PIAT sticking out from the front would, in the dawn light, have looked like a barrel. With daylight would come the realisation that they had been duped.

A cloud suddenly shifted and the brighter rays of the sun made me realise that time had passed. I looked at my watch. It was 0645. We had held out longer than I had expected. I knew that the men behind the wall had taken casualties but we only had four men wounded...so far. Then I heard the rumble of tanks. There was more than one. I peered through the telescope and saw them. There were at least four that I could see. Our plan had worked. These tanks had taken almost an hour to reach us. They had to have come from the road to the north of us. There would be fewer tanks, at least, for the French to clear. The tanks were still deep in the woods. Although the woods was open they still had to travel slower than they would have liked. This was not tank country which was why they had just used infantry to defend it.

I moved the gun until the commander of one Mark IV, with his torso out of the turret, could be seen. It was long range but worth the shot. If the commander was buttoned up then his vision would be restricted and tankers did not like that! I let out my breath as I fired four bullets in quick succession. One must have hit for his body lay half in and half out of the turret. He was dragged back inside and the hatch closed. I moved my sights to the next one but he was safely buttoned up.

"Sergeant Lee, there are some Mark IV tanks. Wait until they are at the edge of the woods. Three rockets for each one, if you please."

"Sir."

The Germans dared not fire yet because of the trees and their branches but they did send smoke up from their mortars. The area before the woods became filled with the smoke of six smoke bombs.

"Watch out for infantry advancing."

Gordy said, "Let's discourage them eh sir?" He aimed the grenade rifle almost vertically. That way he could send a grenade to land just forty yards from us. The range was too far for a hand thrown one but deadly against infantry advancing across an open field.

Sergeant Poulson opened fire with the MG 42. Resting on the wall he traversed left and right, firing in short bursts. Emerson quickly changed the belt when it was empty. I heard the double crack as the two leading tanks fired. They had had to wait until they were close to the edge of the woods. Behind me I saw an M2 half-track explode as a shell hit the engine. Machine gun fire scythed through the bushes and two more Americans fell.

"Medic!"

"Sir! My men can't see anything!"

"Hang tough, sergeant. The tanks will appear any moment now. Look for the big shadows." Even as I spoke the machine gun began to fire above our heads as it tried to hit the half-tracks on the other side of the road. The smoke which impaired our vision did exactly the same for the Germans.

I fired at human shadows which headed towards us. Beaumont hurled a German grenade high into the air and then I saw the barrel of a Mark IV. The machine gun below it which fired marked its position. It was just sixty yards away. Four of the rockets slammed into it. It did not explode but it stopped and smoke and flames could be seen. Billy Hay sprayed the crew with his machine gun as they tried to bail out. Then Lance Sergeant Hewitt, who was standing close to me, fired the section PIAT. He was firing at an oblique angle and I saw his rocket hit the turret. One of the Americans sent his in the same direction and smoke came from the tank which was now, effectively, out of action. I saw the driver attempt to reverse it back to the safety of the woods.

At that moment I heard the roar of aeroplanes. They were coming from the west. I looked and saw that they were Typhoons and a squadron of P47 Thunderbolts. Saner minds had decided not to repeat the mistakes of Operation Cobra. This would not be the sledgehammer of the Halifax or Handley Page but the surgical strike of two of the finest fighter bombers in the world.

"Take cover! Incoming!" I was far closer to the rockets and bombs than I would have liked. I dived to the ground and covered my ears to protect them from the concussion. The proximity of the tanks, just forty yards away meant that the aeroplanes would target them. I took consolation in the fact that I would know nothing at all about it if I was hit by friendly fire.

The explosions seemed to gallop from the west as the waves flew incredibly low to use their rockets and their machine guns as well as cannon to clear the ground. The ground on the other side of the wall seemed to shake as though there was an earthquake. The two tanks we had hit were struck again and their petrol tanks ignited. They rose in the air and struck the ground with such force that I saw a couple of American soldiers fall to the ground with the force of the explosion. The tanks which were deeper in the woods must have been hit too for I heard another two huge explosions. The attack lasted less than fifteen minutes. After they had bombed and used their rockets they returned for one last pass to empty their guns. Wave after wave passed over at tree top height. Nothing remained alive in the woods before us. The smoke cleared slowly and it looked like a scene from Dante. There was nothing moving between us and the woods. Fires were burning and the ground was littered with charred and smoking bodies. The only ones who remained alive were us, on our side of the walls.

"Reload and keep an eye out but I think our job here is done. At 0900 we will head back to the half-tracks."

It was tempting to go into the woods and see if we could advance in that direction but there was no point. The mission was to gain the road to Paris. Our job had been to create a diversion and we had done so. The medics took away the wounded and my men drank their canteens dry. We heard the rumble of tanks to the west of us at 0830. The General was keeping to his timetable. I stood and waved my arm, "Right boys, back to the half-tracks! Well done!"

The Americans went back in high spirits. That was soon dampened when they saw the blanket covered bodies and the burned out half-tracks. The Germans had managed to hit two. I counted the blankets. Twelve Americans had died. Lieutenant Cooper had a soot covered face and his hands were heavily bandaged. His sergeant took the cigarette from between his lips so that he could talk. "That was hell Captain! I don't know how you guys survived the attack."

"Your chaps did well, Coop. They didn't panic and they did their job."

Coop smiled and gestured a thumb at our half-track. It was a good fifty yards back from the wall, "Your guys had more sense than we did. As soon as the mortars began they pulled back."

I nodded, "It is what I would have done. The mortars were firing blind." I pointed to the north. "We had better get after the General. I am not certain he has finished with us."

We clambered aboard the half-track. Emerson shooed Fletcher from the driver's seat, "I hope you were careful with her!"

"I pulled her back didn't I? Gratitude!" He turned to Private Beaumont, "Did you manage to get anything worthwhile?"

Beaumont shook his head, "They were line troops. I felt sorry for them."

I nodded, "I know what you mean."

Lieutenant Lemay said, "I hate them! They have despoiled my country for five years now! I wish them all dead!"

As I settled into the cab I realised that was the difference between fighting in your country and for your country. We had been bombed and burned in

England but Germans had only claimed the tiny Channel Islands. For Lieutenant Lemay it was like being violated.

We had to travel a long way to reach the support vehicles and it was gone noon when we saw the end of the battle. The Germans had fought hard but the heart had been torn from them by our surprise attack and the air attack. The French had lost six tanks and a self-propelled gun. I saw Americans of the 4th Division deploying from their vehicles to go and mop up. We halted at the medical vehicles where doctors were dealing with the wounded.

It was early afternoon when I saw the M3 of Colonel Lanham heading in our direction. It had taken damage and his gunner had his arm in a sling. He dismounted and walked over to Lieutenant Cooper, Sergeant Lee and me. He smiled, "You guys did your job and then some! Well done. What is the body count, Coop?"

"Twelve and we lost two vehicles."

He nodded, "Well you will be pleased to know that Major General Gerow has ordered us to stop here and recuperate for a few days. We are not going on to Paris. At least not yet."

"Does General Leclerc know this?"

The American Colonel shook his head, "He will find out when he returns. He is losing too much armour. We need to take it slower."

I glanced over at Lieutenant Lemay, he was one of many Frenchmen who would not be happy. I remembered the French General's plans. They necessitated Captain Raymond Dronne racing ahead with his armoured company to liberate Paris. I had no idea how he would react to his superior's orders. I had not met the Major General. He was with the main army and that was ten miles behind us. I had no doubt he had good reasons for his decision but it would not sit well with our French allies.

I left the Americans and joined my men. "We had better re-equip ourselves. Fletcher you and Beaumont go on the scrounge! It seems a task for which you are eminently suited."

"If I knew what eminently meant I might be insulted. Come on Rog let the master get to work."

"I thought I heard the Colonel say the advance was halted."

"You did but let's keep that to ourselves. We don't want to upset Lieutenant Lemay We obey orders, as always."

Polly grinned, "Sir, we bend more orders than we actually obey!"

"If this operation is cancelled then it may well be that we go back to Caen. When Fletcher returns I will have him get in touch with Major Foster. In the meantime get as much fuel as you can and replace the ammunition we used."

He turned to go and then smiled, "We managed to get more grenades for the grenade launcher. Gordy is happy!"

"If we have put a smile on that curmudgeon's face then that, in itself, is a cause for celebration. I think we will finish off Petty Officer Leslie's rum tonight."

We had no showers and so I went to the water bowser to wash off the blacking and clean myself up. Lieutenant Lemay said, "Sir, would it be all right if I went to see the General when he returns. I wish to congratulate him on his great victory."

"Of course. You had a victory yourself today, Lieutenant. You did well and held your nerve. That is to be commended. When you return to your company you can tell them how you fooled the Boche."

"Thank you sir. When this war is over I shall dedicate myself to making my company the equal of yours. You are lions!"

Beaumont and Fletcher returned, laden. They had, not only more .45 ammunition, but also a tin of pork chops. Fletcher shook his head, ruefully, "If you had sent more lads sir, we could've had a ton of stuff! Them Yanks are well looked after!"

"When you have put the ammo in the half-track see if you can get in touch with Major Foster. If this operation is postponed what are our orders?"

Fletcher looked crestfallen, "Postponed? But I had plans for Paris!"

"Get on the radio!"

"Sir." He went off cheerfully. He was a hard man to put down. He returned later with the news that he could not reach Major Foster, "Interference sir and too much traffic. I might try after we have eaten eh sir? A bit quieter then."

I had just started to eat the pork chop when Lieutenant Lemay found me, "Sir, General Leclerc wishes to speak with you."

I was enjoying the chop. We had even found some apples. They had not been ripe but pork and apple sauce was to be savoured, no matter how tart they were. "Now?"

He looked at me in surprise as though he could not understand why I was not running to the General. "Yes sir. He said it was important."

I stood, "Sergeant Poulson, keep your eye on that chop! I am not finished with it!"

My men laughed, "Yes sir."

There was a heated debate when I reached the General's tent. Colonel Lanham was there too and he looked to be agitated. General Leclerc saw our approach and shouted, "Silence! I will speak and you will all listen!"

There was silence. I saw Colonel Lanham stiffen, "Sir, we have had orders from Major General Leonard Gerow that we are not to advance on Paris. The orders are that we wait here for him."

Some of his officers began to shout and the General said, "Silence." He looked at me and smiled, "Thank you Captain for what you did today. I

179

have already thanked Colonel Lanham but he assures me that it was you who made it work. You saved many lives today."

"Thank you sir, I had good men under my command. Lieutenant Lemay is a credit to the Fusilier-Marins."

"Sit, please. Thank you for your comments. They show that you are a gentleman." The look he flashed Colonel Lanham suggested that he was not included in that description. "Napoleon once asked if a general was lucky. He said, *'I know the man is good but is he lucky?'* You, Captain, appear to be lucky and that is not to be ignored."

"Thank you for the compliment sir." I waited. I knew he had not finished and had used his conversation with me to calm himself down and to give himself thinking time. Dad had told me of officers in the Great War who had used a pipe for the same purpose.

He turned to face Colonel Lanham, "I will not be heading for Paris tomorrow. I will wait here for Major General Gerow." His officers jumped up and began to shout. He held up his hand and they subsided. "Captain Dronne, however will go ahead with the plan we outlined yesterday. The difference is that the 22nd will not be with him."

"Sir, you are disobeying orders!"

"Then I will take the consequences! But I will not allow my countrymen to bleed for my city while I sit less than twenty miles away twiddling my thumbs!" Colonel Lanham nodded. "Captain Harsker I will not order you to go with Captain Dronne but I will ask if you would accompany my flying column. They might need your luck and you also seem to have skills which we need."

I nodded, "Of course sir. I would be honoured to help Captain Dronne."

"Then we need detain you no longer. Lieutenant Lemay will bring your orders. I am sorry for having to interrupt your dinner."

Colonel Lanham stood too, "I will leave now, General. I am sorry if I offended you."

"You did not but your General is a different matter."

As we walked back he said, " General Leclerc flew the other day to meet with Bradley. He was told he could advance to here but no further. That was why we camped the other day. Then we heard that the Germans in Paris are hurting the resistance. The General was not happy. You could be heading for a court martial here, son."

"I doubt it. I am just obeying a general's orders sir. We English are very pragmatic. You fight when you have to. If there is no point then go along with it and make the best of a bad job. I understand the French. If this was Washington, say the British had captured it, wouldn't you want it back in your hands, sir?"

180

He grinned, "I guess I would but I understand what the Major General means. We are out on a limb here. We have out run our supply lines and there are Germans all around us. We could be like the Germans in Falaise, surrounded and cut off if the Germans chose to attack us. You will have to fight your way in."

"I know but this time we will have armour with us. For my men that will be a first. Normally we are using whatever we can against the enemy tanks. This will be fine."

We had reached my camp. "You are a damned good fellow. Hemingway will be sorry he has missed you."

"Where is he? Still with the resistance?"

"Apparently. I have sent one of my men for him. Perhaps the thought of liberating Paris might appeal to him eh?"

When I reached the half-track I said, "We leave tomorrow for Paris. We are going in with the French again."

Even though there was danger involved they all seemed remarkably happy about the whole thing.

"Great sir!"

"We are all fuelled and ready to go."

"We have supplies!"

Sergeant Poulson came over and handed me my plate. "Here you are sir, we kept it by the fire. It is still warm."

"Thanks Sergeant, oh Fletcher, get Major Foster on the radio, if you can. Tell him that General Leclerc wishes me to remain attached to his division for the next week or so."

"Right sir."

Private Beaumont was the one who could join dots and see the bigger picture. He nodded and said, "Rather reminds me of Nelson at Copenhagen, sir, *'I see no ships!'*"

Sergeant Poulson frowned, "I don't get it."

I explained, "It means I am disobeying the order of a superior by pretending I didn't hear it. General Leclerc has asked us to go to Paris but Major General Gerow has ordered the whole unit to stay put."

"Ah. Will you get in trouble sir?"

"Only if we fail, Sergeant, only if we fail. Fortune favours the brave or, in our case, the foolhardy."

Captain Dronne arrived at our camp just after I had finished eating. He had with him a pair of swarthy looking men, one a sergeant and one a private. He held out his hand, "Captain Harsker, I have heard much about you and I am pleased to be fighting alongside you."

I could tell that he struggled with English and I answered him in French, "It is an honour and I shall enjoy telling the tale to my children."

"You have children?"

"Not yet. That rather depends upon tomorrow does it not?"

He laughed, "These are two of my men. As you can see my unit was formed in Africa and most of my men are Spanish. Pablo here acts as my adjutant. If there is anything you need then tell him. He will be in *'Madrid'*."

"Madrid?"

The Captain smiled, "Yes, my men have named our vehicles. We have three armoured cars, *'Guadalajara'*, *'Madrid'* and *'Ebro'* and three Shermans, *'Montmirail'*, *'Romilly'* and *'Chaumpaubert'*. We did not name the self-propelled gun and the two half-tracks."

I nodded, "I have a man who likes to do such things. Private Emerson has named our German half-track 'Bertha'!"

He laughed, "We will get on. I intend to leave before dawn. I would like your vehicle to go first until we see Paris. You will understand that it has to be a French vehicle and officer which liberates our city."

"Of course. And which route will you take?"

"We take the Paris road. Pablo, the flag." The Sergeant handed me a tricolour. "The resistance is expecting us but they are wary of armour. We will drape our vehicles in these flags. It will prevent confusion."

"And make us a target for any Germans. We normally like to sneak around."

"And usually I would agree but tomorrow is different eh, my friend? Tomorrow we make history and for that I think we can all take a risk or two. We will meet you at the road to the north west, by the bombed out Sherman."

After they had gone I gathered my men around me and told them what the Captain had said. Surprisingly the prospect of driving in with a flag did not bother them in the least. Fletcher seemed quite upbeat about it. "The French women will throw themselves at us sir! I might even have a shave!"

"Get on the radio to Major Foster would you? The rest of you better get your heads down. Tomorrow will be a long day."

I had already reloaded my weapons and so I went to check the vehicle. We could not afford that to let us down. We were sticking our neck a long way out and Major General Gerow had made it quite obvious there would be no support... unless we succeeded. Private Emerson saw what I was doing and joined me, "She is sound as a pound sir. I filled the radiator and topped up the oil. We have spare fuel and I managed to find a second spare tyre. We can afford two punctures. She won't let you down."

"I know Fred but if tomorrow goes well then we will be due a rest. The lads need it. We have barely stopped since D-Day and now it is almost the end of August."

182

"Aye sir. You mean the war might be over soon?"

"The Americans and French invaded the south of France a week or so ago and are driving north. I think the war in France will be over by autumn. As for the whole war... I don't know. Don't forget we have Germany and the Low Countries to go yet."

"Don't worry, sir. So long as you are the boss the lads'll be happy!"

I had just finished my inspection of the weapons in the half-track when Fletcher found me. He was grinning, "Just had Major Foster on the radio sir. He is a rum bugger sir, if you'll pardon my French. He said *'Tell the Captain to keep on riding his luck! We have his back!'* I think we are all right sir. By we does he mean your dad?"

"I think so. Early start tomorrow, Fletcher, you will need to keep in touch with Colonel Lanham. You still have the frequencies they use?"

"Yes sir and Delbert, their radio man, can understand me!"

"Good."

When we started the heavy half-track engine at 0400 there were moans and groans from the Americans sleeping close by. Emerson grumbled, "They get a lie in and they are complaining!"

Chapter 21

Captain Dronne and his men were waiting for us and we took the lead. We were travelling along the D370 and it was a god job we had tracks for there was much rubble on the road. We were close to Rennemoulin when we encountered our first Germans. They had troops dug in on both sides of the road. Emerson had quick reactions and as the Germans opened fire he ducked behind a convenient building. The bullets rattled off the wall. It was *'Ebro'* behind us and it did not take evasive action quickly enough. Its front left tyre was shredded.

"Outside and bring the PIAT."

I took my Mauser as bullets continued to smash against the French armoured car. The first of the Shermans was lumbering to support us. The Germans were focussed on the armoured car and I brought up the rifle while Bill Hay and Ken Shepherd set up the PIAT. I shot the only head I could see. It was the gunner on one of the machine guns. The gun stopped firing but it drew every bullet to my position. Luckily I had ducked my head before they hit. Shepherd tapped Bill on the shoulder and there was a whoosh as the rocket sped towards the machine gun. The explosion bought the Sherman time and it fired both its main gun and machine guns.

"Right lads, back on board."

As we boarded the other two tanks added their fire power and the Germans fled. Waving to the crew of the armoured car who were replacing the wheel we overtook the Shermans and headed down the road again.

"That was quick thinking, Emerson. Well done."

We had a largely empty road until we hit Bailly and, once again we encountered Germans. This time they had one of their small armoured cars blocking the road.

"Floor it Emerson!" Fred had not been driving at full speed and when he used the accelerator we leapt across the road. "Poulson, machine gun!" The shell struck the space we had recently occupied.

Sergeant Poulson opened fire with the MG 42 to buy us time while the armoured car reloaded and traversed its turret. The infantry opened fire too but their bullets clanged off the armour of the German half-track. Behind us I heard the crack of the French Sherman. It hit the armoured car's side. The shell tore inside and it exploded. Sergeant Poulson mopped up the infantry who had been around it.

Lieutenant Lemay shouted, "Sir, the Captain has been on the radio. The General has been given permission to follow us and the Americans. There are strong points ahead. We are ordered to turn right at Rocquencourt and head for the Pont de Sèvres."

"Tell them that we will do so."

That was easier said than done. There was a tank and a pair of armoured cars waiting for us at Rocquencourt. This time they alerted us to their presence by firing at us when we turned a bend and were just eight hundred yards from them. Our speed saved us again. The shell whizzed over the top of the half-track and Emerson, without waiting for orders, took us behind a half demolished wall. I jumped from the cab. Hay and Shepherd were already unpacking the PIAT. The 75mm shell smashed into the wall. I was covered in brick dust while a section of the wall fell on to the half-track. Emerson leapt from the cab to clear it.

I took my rifle but I had no target save the tyres of the armoured car. It was a target and I took it. As another shell threatened to demolish the wall completely I popped first one and then a second tyre. Sergeant Poulson, who was firing the MG 42 , said, "Any time soon lads!"

"Ready!"

The rocket whooshed away and struck the tank on the right front track. The track came off. At that range it was as good as we might have hoped. Two of the Shermans fired at the damaged tank. Head to head they might have struggled but they could manage a flank shot and the tank began to burn. The undamaged armoured car tried to escape but the third Sherman hit it and it exploded in a huge fire ball. The crew of the second one held their hands up.

"Sir, we need to clear this rubble or Bertha is going nowhere."

"Right lads give him a hand."

I was about to step out when a shot rang out and the commander of 'Romilly' slumped dead. He had been shot. The machine gunner just reacted and the Germans who had surrendered were machine gunned. The tanks then began firing , blindly, at the buildings in case they held more Germans. It was a waste of ammunition. I used the telescopic sight to search for the shooter. It had to be a sniper and that mean height. There was just one building. It was a church tower. Not particularly high it rose about ten feet above the surrounding buildings. It was almost eight hundred yards from me. I aimed my rifle and waited. I doubted that the sniper would flee for he was in little danger. The tanks were firing in the wrong place.

'Madrid' pulled up ahead of the tank and the gunner used his machine gun to sweep the buildings. I saw the flash and then heard the report of the bullet. The gunner fell as it hit him. I had been right. He was in the tower. I focussed in on the aperture at the top. He was well camouflaged but when he moved to reload then I saw him. I squeezed the trigger. I quickly emptied the clip. The sniper's body sagged out of the tower. He was dead. I continued to scan the roof tops but there were no more snipers.

I hurried over to the armoured cars. Captain Dronne joined me, "Thank you for that Captain Harsker. Juan had been with me since North Africa."

I pointed to the half-track, "We will need to dig Bertha out."

"We will push on. Join us when you can."

He was impatient but I wondered if he knew what he was taking on. When I reached the half-track I saw that they were jacking up one side. "A bullet sir, in the tyre."

"Can't be helped. Fletcher get on to Colonel Lanham and tell them what has happened. Beaumont, take Shepherd and see if you can find a spare on the German armoured cars."

I did not need to tell the others to take on water and food. They did so automatically. As I wiped my mouth I wondered when I would taste water which did not taste of chemical and metal.

It took twenty minutes to change the tyre and clear all of the debris from the vehicle. As we set off Emerson said, "They'll be in Paris by now sir! Sorry about the tyre."

"Not your fault and I am not so sure."

Not far from Ville-d'Avray we saw '*Ebro*'. It was burned out. It looked like there had been another fire fight. There were German bodies but the French had taken their dead with them. They would see Paris! We were passing Sèvres when we heard the sound of heavy ordnance.

"Foot down Emerson!"

We did not get as far as the bridge. '*Guadalajara*' was on fire and one of the Shermans had lost a track. I saw that the troops had left the lorries and were firing at, as yet, unseen Germans. The self-propelled gun and the two other Shermans were firing at the Germans who were on the other side of the Seine.

"Find some shelter."

There was plenty of that. The two damaged vehicles partly blocked the road and shells from the other side of the bridge had brought down part of a wall. The two surviving Shermans had taken cover behind a half demolished wall. Taking out my binoculars I saw that there were two Mark IV tanks on the other side of the bridge. They would take some shifting. Grabbing my Mauser I ran towards Captain Dronne's tank. Lieutenant Lemay was glued to my side.

"Sorry we took so long."

"We have to shift those two big beasts and they have the bridge wired to explode." He pointed to the left of the bridge. "The resistance is doing their best but they cannot get close."

"Have you a PIAT or a grenade launcher?"

The Captain shook his head. "We did not think we would need them."

"Lieutenant, go and fetch my men." He turned and ran off. I pointed to the bridge. "It is what, a hundred metres across and perhaps thirty wide?"

"Something like that, why?"

"If we can get to the end of the bridge here the natural curve on the bridge and the abutments will give us some shelter. It is dead ground. If you and your tanks can keep their tanks occupied we will try to get to the edge of the bridge. I think we can clear away the infantry there. If we can get close enough the PIAT can immobilise a tank. Then it would be up to you. Perhaps you should use H.E. with the self-propelled gun. The armour piercing is not working. I can get you the bridge. The rest is up to you."

"Give me that and all of France will be in your debt."

My men arrived. "Captain, lay down smoke and have your big gun make a killing ground of the far side of the bridge. Your armoured car's gun can make a nuisance of himself too." I turned to brief my men. "We are going to run the hundred yards or so to the end of the bridge. I want to clear away the infantry and then get the PIAT close enough to destroy one of the tanks. The Captain will take on the other."

Beaumont said, "Sir, the PIAT can do some damage at that range."

"Right. Fletcher you stay here with the radio. Emerson get back to the half-track. When the tanks cross I want you to pick up Fletcher and then us. Gordy you and Shepherd on the grenade launcher. Bill you and Hewitt on the PIAT. Lieutenant, you can load for the Sergeant."

"And what about you sir?"

"Me, Lieutenant? I am going to go first and see if I can do some damage with this rifle. If I can attract their attention then you lads can follow. Sergeant, it is your call."

"Right sir."

"Covering fire. Gordy, have you a smoke grenade?"

"Just the one sir and I am afraid it is red!"

I laughed, "Perhaps they will think we are calling fighter support! Send it as far over to the other side as you can."

Gordy had become as proficient with the launcher as Crowe and he laid the smoke grenade in between the two machine guns and tanks at the far end. A furious fusillade followed. I stood and ran, crouching. I moved in a straight line for I wanted to make it as quickly as possible. The French opened fire with their own guns and smoke also filled the bridge. I hurled myself against the reassuringly solid end of the bridge. I was safe. I lay down and rolled so that I could see across the bridge. Annoyingly there was no ledge for me to use and so I crawled along the pavement side. As I could not see the machine guns I guessed that they could not see me. When the top of the tank came into sight I slowed and edged my way forward.

The self-propelled gun was now lobbing H.E.at the Germans while the two Shermans, I could see, had ventured a little further forward. They were both firing blind but the French knew where the Germans were, in the middle of the bridge. I crept further forward as a shell exploded eighty yards from me in the middle of the two tanks and two machine guns. The shells were not intended to pierce armour but they manage to damage one of the tank's tracks. When I heard grenades exploding then I knew that Gordy had the range.

I looked through the sights of the rifle. The swirling smoke brought my targets into and out of view. I took a breath and squeezed into the smoke. As it cleared I saw that I had wounded a machine gunner. They could not see me and I fired again. I heard movement behind me as Beaumont and Bill Hay joined me. "It seemed safe enough, sir, so we thought we would join you."

"I can only see the top half of the tank and if you lift your body to get a better shot then the machine will have you." Just then I heard the chatter of a German machine gun. I looked across the bridge and saw that it was Poulson and the young French Lieutenant. They had taken their chances too. "I will try to hit the machine gun opposite. It will give you a shot."

"Right sir. Beaumont, load!"

I raised my head and aimed at the far machine gun position. Sergeant Poulson was still keeping the second one occupied. I fired all five bullets at the occupants of the machine gun. They were changing belts and I caught two of them.

"Now!"

The PIAT belched flames and, at eighty yards range the rocket penetrated the tank by zipping through the driver's visor. The turret lifted off and smoke and flames ripped across the bridge. I stood, "Come on, let's close while they are in the smoke!"

As we started to run I heard a cry and saw Lieutenant Lemay hit. I could do nothing to help him. We ran into the smoke and I saw, less than fifty yards from us, the remaining Mark IV. I knelt and aimed at the machine gunners. The tank was busy firing at the Shermans which were now advancing but the machine gunners had been protected by the tank. I fired one clip and hit one of them. I saw more Germans running to take the dead man's place. Then Gordy hit the machine gun with a direct hit. The nest became a death trap and I heard ammunition exploding.

"Now Hay! You will never get a better chance!"

They were behind me and the rocket sped towards the tank. At the same time the two Shermans concentrated their fire on it as well. It was ripped apart by the combination of three direct hits. "Come on!"

I ran to the other end of the bridge, drawing my Luger as I did so. A German rose from the far machine gun post with a rifle in his hands. As he raised it I fired four shots. He was pitched over the parapet. A German was climbing from the first tank we had hit with a gun in his hand. He was less than ten yards from me and I emptied my gun into him. A handful of Germans who had survived stood and began firing. I was a dead man. Then two sub machine guns opened up behind me as Beaumont and Hay came to my rescue. We reached the end of the bridge and I held up my hand.

"We stop here."

"Here sir?"

"Here, Lance Sergeant Hay. That is Paris and the first Allied officer who steps on to it will be French. We wait for Captain Dronne. Bill, go and fetch Poulson. See how the French Lieutenant is doing." I noticed Beaumont rooting around in the carnage of the machine gun emplacement. "What on earth are you doing?"

"Fletcher asked me to keep my eye open for good stuff." He flourished a Nazi flag. "Gold dust."

A Sherman pulled up behind me. Captain Dronne pushed up his goggles, "You could have been the officer who liberated Paris, my friend."

I shook my head, "The honour is yours. Besides I have wounded men to see to."

He saluted, "You, Captain Harsker, are a gentleman!"

The Sherman crossed to the other side of the Seine. There was nothing dramatic to be seen but the French resistance fighters who rushed towards him didn't care. He and his crew were mobbed. Sergeant Poulson joined me, he was limping, "Wounded?"

"Turned my ankle sir. Stupid injury!"

"How is the lad?"

"Hit in the arm sir. Hewitt has him fixed up but he refuses to go to hospital. He says he wants to be in at the finish."

"And I can understand that. As soon as Emerson arrives load up the half-track. I will go and find out what we are doing."

The rest of the French column had now crossed and it was like a party. I saw Captain Dronne speaking on the radio. Then he hurried to me. "The General is heading for the Pont D'Austerlitz. He wants us to get to the Hotel de Ville. It is nine miles away."

"Through streets held by Germans."

He grinned, "There is a cease fire. Your young Lieutenant knows Paris well. Ask him to guide us through the back streets and we will get there unseen."

"With just a couple of Shermans?"

He shrugged, "Why not? Will you do it?"

"Of course!"

Lieutenant Lemay was already in the cab of the half-track. I nodded, "You did well. The Captain wants you to take us to the Hotel de Ville. We have to use small roads but they have to be big enough for the Shermans. Can you do that?"

He smiled. "It is my city, sir, and I would be honoured."

"Emerson follow the Lieutenant's orders to the letter. I shall be up top."

I took my rifle and joined Poulson. There might be a cease fire but we would take no chances. I heard Gordy from the back, "Sir, you are not going to believe this but there are a bunch of civilians on the front of the Sherman!"

"They have been fighting the Germans all week with nothing more than rifles and hope. Let them enjoy a ride on a Sherman."

Julian knew his Paris. We twisted and turned as we made our way north and east. I was grateful when darkness began to fall and then there was the crack of a rifle and a cry from behind. "Sir, one of the civilians has been shot."

I took my Mauser and went to the back where it was open. A second shot rang out and another French resistance fighter fell. "Over there sir, in the trees by that little park."

I leaned my rifle over the side and moved it slowly from side to side. I could see nothing. Then the sniper fired a third time and I saw the muzzle flash. Before I could fire Sergeant Poulson had let fly with the MG 42. He took out the top of the trees and two Germans fell dead. "Well done Sergeant."

The French resistance took to sheltering behind the slow moving Shermans. I smiled when Fletcher said. "Is that the Eiffel tower there sir? It looks a bit bigger than Blackpool Tower."

"The answer is yes to both questions. It is the Eiffel Tower and it is bigger." I noticed that the tricolour now flew from it but the bridge across the river had been damaged. As darkness proper took over I saw flashes from the east and the west as the other two columns advanced on this historic city. I knew that the Hotel de Ville was close to the cathedral of Notre Dame and when I saw it loom up in the dark I began to hope that we would succeed.

A small German detachment in the Tuileries tried to spoil the party. They opened fire on the half-track as we passed. The armour of the half-track deflected the bullets but, before we could return fire, the two Shermans behind us let rip with their machine guns, augmented by the resistance fighters. It was the last obstacle before we entered the huge square by the Hotel de Ville. It was five to midnight, The two tanks parked on either side of us and I helped the Lieutenant from the cab. Captain Dronne waited for him and the two of them walked up the steps of the town hall to be greeted by the resistance fighters who had occupied it. A huge cheer went up and then, from behind us, we heard the bells of Notre Dame as they were pealed. Soon I could hear bells all over Paris. Against the odds we had succeeded. We had helped to liberate Paris.

Epilogue

We slept under the half-track in the square although we did not get to bed until the early hours. The restaurants and bars brought us food and wine to celebrate the liberation of Paris. We were treated as heroes. The food and the drink helped us to sleep well. When I awoke I got on the radio and discovered that there were just two pockets of Germans left in Paris. There were two thousand Germans in the Bois de Boulogne and seven hundred in the Luxembourg gardens, The rest had surrendered. General Choltitz had disobeyed Adolf Hitler and refused to destroy Paris. The 2nd Armoured Division and the 4th Division were clearing the last pockets of resistance. Our orders were simple. We were to wait for the British contingent to arrive. Until then we were the representatives of Great Britain.

So it was that I met General Charles de Gaulle. General Leclerc introduced us and his natural distaste for all things English was mitigated by the work I had done for the French. He seemed to appreciate the gesture I had made in allowing Captain Dronne to be the first allied officer into Paris.

He spoke briefly to me, "I thank you, Captain Harsker. I have heard of you before and know that you are a gentleman and a good soldier. If ever you need my help then please do not hesitate to ask."

"Thank you sir but I am happy to serve my country."

He nodded, "As I serve mine. You will be present this afternoon when I make my speech. You will find it interesting, I think."

The square was packed and the atmosphere party like as the General spoke, "Why do you wish us to hide the emotion which seizes us all, men and women, who are here, at home, in Paris that stood up to liberate itself and that succeeded in doing this with its own hands?

No! We will not hide this deep and sacred emotion. These are minutes which go beyond each of our poor lives. Paris! Paris outraged! Paris broken! Paris martyred! But Paris liberated! Liberated by itself, liberated by its people with the help of the French armies, with the support and the help of all France, of the France that fights, of the only France, of the real France, of the eternal France!..."

I turned away at that point for he seemed to be saying that it had been the French who had been responsible for the victory. I thought of all those Americans, Canadians and British who had died on the beaches of Normandy, or at Bréville. I thought of the Poles who had defended their hill to the last. It had not been a French victory but an allied one yet his words were political. Was this war, fought for the right reasons, now going to degenerate into a political fight?

I turned to leave and Lieutenant Lemay said, "Listen to the end, sir, I beg of you. Stay for me."

"Very well."

I returned as he concluded his speech, " This is why the French vanguard has entered Paris with guns blazing. This is why the great French army from Italy has landed in the south and is advancing rapidly up the Rhône valley. This is why our brave and dear Forces of the interior will arm themselves with modern weapons. It is for this revenge, this vengeance and justice, that we will keep fighting until the final day, until the day of total and complete victory.

This duty of war, all the men who are here and all those who hear us in France know that it demands national unity. We, who have lived the greatest hours of our History, we have nothing else to wish than to show ourselves, up to the end, worthy of France. Long live France!"

Lieutenant Lemay was beaming, "Do you see sir, he acknowledges you? You were the vanguard."

I shook my head, "You will learn, my young friend, that war is about every man doing their job. It is not just the vanguard but everyone. If Emerson didn't look after Bertha we would not be here. If Beaumont wasn't a whizz with explosives we would not be here and we are the tip of the iceberg. I am proud to be here today but that is because I represent all those who can't be here. The job isn't done yet but, by God, I will make damn sure that I am there at the end!"

The End

Glossary

Abwehr- German Intelligence

ATS- Auxiliary Territorial Service- Women's Branch of the British Army during WW2

Bisht- Arab cloak

Bob on- Very accurate (slang) from a plumber's bob

Butchers- Look (Cockney slang Butcher's Hook- Look)

Butties- sandwiches (slang)

Chah- tea (slang)

Comforter- the lining for the helmet; a sort of woollen hat

Conflab- discussion (slang)

Corned dog- Corned Beef (slang)

Dhobi- washing (slang from the Hindi word)

Ercs- aircraftsman (slang- from Cockney)

Ewbank- Mechanical carpet cleaner

Fruit salad- medal ribbons (slang)

Full English- English breakfast (bacon, sausage, eggs, fried tomato and black pudding)

Gash- spare (slang)

Gauloise- French cigarette

Gib- Gibraltar (slang)

Glasshouse- Military prison

Goon- Guard in a POW camp (slang)- comes from a 19thirties Popeye cartoon

Hurries- Hawker Hurricane (slang)

Jankers- field punishment

Jimmy the One- First Lieutenant on a warship

Kettenhunde - Chained dogs. Nickname for German field police. From the gorget worn around their necks

Killick- leading hand (Navy) (slang)

Kip- sleep (slang)

LRDG- Long Range Desert group (Commandos operating from the desert behind enemy lines.)

Marge- Margarine (butter substitute- slang)

MGB- Motor Gun Boat

Mossy- De Havilland Mosquito (slang)

Mickey- *'taking the mickey'*, making fun of (slang)

Micks- Irishmen (slang)

MTB- Motor Torpedo Boat

ML- Motor Launch

Narked- annoyed (slang)

Neaters- undiluted naval rum (slang)

Oik- worthless person (slang)

Oppo/oppos- pals/comrades (slang)

Piccadilly Commandos- Prostitutes in London

PLUTO- Pipe Line Under The Ocean

Pom-pom- Quick Firing 2lb (40mm) Maxim cannon

Pongo (es)- soldier (slang)

Potato mashers- German Hand Grenades (slang)

PTI- Physical Training Instructor

QM- Quarter Master (stores)

Recce- Reconnoitre (slang)

SBA- Sick Bay Attendant

Schnellboote -German for E-boat (literally translated as fast boat)
Schtum -keep quiet (German)
Scragging - roughing someone up (slang)
Scrumpy- farm cider
Shooting brake- an estate car
SOE- Special Operations Executive (agents sent behind enemy lines)
SP- Starting price (slang)- what's going on
SNAFU- Situation Normal All Fucked Up (acronym and slang)
Snug- a small lounge in a pub (slang)
Spiv- A black marketeer/criminal (slang)
Sprogs- children or young soldiers (slang)
Squaddy- ordinary soldier (slang)
Stag- sentry duty (slang)
Stand your corner- get a round of drinks in (slang)
Subbie- Sub-lieutenant (slang)
Tatties- potatoes (slang)
Thobe- Arab garment
Tiffy- Hawker Typhoon (slang)
Tommy (Atkins)- Ordinary British soldier
Two penn'orth- two pennies worth (slang for opinion)
Wavy Navy- Royal Naval Reserve (slang)
WVS- Women's Voluntary Service

Historical note

The first person I would like to thank for this particular book and series is my Dad. He was in the Royal Navy but served in Combined Operations. He was at Dieppe, D-Day and Walcheren. His boat: LCA(I) 523 was the one which took in the French Commandos on D-Day. He was proud that his flotilla had taken in Bill Millens and Lord Lovat. I wish that, before he died, I had learned more in detail about life in Combined Operations but like many heroes he was reluctant to speak of the war. He is the character in the book called Bill Leslie. Dad ended the war as Leading Seaman- I promoted him! I reckon he deserved it.

'Bill Leslie' **1941**
Author's collection

I went to Normandy in 1994, with my Dad, to Sword Beach and he took me through that day on June 6th 1944. He pointed out the position which took the head from the Oerlikon gunner who stood next to him. He also told me about the raid on Dieppe. He had taken the Canadians in. We even found the grave of his cousin George Hogan who died on D-Day. As far as I know we were the only members of the family ever to do so. Sadly that was Dad's only visit but we planted forget-me-nots on the grave of George. Wally Friedmann is a real Canadian who served in WW2 with my Uncle Ted. The description of Wally is perfect- I lived with Wally and his family for three months in 1972. He was a real gentleman. As far as I now he did not serve with the Saskatchewan regiment, he came from Ontario but he did serve in the war. As I keep saying, it is my story and my imagination. God bless, Wally.

I would also like to thank Roger who is my railway expert. The train Tom and the Major catch from Paddington to Oswestry ran until 1961. The details of the livery, the compartments and the engine are all, hopefully accurate. I would certainly not argue with Roger! Thanks also to John Dinsdale, another railway buff and a scientist. It was he who advised on the use of explosives . Not the sort of thing to Google these days!

I used a number of books in the research. The list is at the end of this historical section. However the best book, by far, was the actual

196

Commando handbook which was reprinted in 2012. All of the details about hand to hand, explosives, esprit de corps etc were taken directly from it. The advice about salt, oatmeal and water is taken from the book. It even says that taking too much salt is not a bad thing! I shall use the book as a Bible for the rest of the series. The Commandos were expected to find their own accommodation. Some even saved the money for lodgings and slept rough. That did not mean that standards of discipline and presentation were neglected; they were not.

LC(I)523 leaving Southampton taken (I think) from LC(I)527 the Flotilla leader. From my Dad's Collection

Reference Books used

- The Commando Pocket Manual 1949-45- Christopher Westhorp
- The Second World War Miscellany- Norman Ferguson
- Army Commandos 1940-45- Mike Chappell
- Military Slang- Lee Pemberton
- World War II- Donald Sommerville
- The Historical Atlas of World War II-Swanston and Swanston
- The Battle of Britain- Hough and Richards
- The Hardest Day- Price
- Overlord Coastline- Stephen Chicken
- Disaster at D-Day- Peter Tsouras
- Michelin Map #102 Battle of Normandy (1947 Edition).

Griff Hosker September 2016

Other books

by

Griff Hosker

If you enjoyed reading this book, then why not read another one by the author?
Ancient History

The Sword of Cartimandua Series (Germania and Britannia 50A.D. – 128 A.D.)
Ulpius Felix- Roman Warrior (prequel)
Book 1 The Sword of Cartimandua
Book 2 The Horse Warriors
Book 3 Invasion Caledonia
Book 4 Roman Retreat
Book 5 Revolt of the Red Witch
Book 6 Druid's Gold
Book 7 Trajan's Hunters
Book 8 The Last Frontier
Book 9 Hero of Rome
Book 10 Roman Hawk
Book 11 Roman Treachery
Book 12 Roman Wall
Book 13 Roman Courage

The Aelfraed Series (Britain and Byzantium 1050 A.D. - 1085 A.D.)
Book 1 Housecarl
Book 2 Outlaw
Book 3 Varangian

The Wolf Warrior series (Britain in the late 6th Century)
Book 1 Saxon Dawn
Book 2 Saxon Revenge
Book 3 Saxon England
Book 4 Saxon Blood
Book 5 Saxon Slayer
Book 6 Saxon Slaughter
Book 7 Saxon Bane
Book 8 Saxon Fall: Rise of the Warlord
Book 9 Saxon Throne

The Dragon Heart Series
Book 1 Viking Slave
Book 2 Viking Warrior
Book 3 Viking Jarl
Book 4 Viking Kingdom
Book 5 Viking Wolf
Book 6 Viking War
Book 7 Viking Sword
Book 8 Viking Wrath
Book 9 Viking Raid
Book 10 Viking Legend
Book 11 Viking Vengeance
Book 12 Viking Dragon

Book 13 Viking Treasure
Book 14 Viking Enemy
Book 15 Viking Witch
Book 16 Viking Blood
Book 17 Viking Weregeld
Book 18 Viking Storm
Book 19 Viking Warband
Book 20 Viking Shadow
Book 21 Viking Legacy

The Norman Genesis Series
Hrolf the Viking
Horseman
The Battle for a Home
Revenge of the Franks
The Land of the Northmen
Ragnvald Hrolfsson
Brothers in Blood
Lord of Rouen
Drekar in the Seine

The Anarchy Series England 1120-1180
English Knight
Knight of the Empress
Northern Knight
Baron of the North
Earl
King Henry's Champion
The King is Dead
Warlord of the North
Enemy at the Gate
The Fallen Crown
Warlord's War
Kingmaker
Henry II
Crusader
The Welsh Marches
Irish War
Poisonous Plots
The Princes' Revolt

Border Knight 1182-1300
Sword for Hire
Return of the Knight
Baron's War
Magna Carta

Modern History
The Napoleonic Horseman Series

198

Book 1 Chasseur a Cheval
Book 2 Napoleon's Guard
Book 3 British Light Dragoon
Book 4 Soldier Spy
Book 5 1808: The Road to Corunna
Waterloo

The Lucky Jack American Civil War series
Rebel Raiders
Confederate Rangers
The Road to Gettysburg

The British Ace Series
1914
1915 Fokker Scourge
1916 Angels over the Somme
1917 Eagles Fall
1918 We will remember them
From Arctic Snow to Desert Sand

Wings over Persia

Combined Operations series 1940-1945
Commando
Raider
Behind Enemy Lines
Dieppe
Toehold in Europe
Sword Beach
Breakout
The Battle for Antwerp
King Tiger
Beyond the Rhine

Other Books
Carnage at Cannes (a thriller)
Great Granny's Ghost (Aimed at 9-14-year-old young people)
Adventure at 63-Backpacking to Istanbul

For more information on all of the books then please visit the author's web site at http://www.griffhosker.com where there is a link to contact him or you can Tweet him @HoskerGriff

CPSIA information can be obtained
at www.ICGtesting.com
Printed in the USA
BVHW041255121119
563595BV00009B/46/P

9 781724 437310